HOMER'S ILL ILIAD

HOMER'S ILL ILIAD

Jay Dubya

www.bookstandpublishing.com

Published by
Bookstand Publishing
Pasadena, CA 91101
4932_6

ISBN 978-1-956785-26-5

For Homer (but not Jethro)

Other Books by Jay Dubya

Adult Fiction

Black Leather and Blue Denim, A '50s Novel
The Great Teen Fruit War, A 1960' Novel
Frat' Brats, A '60s Novel
Ron Coyote, Man of La Mangia
Pieces of Eight
Pieces of Eight, Part II
Pieces of Eight, Part III
Pieces of Eight, Part IV
The Wholly Book of Genesis
The Wholly Book of Exodus
The Wholly Book of Doo-Doo-Rot-on-Me
Thirteen Sick Tasteless Classics
Thirteen Sick Tasteless Classics, Part II
Thirteen Sick Tasteless Classics, Part III
Thirteen Sick Tasteless Classics, Part IV
Thirteen Sick Tasteless Classics, Part V
So Ya' Wanna' Be A Teacher
RAM: Random Articles and Manuscripts
Mauled Maimed Mangled Mutilated Mythology
Fractured Frazzled Folk Fables and Fairy Farces
FFFF&FF, Part II
Nine New Novellas
Nine New Novellas, Part II
Nine New Novellas, Part III
Nine New Novellas, Part IV
One Baker's Dozen
Two Baker's Dozen
Shakespeare: Slammed, Smeared, Savaged & Slaughtered
Shakespeare: Slammed, Smeared, Savaged & Slaughtered, Part II
Suite 16
Time Travel Tales
Snake Eyes and Boxcars
Snake Eyes and Boxcars, Part II
UFO: Utterly Fantastic Occurrences
The Psychic Dimension

Young Adult Fantasy Novels

Content Chapters

Background

Homer did not invent the game of baseball. Instead, the popular sport had been organized by a fellow named Abner Doubleplay.

The poet/bard Homer, reputed to have been blind, is credited with orally describing the *Iliad* (the story of the end of the ten-year Trojan War), and the *Odyssey,* the epic tale of the Greek hero Odysseus, who had been punished by Poseidon (Neptune, the sea god) for ten-long-years after the Trojan War. Homer had lived during the time when alphabets and writing were being developed (around 1,000 BC), so his epic poems were later recorded by educated scribes and both stories exist today in their present forms.

Around 1184 BC, King Agamemnon of Mycenae, and his brother, King Menelaus of Sparta, had led the great expedition of a thousand Greek ships and 50,000 warriors against the Asia Minor city of Troy. The kings of the Greek city states were notorious pirates and marauders, but to glamorize their siege upon Troy, a mythological story involving Helen of Sparta, wife of King Menelaus, claimed that she had been wooed by Prince Paris of Troy to elope to Asia Minor. Thus, Helen of Sparta soon became Helen of Troy, and her abduction became the principal cause of the Trojan War.

The Trojan War had taken almost ten-long-years to fight, and the lengthy conflict was finally won when Odysseus, a brilliant schemer and ball-breaker, had a magnificent Wooden Trojan Horse built, and then had the Greek warriors situate the structure outside the main gates of Troy. The city was strategically located at the Hellespont Channel between Greece and Persia (now Turkey). Greek heroes were hidden inside the stomach of the colossal horse, and during the night, the warriors stealthily climbed-down a rope, opened the gates to Troy, and allowed thousands of Greek warriors to enter, rampage, sack and plunder. The Trojan War was fought during the late Bronze Age, which according to historical records, was around 1184 BC.

Mythological Background

Zeus, king of the Mt. Olympus gods and ruler of Heaven and Earth, and his brother Poseidon, king of the sea, both loved and desired Thetis, a beautiful sea-nymph. Zeus was aware of a prophecy that a son would be born to Thetis who would be mightier than Zeus himself, and *that* son would be capable of overthrowing the king god, just like Zeus had rebelled against his Titan father Cronus. In order to prevent that possible insurrection from happening, mighty god Zeus arranged a marriage between Thetis and a common mortal, a fellow named Peleus.

"It is not right for either my brother Poseidon or myself to sire *that* foretold rebellious child," Zeus thundered to his wife Hera. "We'll invite all of the gods to the wedding of Thetis and Peleus." But one particular goddess, Eris (goddess of discord), was overlooked and not invited. Eris appeared at the reception and rolled a golden apple onto the marble floor.

"This apple will go to the fairest goddess of all," Eris coyly announced. "The leading candidates are Hera, Athena and Aphrodite. And Prince Paris of Troy is to be the judge whose selection will be final!"

"I'll offer you the most gorgeous woman on Earth!" Aphrodite promised Paris, without revealing to the knucklehead that Helen of Sparta had already been married to King Menelaus. "My prize will be more valuable to you than the power and fame that Hera and Athena have offered."

Cunning Aphrodite, goddess of love and beauty, assisted Prince Paris in journeying to Sparta and seducing Helen, bringing her to Troy. Sometime later, Menelaus, and his brother King Agamemnon of Mycenae, assembled an armada of one-thousand ships to depart to Asia Minor to retrieve Helen of Sparta, who then had auspiciously become Helen of Troy.

But the sea-nymph Thetis and Peleus did have a very famous son, whose immortal and legendary name was the Greek champion Achilles.

Greek Name	Roman Name
Zeus	Jupiter
Poseidon	Neptune
Hades	Pluto
Athena	Minerva
Hera	Juno
Aphrodite	Venus
Apollo	Apollo
Hermes	Mercury
Ares	Mars
Cronus	Saturn
Hephaestus	Vulcan
Artemis	Diana
Thetis	Thetis
Odysseus	Ulysses

Gods Supporting Greeks	Gods Supporting Trojans	Neutral
Athena	Aphrodite	Zeus
Hera	Apollo	
Poseidon	Ares	
Hermes	Artemis	

Chapter 1
"ACHILLES AND AGAMEMNON ARGUE"

Brain-dead-but-awesome Ancient Muse, amuse and speak to me now of those intrepid heroes who had pillaged and looted the corrupt bordellos and brothels of Troy. You can begin your unique narrative with the verbal dispute occurring between King Agamemnon, leader of the Greek armies against Troy, and the mighty hero from antiquity, Achilles.

"Agamemnon, you' totally obnoxious bastard," Achilles brazenly insisted. "You've caused plenty of anger from Lord Apollo for insolently yelling-up to high heaven, 'A-pollo is a chicken! A-pollo is a chicken'!"

"Get real, Achilles," Agamemnon vehemently maintained. "True, I have been a trifle irreverent. All I did was create a minor crisis by mildly offending Chryses, Apollo's favored high priest, who is only four-foot-tall!"

"We have been plagued with various plagues ever since your mounting arrogance had insulted Phoebus Apollo," Achilles screamed, almost rupturing his tonsils and adenoids. "Lord Apollo had heard Chryses' pleas for retribution, and the dispassionate god shot thousands of arrows of death and disease down-upon our afflicted Achaean armies. You're to blame for all of the recent destruction and devastation to our apprehensive troops," alleged Achilles. "For nine whole days and nights, Apollo's silver arrows came-down like torrential rain, killing good warriors, and having us cremating the corpses upon makeshift funeral pyres. The bodies were easy to burn because your defiance of Apollo and his lethal arrows had already scared the shit out of thousands of our brave warriors, making our enemy, the Trojans, both jealous and envious of the sky chariot god's awesome shooting ability. No mortal in his right mind wants to have Apollo as an enema, or, I meant to say 'as an enemy'!"

On the tenth day of massive death, Achilles called all of the Greek captains to a general council and firmly stated that under Agamemnon's dangerous leadership, the Achaean military campaign against King Priam and his Trojan minions was doomed to utter failure. "The Trojans cannot defeat us, but Apollo's wrath very easily can slaughter our' frustrated soldiers. I suggest that we forget this unproductive siege upon Troy, unless one of you morons can reveal to this assembly exactly why the immortal gods have apparently sided against us!"

"I'll tell you precisely what you desire learning," Calchas calculated and volunteered a viable answer to Achilles' imperative request. "But first, you must guarantee me safety from the wrath of a bitter rival. I need inclusion in your secret government protection program."

"Look, Calchas!" Achilles yelled. "Even if your alluded-to foe happens to be King Agamemnon himself, I'll kick his royal ass good, along with easily crushing his tiny testicles bouncing-around inside his miniature scrotum sac!"

"Lord Achilles; Phoebus Apollo is especially angry on two counts," Calchas anxiously disclosed. "First, our leader against Troy called all-powerful A-pollo 'a chicken', rather repeatedly; and second, your adversary Agamemnon refused to surrender his handsome ransom Chryseis, high priest Chryses' beautiful daughter. Apollo will not stop shooting silver arrows into our vulnerable assholes and puncturing our' delicate scrotum sacs until Chryseis is safely returned to Chryses! It's that plainly simple! What a fully fucked-up situation this Chryses/Chryseis crisis is! After you return Chryseis to Chryses to avoid further crisis, I suggest that we alter our errant ways and make abundant sacrifices to Lord Apollo upon a newly constructed altar!"

But Agamemnon, king of Mycenae and the Achaean leader against Troy, became infuriated at Calchas' Chryses/Chryses commentary. "Look, Calchas, you feckless wimp," the king of Mycenae bellowed. "All of your prophecies are basically doom and gloom in nature. Chryseis is a tremendous piece of ass, and she's better in bed than my wife Clytemnestra is at daily humping and pumping. And as you know, my captains. My brother King Menelaus of Sparta had married that cold-hearted bitch Helen, and I have regrettably married Helen's frigid sister, Clytemnestra!"

"Do you value this religious-freak girl Chryseis over your entire army of fifty-thousand men?" Achilles audaciously challenged Agamemnon. "Surely, you should not jeopardize all of us simply over a well-endowed whore. But first, you must scream-up to the sky, 'A-pollo is *NOT* a chicken! A-pollo is *not* a chicken!"

"I shall surrender my pride and obey Apollo's greedy will," Agamemnon reluctantly agreed. "But then it would look like I am weak if I must surrender my prize at a belligerent underling's prompting. Now Achilles; I assert that I must be given another horny harlot in the place of me giving-up Chryseis."

"What woman do you wish to pump the poop out of?" Achilles demanded of Agamemnon. "You might just lose your confused head over a stupid piece of ass!"

"I might just consider possessing your prized concubine, Briseis, Achilles, or perhaps instead, I'll decide to confiscate Ajax's prized hussy. I can't emphasize how terrific it is for me being the chief chauvinist with absolute authority on this military expedition. There's plenty of time for my' heart to determine which sexy bitch I'll choose for my personal gratification! But first, I must avoid future crises by appeasing Apollo by giving that excellent piece of ass Chryseis back to that lunatic dumb-dick priest Chryses."

"You dare belittle super-strong Ajax, the great warrior who had cleaned-out several Trojan platoons like an ivory-skinned white tornado!" Achilles loudly challenged.

"As leader of the forces against Troy, I can do whatever I please," Agamemnon articulated, using the rank card. "Your might is no defense to my acclaimed and established wisdom!"

"You're a very greedy bastard," Achilles accused the Mycenae King. "Quite truthfully, I have no particular grievances or quarrel against the Trojans. I had led my troops here to Troy to help your brother Menelaus retrieve your sister-in-law Helen from the clutches of Prince Paris. In fact, I've contributed more to this battle than you have. Just look at all the cities I've sacked, and all of the promiscuous whores I've bagged! Yet, you; you stubborn asshole, get to keep all of the plunder to your own avaricious self! Frankly, I've had enough of your abusive bullshit!" livid Achilles screamed. "I'm inclined to gladly sail for home and return to Phthia in my native Thessaly, and leave you to fight Paris, Hector, Priam and the rest of the Trojans over the stolen wife of Menelaus, who is reputed from Greek gossip to be a third-class piece of ass!"

Agamemnon then accused Achilles of being an emboldened coward, and to demonstrate his supreme authority, deliberately belittled the greatest of Greek warriors. "Achilles; enough of your snarky innuendo; now hear me out! You cannot defy the will of the Lord King, namely myself, captaining this formidable armada! Since I shall give Chryseis back to the short high-priest Chryses, I demand that you make a reasonable concession before this military council and give me your prized female, Briseis, to compensate for Chryseis, in order to avoid more crises with Chryses, the dwarfish high-priest of Apollo."

When Achilles and Agamemnon were about to commence dueling with bronze swords, Hera, wife of Zeus, urgently dispatched Athena, daughter of Almighty Zeus, to whisper powerful words into enraged Achilles' ear.

"Hold your hand from your' sword, dear Achilles, and I urge you to forget about using your bronze weapon at this moment," Athena softly and discreetly recommended. "For your exhibition of self-control, I assure you, brave warrior, that soon you'll be fully rewarded with endless fame and glory, if you just wisely practice self-control and restraint against Agamemnon. Slice the garrulous asshole with your clever language, but not with your awesome sword!"

"As is our tradition, the meeting scepter has been passed along to me, and as you all know, I am the only one entitled to speak at this moment," the Phthian prince insisted. "Now Agamemnon; here is my general evaluation of our' impasse! I've concluded that I shall refuse to fight on your behalf," Achilles boldly addressed Agamemnon while standing erect before the other noble captains attending the assembly. "As Hector and Paris courageously lead their soldiers against *your* invading armies, I will not participate any further in *your* futile battle!"

Elderly Nestor was then handed the scepter by Achilles, and the old fart slowly addressed the aggregate of Greek commanders. "I am the oldest one here, and had once fought with the hero Theseus, slayer of the Minotaur on the island of Crete. But I must confess to you, King Agamemnon, that this is indeed a black day! I advise that you give-up Chryseis to Chryses and not take Briseis from Achilles. And I say to you, Lord Achilles; I further extend this fair compromise as a viable solution to this ongoing argument. Please help us to defeat the Trojans and not sail back to your homeland with your battle-proven Myrmidons!"

"Well said, Nestor," Agamemnon complimented the distinguished philosopher from Pylos. "But Achilles is obviously extremely envious of my prowess, and the covetous fool evilly wishes to pilfer my authority! I shall never relinquish my newly acquired prize Briseis to *his* jealous disposal, and if the son-of-a-bitch dares to double-cross me, *his* pathetic blood will soak my trusty sword!"

Fearing the infamous wrath of Achilles, double-talking Agamemnon quickly relented from his demand, and the King of Mycenae instructed Odysseus of Ithaca to transport Chryseis back to her father, the midget high priest Chryses, in order to avert continuing crisis involving Apollo's revenge. But soon thereafter, Agamemnon instructed two guards, Eurybates, brother of Eurabadass, and Talthybius, father of the pygmy-runt

Tallthebes, to escort Briseis from Achilles' tent and transferred into *his* personal custody.

"Lord King; can't I sail to Lesbos instead and eagerly watch some kinky lesbians in action?" Odysseus begged and asked Agamemnon. "I understand that there are some tri-sexuals living on that bizarre island, in addition to the notorious female homos!"

Meanwhile, aggrieved and thwarted Achilles, suffering from emotional distress, ventured to the distant seashore and beckoned his petulance to his mother, the sea nymph Thetis.

"Why do you sorrow so extensively, my dear son?" Thetis curiously inquired. "Did that antagonistic heel Apollo castrate your exposed testicles with one of his silver arrows? I've heard that the chariot sky rider's major beef is when a mere mortal like yourself yells-up to the clouds, 'A-pollo is a chicken'!"

"You already know the reason for my demeanor being quite disconsolate," Achilles replied to his immortal mother. "I've been horribly disgraced by Agamemnon, and have currently lost my slave girl Briseis to *his* imperial command. Now mother; I understand through hearsay that Almighty Zeus owes you a colossal favor. I'd like you to intervene for me and ask Lord Zeus to side with the home-team Trojans against the visiting Achaeans, and let all the Greek Captains finally realize the abundant crazed madness of Agamemnon! The Trojans must temporarily gain the upper-hand in the ongoing conflict! Then, the Greek Captains will finally comprehend exactly how important I am, and how unimportant Agamemnon really is!"

"My son, I see on the horizon a dim future for you as a mortal being. Confidentially, you have so little sand left falling inside your hourglass. Zeus and several other Mt. Olympus gods are presently attending a major feast in Ethiopia, but when they return from their merry festival, I'll plan to speak to him on your behalf."

Fulfilling his vital errand, Lord Odysseus reunited Chryseis with her father Chryses, and in the process, the current ever-escalating crisis with vindictive and arrow-gant Apollo had been successfully averted.

"In the future," the midget high priest/prophet commended, "I see you, Odysseus, going-down in history and standing next to fantastic contributors to world civilization such as the great Michelangelo, the magnificent Leonardo da Vinci, and a political genius with the weird appellation Thomas Jefferson," Chryses articulated and informed.

"Who the hell are those three anonymous assholes that you've just mentioned?" the King of Ithaca instinctively asked the tiny high-priest. "Those jerk-offs you've just indicated don't sound like ordinary Greeks or Trojans to me! Are the three others you've just mentioned distrustful Etruscans, or perhaps itinerant, fucked-up Chinese cavemen?"

Chryses ignored Odysseus's dumb-ass comments and solemnly proceeded with his preferred reverence to *his* adored god, Lord Apollo. The senile priest then offered monotonous prayers, dissonant songs, and cheap libations in the form of watered-down wine to satisfy the god's enormous ego.

"Odysseus, I bless you, valiant hero, in your gallant pursuit of evasive glory," Chryses advised. "The future of civilization depends on your genius in bringing the Trojan War of East versus West to a reputable end! Go now, oh illustrious champion; go in quest of your honorable destiny!"

And then Odysseus, with his essential mission of delivering Chryseis to Chryses being fully accomplished, sailed back to the shores of Troy with his crew upon his reliable Bireme.

On the twelfth day after the initial argument between Achilles and Agamemnon, Zeus had merrily returned to Mt. Olympus and granted an audience to Thetis, obsessively representing her tantrum-plagued son Achilles. But learning of the sea-nymph's visit, Hera, wife of Zeus, boldly confronted and challenged her husband's fidelity.

"I had witnessed you submissively bowing your head to that sea-whore Thetis, so what the Hades did you ever promise that conniving strumpet? I think, husband, that I already know the correct answer. You'll create a convoluted scenario where the Trojans will drive the Argives back to their anchored black ships upon the shoreline, just to satisfy the will of that over-ambitious heel, Achilles, son of Thetis."

"Leave me the fuck alone, wife!" Zeus boomed. "If you continue goading my sensitive ass, I'll turn you into a horny frog who is de-evolving-down into an insignificant tadpole. Depart from this chamber immediately, or else woman, you'll most certainly feel my tempestuous anger when I become excessively pissed-off!"

Upon Hera exiting the Mt. Olympus throne room, Zeus snapped his fingers and suddenly, his devout attendant Dream appeared to honor his master's imperative command, which happened several dozen times a day atop Mt. Olympus.

"Dream; I want you to take a brief trip to the distant shores of Troy and visit beleaguered King Agamemnon while the idiot's still sound asleep.

Instruct the dumb-fuck to wildly attack the city with his entire force. Whisper into his defective brain that the day of the Achaean victory will soon arrive. This activity, meaning the power of suggestion as enacted by you, will be phase one of my most recent war game scheme. Now Dream, I hereby insist that you get your shit together and complete your assignment in forty-winks!"

"Yes, Master Zeus. I see much merit in your most-recent canard. As always, your imaginative wish is my loyal instruction!" Dream obediently declared. "But honestly, my dear Lord Zeus. You could call me by my other popular name if you'd like: Mr. Sandman!"

Chapter 2

"RALLYING THE WARRIORS"

The following morning, Agamemnon summoned his captains to an important assembly to reveal the detailed essence of the deceitful dream that unscrupulous Zeus had fabricated, and that Dream had deposited deep inside *his* thick skull.

"Captains," the King of Mycenae prefaced his remarks. "Last night Mighty Zeus had sent me a dream, but unfortunately, it wasn't a marvelous white one. The king god had informed my subconscious mind that *our* day of triumph has finally arrived, and that a phenomenal victory will soon be within our grasp. The walls of Troy will soon topple and disintegrate into dust, for Zeus now favors us Achaeans; the chief deity wants us to stop kissing butt and to start kicking ass!"

Agamemnon then held a brief private side-bar conference with Odysseus and Nestor, the two captains that he most trusted. "The under-ranking men's loyalty must be tested. I'll feign honesty and announce that the troops should board their boats and be ready to sail back to their native lands. If the idiots desire to be reunited with their wives' smelly crotches and with their aberrant, wise-ass kids' undisciplined antics and semantics, then I command that you, Odysseus and Nestor, convince your loyal confederates to rally the lower-echelon morons if the ridiculous dolts appear to be succumbing to my brain-dead test."

"This is an idiotic notion that you're foolishly commanding us to implement," Odysseus complained to the expedition's leader. "Do you think that the fifty-thousand soldiers in our landing party will facetiously obey your silly intent and stay on the battlefield, risking their lives fighting against the rabid Trojans?"

"Odysseus is absolutely right!" Nestor chimed-in. "Your plan, Lord Agamemnon, is evidently more fucked-up than the fucked-up gods on Mt. Olympus are!"

"Do as I command, for although the dumb-ass plan sounds like a dumb-ass plan, the fucked-up scheme had originated from Zeus, who might be a dumb-ass, but whose electric lightning bolts are notorious for cauterizing mortals' assholes so that the afflicted victims die because they can no longer shit or fart!"

Agamemnon then climbed to the top of a recently reinforced rickety platform and non-persuasively spoke gibberish to his assembled minions. "Achaeans; for nine difficult years we've battled the enemy outside the walls of Troy, and have suffered misery, plagues and persistent heartache. I know that you dumb-shits miss your bratty delinquent kids along with your sex-starved wives' stinking vaginas. The riggings and hulls of our ships are slowly rotting away, and the Biremes all smell worse than your spouses' pungent pussy holes. Now, we happen to outnumber the Trojans ten-to-one, but please remember; we had to also fight surreptitious sneak attacks from their myriad allies arriving on the battlefield from neighboring cities."

"What the fuck are you saying? What the fuck are you saying?" the fifty-thousand soldiers all amazingly chanted in unison. "Stop speaking nonsense out of your asshole! Stop speaking nonsense out of your asshole!" the irate contingent of exhausted soldiers continued yelling and cursing their leader.

Agamemnon raised his hands to achieve silence, which was finally accomplished after a half-hour of incessant wild protesting. "Men," the King of Mycenae resumed his address. "I do not disparage you! I now ascertain that Zeus has lied to me in my dream, where the villainous immortal has deceitfully promised us victory. Let's euphorically board our awaiting ships, and depart from accursed Troy in defeat."

The Achaeans leaped up and down in joyful celebration, and jubilantly dashed across the arid plain to their respective ships, eagerly scrambling on board their separate Biremes. But Athena, who for sheer mental diversion favored her mortal champion Odysseus, placed courage into the Ithacan king's heart, enough strength to settle-down his rambunctious troops and to encourage the fatigued warriors to not obey Agamemnon's dumb-ass frivolous command.

"Attention, all you goons and loons. Our erudite leader has tested your fidelity to our Greek cause. Stupid-shit assholes, you have failed the challenge by complying with his preposterous orders!" Odysseus admonished his confused troops. "Get back in line, and stop behaving and acting out of line! Your deplorable deportment is both shameful and cowardly!"

And then, Odysseus screamed-up to Agamemnon, still standing atop his rickety platform that was swaying back and forth in the heavy, gusting wind. "Mighty King and Fearless Leader! Your men have forgotten their oath to you and to our absurd mission to not leave these foreign shores until they have plundered Troy, and have raped and screwed at least a dozen gorgeous women each. Men," Odysseus then shouted to the fifty-thousand soldiers. "Wouldn't you like humping and pumping fresh, young pussy rather than returning to your haggard wives with their crotches that smell like rotten tuna? I insist that you dunce-like dimwits remember the prophecy of Calchas, where a tremendous red snake had surfaced from behind the pedophile priest's altar. The slimy reptile slithered up a tall tree, and ravenously swallowed-down eight tiny birds, that weren't swallows, but actually sparrows, I believe. After digesting the eight defenseless chicks, the voracious snake then lurched-out and caught the alarmed mother sparrow, and upon lunging at the panicky wing-flapping bird, devoured the cawing mother, but as a result of the viper's appetite, the venomous red snake, according to Calchas, immediately turned to stone."

"What nincompoop puts credence in such totally bullshit mythology?" a cynical witness named Thersites yelled-out in opposition. "That dumb-fuck story lacks credibility! It's truly the mantra of a born loser! And old fart Agamemnon; you are completely wrong in your fucked-up quarrel with indispensable Achilles, the whole argument being over a dumb-cunt kinky slave girl!"

Odysseus was not deterred by the critical objector's negative comments. "Calchas had told me to interpret those nebulous signs, and I suddenly became inspired to perform some basic analysis. The nine devoured sparrows symbolically indicated our nine years fighting our bitter enemy here outside Troy. The serpent turning to stone indicates that soon, the stone walls of Troy will fall to our fierce onslaught, and despite the petty interference of the Greek gods on either side of the war, the Argives shall prevail and win this fucked-up hostility being fought over Helen, Menelaus's whoring wife!"

The troops, encouraged by Odysseus's plausible explanation of the snake and birds' parable, all yelled in accord: "Yaaa!" and "Hooray!" Their boisterous exclamations were hollered in loud appreciation of the prospect of each soldier screwing at least a dozen hairy slit holes.

"Ha, ha, ha!" Nestor congenially laughed to Ajax. "Odysseus had once told me that existing on his stranger-than-fiction island of Ithaca, there grows a fabulous Cunt Tree Shrine out in the country, that a man's nostrils could smell from miles away!"

"Ha, ha, ha!" the gargantuan Ajax jollily answered the famed philosopher, Nestor of Pylos. "That remarkable Ithacan Cunt Tree out in the country must stink worse than the world's largest rotten fish market. I suspect that the emanating malodor would be so bad that the filthy stench would both attract and 'deter gents' who would be alertly coming to the shrine from all directions! Ha, ha, ha!" Ajax replied.

Nestor suggested that the time was ripe to organize the various clans and tribes into attack groups, and to then prepare for the mighty battle awaiting them. Agamemnon, feeling relieved from not being assassinated by Achilles and his allies, praised Odysseus and Nestor for their wisdom and military strategy.

"Let's have an ox slaughtered, and then wrap its corpulent thighbones in greasy fat. We'll burn a wholly wonderful sacrifice to Almighty Zeus, who, according to tradition, is basically carnivorous, and definitely not an avowed vegetarian. Then, let's have the various, skilled brigade butchers' carve-up the thousand fattened steers that we had stolen in previous raids, and thereafter, we'll excitedly feast on the beasts. And gentleman," Agamemnon continued his exposition. "Make sure that the butchered meat has been pounded correctly, because our sex-deprived butchers have been seen pounding their own meat for lack of accessible pussy."

After feasting and anticipating their forthcoming victory following nine years of frustration, the heralds announced for the fifty-thousand or so remaining troops to muster upon the open plain situated between the narrow sea and Troy. In what later in history became known as a Homeric Catalogue, Agamemnon of Mycenae had brought a hundred ships from Mycenae; Menelaus had led sixty; Nestor of Pylos ninety vessels; Diomedes of Argos eighty Biremes; Idomenus of Crete had amassed eighty ships for the war effort, and Agapenor of Arcadia, where primitive versions of simplistic amusement games had been invented, led an armada of sixty Biremes. Some of the other captains who had navigated their vessels in lesser numbers were Odysseus, twelve ships; the giant Ajax, the detergent king, a dozen also; Tlepolemus of Rhodes, an academic scholar and the son of Hercules, had aggregated nine ships, and delirious Podalirius from Thessaly, who was green in complexion, and according to mythology, had been miraculously born inside a four-foot-long peapod, had assembled thirty vessels.

Of course, because of his ongoing personal dispute and conflict with King Agamemnon, Achilles, proud commander of fifty sea-worthy Biremes, and his famed Myrmidons, who incidentally looked a bit like prehistoric Trachodons, all refrained from participating in the battle preparations just to deliberately spite Agamemnon. The classic story of the acclaimed Achaean assault on the wealthy Asia Minor citadel was about to be finally fought and chronicled. "We shall destroy Troy!" became the

Greeks redundant battle-cry. "We each can't wait to get laid with a dozen hairy-holed Trojan whores!"

Back on Mt. Olympus, unscrupulous Zeus was now temporarily allied with the Trojans, since the king of the gods had promised the alluring sea-nymph Thetis that the Greek army would eventually realize how essential her son Achilles would have been in the ensuing battle, and that Agamemnon was not nearly as intrepid or audacious as the renowned Phthian hero was to winning the Argives' cause.

In the interim, Iris, the irascible Goddess of the Rainbow, and also a dependable disciple and pupil of devious Aphrodite, (who obviously had sided with Prince Paris), upon Aphrodite's insistence, disguised herself as King Priam, who then instructed the Trojan captains to be vigilant and to keep a lookout for the impending Greek siege upon the city.

'Paris must be favored, since the handsome prince had chosen me over Hera and Athena in the fairest of goddesses beauty contest at the wedding of Peleus and Thetis,' Aphrodite imagined and recalled. 'My will and the Trojan cause must ultimately prevail! I have had the upper-hand ever since Eris's golden apple got rolling upon that ancient dance floor! I respect and admire both Eris and Iris's allegiance to my imperial will!'

Chapter 3

"PARIS DUELS MENELAUS"

The impressive battle scene was now set for a spectacular confrontation. The dedicated Trojans and their allies flowed-out of the city's main gates, screaming war cries as the soldiers hustled forward through a dense cloud of dust, all troops dressed in full battle array. King Priam's warriors were loud and clamorous, while on the contrary, the Greek advance was deliberate and methodical, with the silent Argives moving shoulder-to-shoulder in strict military fashion.

Feeling responsible for the tremendous loss of life on both sides, Paris boldly stepped-out and challenged any of the reticent Achaeans to fight him in mano-to-mano combat. Seizing the opportunity, Menelaus, recognizing the abductor of his wife Helen, accepted the fortuitous invitation. But when Prince Paris realized that his forthcoming opponent would be the red-headed King of Sparta, the youth scampered like a frightened rabbit back into the Trojan ranks, where his older brother Hector began berating his cowardly sibling.

"I feel disgraced and ashamed in calling you my brother," Hector adamantly criticized. "Inspired by Aphrodite, you had sailed to Sparta on a prospective good will mission, and soon wound-up abducting King Menelaus' wife. Your grotesque greed has brought-down a perilous wasp nest upon all our heads, including the damned innocent Achaeans. Now Little Brother, you cravenly state that you'll duel with any of the Greeks, and when Menelaus agreed to honor your terms of engagement, you speedily retreat and are gone with the wind into the shadows, as if you were a frightened antelope."

"You're correct in verbally rebuking and hectoring me, Hector," Paris reluctantly admitted. "But Aphrodite had afforded me the enticing gift of love, but regrettably, not that of courage. Right now, Hector; I wish that I had remained a common shepherd boy tending my lambs and sheep out on the non-fruitive plains, and not be acting as the bragging warrior that I have pretended to be!"

"You're scared shitless of Menelaus, aren't you?" Hector asserted to Paris. "If you foolishly duel with the livid King of Sparta, I believe that you'll soon be wasting-away in Diarrheaville! Indeed, Little Brother Paris;

Menelaus will most certainly plaster you! You'll be pounded so brutally hard that you'll think that you're a slab of veal cutlet on a table inside a butcher shop!"

"Please Hector. Show respect for my sensitive ego that has been severely damaged. In all honesty, I feel like a disintegrating snowflake quickly melting-away in the hot sun. What constructive wisdom can you advise besides constantly belittling my vulnerable self-esteem? Why can't you be my substitute high school guidance counselor?"

"Look here, you disoriented juvenile asshole! Your eighty-pound, spastic sister Cassandra has always beaten your' ass in basic arm-wrestling; and numerous times, the nasty bitch has easily pinned your butt to the mat in two out of three falls. And also, everyone residing and gossiping inside Priam's palace secretly knows that Cassandra is a neurotic heroine on heroin!"

"Okay, you win this totally peculiar discussion," Paris conceded. "I'll duel with formidable Menelaus to the death, and in so doing, I hope to end this absurd ancient war and save Troy from utter destruction. Whoever triumphs in the ensuing death struggle, then that victor will get to keep Helen, along with all of her wealth and precious jewels. Then, the soldiers in both armies will put-down their spears and bows, with the Greeks merrily voyaging back to their homeland, and the Trojans re-entering the gates of their city, and hopefully, co-existing in harmonious friendship with the asshole Achaeans. But first, a fight to the death must commence in order to attain such an honorable solution. I want to be a 'victor', Hector, even though my name is Paris!"

Hector then yelled and commanded for his expert battalions to halt from advancing ahead, and in a matter of seconds, Agamemnon hollered similar instructions to the Argives, stating that the troops should cease mechanically marching forward. Hector proudly stood between the two armies and orated directions to both the Greek and Trojan warriors, whose keen ears listened attentively to his specified rules.

"Trojans and Argives!" Hector loudly enunciated. "Paris now officially challenges King Menelaus to wage single combat, even though only Menelaus is presently married. All warriors on both sides should put-down their spears, and other weapons and paraphernalia, while these two pugnacious pugilists desperately fight for Helen and her Spartan gold."

"I'm the afflicted party here, and I accept the adolescent punk's proposal to fight to the death!" red-bearded Menelaus confirmed. "Enough strife has already occurred between our armies over these past nine years! I submit that there will be no compromises during this lethal altercation. After my imminent vanquishing of my callow opponent, let the Greeks peacefully depart from this non-fruitive Troad Plain, accompanied by my purloined-back wife Helen. Now, before the confrontation happens, we should seal the deal by slaughtering a black and blue ewe and a white, rambunctious ram, both of which to sacrifice to all the gods, some of whom favor the Greeks, and others that staunchly support Troy. And I believe that King Priam should arrive and attend the upcoming bout, so that His Imperial Majesty can verify the oath of peace after my swift triumph is easily attained. For, in all sincerity, I am sagacious enough *not* to trust one iota the statements of Priam's two wild and crazy sons!"

The thousands of tanned warriors representing both sides knelt-down, placed their weapons and shields upon the hot sand, and quietly sat upon the dusty plain, hoping that death to either Menelaus or Paris would finally terminate the near decade-long conflict.

* * * * * * * * * * * *

Meanwhile, Queen Hecuba, King Priam's corpulent wife, called Helen over to the palace's high ramparts to witness a "marvelous spectacle". "Look-out onto yonder battlefield, my dear. The soldiers on both sides are getting sand fleas stuck inside their assholes by stupidly sitting upon the hot desert sand. Yes, the men have ceased fighting; have thrust their sharp spears into the dry earth, and the pathetic fools are so moronic that they're leaning on their shields instead of intelligently sitting upon them!"

"Come and join the Queen and me to witness mythology in the making," King Priam beckoned to Helen. "After all; you have caused all of this needless bullshit to occur! You cannot claim irresponsibility for all of the mayhem your lust for Paris has generated!"

"I love you as if you were my biological father, whom I had despised and never either listened-to or cared about!" wily Helen prevaricated. "I wish that my vindictive brother-in-law and my jealous husband had not come here to reclaim me for their own greed, which has been cunningly disguised as being 'glory for all of Greece'."

"My blurry eyes are not quite as sharp as my peepers once were," Priam revealed while squinting his dilated pupils. "I think that my cataracts are bigger than the fabled ones existing at the source of the Nile River over in Egypt, or is it Ethiopia? Anyway, my child, who most-definitely is not my biological child. Inform me; who is that awesome-looking figure on the *far left?* He doesn't look like a political conservative to me!"

"That idiotic antagonist is my husband's bastard brother, King Agamemnon of Mycenae. He is the son of Atreus, who was quite renowned for designing and building magnificent atriums in various Greek palaces. Vindictive Agamemnon is the elected leader of the Argive expedition to retrieve me and my face, that has launched a thousand ships to Troy, organized to conduct me back to Sparta. Oh, King Priam. I absolutely love living my dream in fabulous luxury here inside your opulent palace, and I totally despise my former nightmare Spartan existence!"

"Pardon my rather impulsive histrionics, Helen. King Agamemnon commands the greatest army ever assembled in history, er, I mean 'in mythology'," Priam declared and clarified. "I've noticed that the Argive captains are all standing erect and not crouched-down, squatting in the hot sand. And who is that portly, psychotic fellow standing next to Agamemnon. He looks as strong as a beastly ox, and as dumb as one, also."

"Don't allow first appearances to deceive you," Helen mildly reprimanded elderly Priam. "That hero you're referring-to is the inimitable Odysseus of Ithaca, son of Laertes. No one on either side can match his genius at practicing shrewd trickery and clever military strategy!"

"And who is that five-hundred-pound giant who towers over everyone else?" astonished Priam asked. "The very imposing ogre looks more powerful than a white tornado! He's probably here to do some ethnic cleansing!"

"That humongous individual is Ajax, who the roads scholars on Rhodes plan to model a colossal statue after, which after being financed by means of exorbitant taxes, will become one of the Seven Wonders of the Ancient World. And standing beside Ajax is famous Idiomeneus of Crete, who metaphorically speaks jabberwocky, mostly mumbled and stuttered in dumb-ass cliches. However, I do not see among the Greek captains my brother Castor, who had perfected manufacturing a certain type of oil, and his twin, Polydeuces, who liked to play poker with the number two cards being wild!" Helen elaborated. "According to recent palace scuttlebutt, I now sadly understand that both of my mentally deficient brothers, who in real life were actual called by others 'mothers', are now the exclusive properties of morbid King Hades and Queen Persephone, with both my brothers now dual disconsolate and miserable spirits mutually residing in dark and dismal Hades!"

The conversation between King Priam and Helen was suddenly interrupted when a gay messenger arrived and announced in a high-pitched voice that Prince Hector desired a black ewe and a white ram to be religiously sacrificed to appease the gods before a specially scheduled duel was to transpire. "Prince Paris and King Menelaus will soon wage hand-to-hand combat. The sought-after prize will be Helen along with her gold and jewels' fortune. And after the contest's victor is determined, the Greeks promise to leave in peace, regardless of the outcome," the staccato-voiced courier divulged.

Priam hobbled out of the palace and was soon escorted onto the Troad Plain battlefield in a well-designed miniature chariot. The Trojan King somberly presented the black ewe and the white ram to grim-faced Agamemnon, who swiftly used his dagger to cut tufts of fleece from the designated animals in order to distribute the sacred wool among his captains. Then, the Ruler of Mycenae orated a short speech to further inspire, perspiring and revenge-minded Menelaus.

"Father Goose, er, I meant to say, Zeus," Agamemnon reflexively corrected his faulty pronunciation. "And also, Lord Poseidon, Lord Hades, and all of you other mercurial-minded Mt. Olympus gods. I hereby request that you very bored deities stay out of this lengthy conflict, despite the fact that many of you have already taken sides. If Paris luckily kills Menelaus, allow the juvenile delinquent to retain possession of Helen, along with her incomparable wealth, and then we melancholy Greeks will dejectedly sail back to our native cities. But if Menelaus plasters Paris and sends the puny punk's skinny ass down to Hades, the Trojans will be obligated to surrender Helen and her fantastic gold as just compensation to my brother, the King of Sparta, and also to my avaricious self. And so, you two royal Trojan dumb-dicks, namely Priam and Hector, you'll both have to invent a new method of birth control in order to rebuild your city's largely-diminished fortune."

The throats of the sacrificial animals were then viciously slit, and the finest of wines was mixed with the ram and ewe blood, and quickly poured-out to pay homage to the generally apathetic Mt. Olympus gods. Every Greek warrior solemnly prayed for Menelaus's victory, to be followed by *their* safe voyage back home.

Priam, in a raspy tone of utterance, then spoke as loudly as the old fart could to aggrieved Agamemnon. "Eminent King; I must take my leave from this impending assassination of my wimpy son. Although I'm not a carnivorous ursa, I cannot bear to witness my dear scrawny and feckless son

Paris die from extensive body mutilation. I'm certain that the gods already know my doomed son's fate and ultimate destiny."

Hector and Odysseus stepped forward and began measuring-out the square perimeter of the proposed (and highly-anticipated) duel. "The inside area of the square must be around one fourth of a hectare," Hector confidently communicated to Odysseus. "And according to my general knowledge of mathematics, there are approximately two and a half acres in a hectare."

"Hector, cut the lousy bullshit!" Odysseus explicitly chided his Trojan adversary. "If Menelaus kicks Paris in his tiny testicles, your younger brother will already be sporting two acres! Ha, ha, ha!"

After the perimeter had been officially established, Odysseus placed two non-building lots inside his bronze helmet to determine which dueler would be the first to hurl his spear at his opponent. Paris's lot was chosen and removed, and the sorrowed Prince discernibly mumbled, "What a lot of fucked-up horse-crap this whole scenario is! I'm in a lot of trouble, and worst of all, being on this raunchy battlefield every day and night, I haven't even yet had the chance to pump the poop out of Helen! Thanks a lot! I can't even get marmalade, let alone get laid!"

The pair of combatants stood a mere fifty-feet apart, and soon, impulsive Paris awkwardly tossed his bronze spear at Menelaus's chest, and the sharp weapon merely deflected off the Greek king's shield, and after the weak carom, harmlessly fell upon the desert plain.

And to Prince Paris's great apprehension, Menelaus frightfully yelled-up to the cloud-laden sky, "Father Zeus! Grant me total revenge upon this skinny wimp who has egregiously wronged me. Let his death be interpreted as a strong message to all of today's witnesses that such a fate as being brutally killed is what awaits any warrior who maliciously betrays another!"

The King of Sparta quickly and accurately hurled his sharp spear at Prince Paris, with the razor-like projectile speeding toward his foe as if it had been a lethal javelin tossed by Hercules himself. The airborne weapon penetrated Paris's sturdy shield, and the abominable tip more-than-grazed the prince's abdomen. The force of the impact immediately knocked the Trojan heir to the sandy ground, and immediately, Menelaus grabbed the hanks of hair extending out from Paris's helmet, and the enraged Spartan proceeded to drag his disgraced victim around the half-hectare outlined perimeter that had been carefully drawn by Odysseus and Hector.

But feeling compelled to intercede on her hero's behalf, beautiful-but-invisible Aphrodite mystically appeared upon the scene and cut Paris's helmet strap, so that her favorite Trojan could continue breathing. And then, the coy Goddess of Beauty enshrouded and enveloped her favored royal Trojan in a dense mist, which hid the prince's form from everyone's scrutiny, while saying to her admired Beauty Contest judge, "Dear Paris; I give you inspiration to inhale so that your respiration will not expire! I shall now mysteriously conduct your lily-white ass to a neutral place of safety, where you, my beloved handsome champion, will adequately recover from your exceptionally bad battlefield encounter!"

"Where the fuck did my craven opponent go?" astounded Menelaus shrieked to the earless heavens. "This whole fucked-up ordeal involving gutless Paris is positively insane! His appearance in this abbreviated duel has resulted in an incredibly dumb-ass, abrupt, magical disappearance!"

Again, employing her supernatural ability, gorgeous Aphrodite miraculously transported Paris to his palace bedchamber and meticulously cleaned the sweat and grime from is entire body, focusing mostly upon his tiny testicles, and also the fatigued prince's limp pussy-plunger. After comforting and caressing her unconscious hero, the devious goddess, disguised as a common palace maid, gracefully flew like a majestic eagle out of the bedroom's open window, and glided over the palace ramparts to visit bewildered Helen.

"Come, Helen of Troy. Paris's privates require your immediate presence inside his private bedroom. His once-abused body is again fresh and fair, but the prince's erratic emotions need immediate solace and comfort. And who the hell knows? Perhaps some perverted pre-marital sex is about to occur?"

'How in the world did Paris ever zoom into the palace after being wounded on the plain by Menelaus?" Helen wanted to know. "I know that the prince sometimes flies off the handle, but he's never before mysteriously flown into his own palace bedroom!"

"Your esoteric wisdom marvelously transcends your splendid beauty!" Aphrodite facetiously complimented and commended Helen. "You are indeed a credit to all of Troy!"

"Holy divine deity shit!" Helen wildly exclaimed. "Ah! Now I understand. You are famed Goddess Aphrodite in wonderful disguise. Why don't you, er, I mean, why *do* you seduce me? Haven't you administered sufficient pain to Paris, to all of Troy, and also to myself? If you love Paris so much, I believe that you should experience inferior sex with him, instead of him having poor sex with me!"

"Do not refuse my generous assistance, ungrateful mortal bitch!" insulted Aphrodite promptly and effectively chastised Helen. "If you ungratefully refuse my liberal favors, then Paris, Hector, Priam, Hecuba and all the combined Trojans and Achaeans alike will be exposed to extreme, powerful hatred coming from all directions, and I emphatically predict Helen, that your dim future will also transform into a very grim one!"

Chapter 4

"THE BATTLEFIELD"

"Lord Zeus, thank you for calling this emergency meeting of the gods," Phoebus Apollo commended. "What particular issues and concerns are presently dominating your superior mind? Are you running out of your supply of thunder and lightning?"

"On the contrary, Apollo," Zeus smugly replied. "I have more lightning bolts at my disposal than you have silver arrows accumulated in your secret personal arsenal. But I do want to review some matters in regard to those pesky mortals meandering-around down on the Earth. As you know, archer god," Zeus stressed, "it is a dumb-ass law of Olympus that once humans acquire a certain knowledge or a particular skill, then the gods are supposed to allow the dimwits to keep their acquisition, without receiving or suffering any major consequences."

"True," Apollo readily confirmed. "But for instance, Almighty Zeus, if mortals ever accidentally discovered the nature and location of nectar and ambrosia, then they too could obtain immortality, and eventually, after developing moderate science and technology, the mischievous race could rival our current dominance over them!"

"Husband, I believe that you are too paranoid worrying about those weak humans down on Earth having a violent rebellion against you," Hera accused Zeus. "And I think that you're afraid that the mortals will someday overthrow you, just like you had an insolent insurrection against your Titan father, Lord Cronus. Do you concur with my assessment?"

'Yes, dear wife. And I've punished Cronus along with his Titan cronies by banishing the whole rebellious group to the dismal black pit of Tartarus, located in the most dark and gruesome center of Hades. My brother Hades and Queen Persephone have made sure that their Titan captives are permanently secured with enormous shackles and chains."

"And just look how you had penalized poor, good-hearted Prometheus," Hera accused and indicted her spouse. "Just because the compassionate Titan felt sorry for the humans living in caves during the winter and had taught the mortals how to make and keep fire, you felt it necessary to severely disciple empathetic Prometheus for all eternity."

"I had tolerated Prometheus after I conducted my usurping of my father Cronus and allowed the Titan to stay here living atop Mt. Olympus. But Prometheus had violated my supreme will by giving mortals vital knowledge that could be used to manufacture metal weapons," Zeus argued. "Now the do-gooder fool is chained to the top of Mt. Etna over in Sicily, where two squawking eagles persistently claw and peck away at his injured heart and tender testicles."

"And don't forget your ongoing quarrel with the Titan Atlas," Hera reminded her volatile-minded husband. "He had been penalized by your verdict to perpetually hold-up the sky from collapsing onto the Earth!"

"Atlas has to be diverted from entertaining a rebellion against me by performing his eternal labor, my wife, so that the temperamental Titan doesn't get any wild ideas about having the other Titans also revolt, with their plan being to again rule the sky along with the entire planet. But now, dear Hera, I would like to change the subject of discussion to what's going on among the Greeks on the nearby shores of Troy!"

"Please be more specific and hurry-up your speech," Apollo assertively butted-in. "Pretty soon I need to get my golden chariot and my four immortal white horses ready to pull the sun across the bright blue sky."

"Gods of Olympus, and I especially mean you, Athena," Zeus commenced, acknowledging the principal reason for convening his special council session. "I've recently been eavesdropping on strange conversations between Odysseus and his five illiterate lieutenants, and I want you other deities to listen-in on their current ass-backwards communications. Just watch my newly installed monitor screen placed by Hephaestus on the side marble wall, and fathom the hilarious full extent of these dumb assholes' oddball comedy dialogue."

"What the hell happened to Prince Paris?" Odysseus forcefully asked his five subordinate lieutenants. "I'm initially asking you, my first-in-line Eurshiddenme. Did the royal Trojan punk apply vanishing cream to his entire body? We all were witnessing and enjoying that King Menelaus was assiduously kicking the Trojan prince's butt really good when all of a sudden, the young loon amazingly disappeared into either thick or thin air!"

"Well, Captain Odysseus," Eurshiddenme replied. "I must state that I've often turned our ship's stern directly into the wind, but I never ever had the Bireme disappear inside the swirling gusts. It seems that Prince Paris had just mysteriously evaporated, like a mystifying vapor trace, integrating right into the atmosphere around him. Maybe the royal Trojan dimwit had been absorbed by a low-drifting cloud."

"What do you think about this conundrum now being discussed, Eurballsourout, my very intelligent second-in command. Do you have any revolutionary theories to explain this confounded disappearing mystery?"

"Well, Captain Odysseus," Eurballsourout uttered. "I truly believe that some sort of divine intervention had incidentally occurred during our' peculiar observation. Perhaps Lord Zeus was performing a demented magic act, but instead of a white rabbit, needed a new available human, namely Prince Paris, to pull out of a high silk hat."

"You're shittin' me?" Odysseus bellowed.

"No, Captain Odysseus. I'm Eurballsourout; the guy standing and farting over to your right is Eurshiddenme!"

"Your balls are not out," the fourth mate Eurdicisin observed and commented to Eurballsourout. "Let's not get testicle, or, I meant to say 'technical'. Perhaps our fifth mate Eurcockisnum has a better answer to contribute to this discussion than I can," Eurdicisin suggested.

"Look, Lard-butt; Eurcockisnum thinks with his dick and not with his dysfunctional cerebrum," Odysseus aptly indicated to Eurdicisin. "Why should I make any inquiry to a dumb-dick like pecker-headed Eurcockisnum?"

"Captain Odysseus," Eurcockisnum ejaculated. "Don't be so hard-on me! How am I ever expected to rise to the occasion?"

"You five dumb-fucks need to become transsexuals and grow inflated tits and massive pink vaginas," Odysseus screamed and commented, "so that after this bizarre Trojan War terminates, my other crew members can enjoy some semi-normal sex instead of perpetual day-and-night, up-the-ass sodomy. When are you' uneducated Danaan jerk-offs ever going to learn that you can't defy the natural laws of biology. An asshole is an exit, and not a friggin entrancing 'entrance!"

"What's wrong with a little up-the-ass pleasurable sodomy?" astute Eurassisgras challenged his four nutcase companions. "I mean, every once in a while, since we're so far from our native Ithaca, I say that we ought to have a little homo-sweet-homo!"

"The ship's doctor has told me that you need more fertilizer up your anus," Odysseus angrily interrupted, "because I think that a cluster of nasty weeds are growing where your ass-like hairs should be showing as artificial turf!" the incensed Ithacan King sarcastically scolded his third mate, Eurassisgras.

"Now fellow deities," Almighty Zeus imperatively stated as the god of thunder and lightning waved his left hand, and successfully canceled-out the

Achaean images off the screen of his visual monitor. "I believe that we immortal gods have nothing to fear or worry about in regard to these earthly nincompoops ever having any organized insurrection successfully waged against us! Lord Apollo. We Mt. Olympus residents have nothing to apologize for to these incompetent, imbecilic Greeks!"

"You're precisely right on target, Lord Zeus," arrow-shooter Apollo praised. "We don't have to worry one scintilla about the inferior human race, simply because the zany dolts are morally corrupt, but more importantly, those defective mortals are, beyond a doubt, mentally retarded."

"As you all well-know," Zeus replied, "I wish to remain neutral in the escalating conflict between the Argives and the city of Troy, as does my brother Hades, who also doesn't give a pregnant fart about who wins the monotonous war, just so that many warriors will die on both sides to populate Hades' underground Kingdom of the Dead. I'm also aware that my daughter Athena; my wife Hera; my brother Poseidon; the blacksmith Hephaestus, and my trusty messenger Hermes have all sided with the Agamemnon and the Greeks. And Aphrodite; Artemis; Ares, and you, Apollo, have sided with Prince Paris and the Trojans. Without objection, and with nothing further scheduled on my short agenda, I'd like to call this meeting to adjourn until there are new developments in the dull and boring Trojan War. Everyone is now free to leave, except Athena, with whom I would like to confidentially confer for a brief-but-constructive exchange of essential ideas."

Zeus privately revealed to Pallas Athene that the Ruler of Olympus was fully aware that Aphrodite had wholeheartedly committed her personal assistance to helping Paris and the Trojans to gain the advantage of soundly defeating the Argives, but then the chief god disclosed to his daughter that he wished to remain neutral, even though Zeus had an inclination to support Thetis's Achilles in his obstinate power-struggle quarrel with Agamemnon. "It's a good thing, Athena, that your Greeks don't have a lot of donkeys in their' camp, or else, your favored Argives might just get their asses kicked!"

"Father, this is no time for merriment or for amateur comedy hour," Athena rebuked. "If I am your favorite goddess who you revere even more than your spouse Hera, then I need your loving allegiance more than ever."

"Dear Athena; allow me to get serious for a moment. I feel that Helen should nostalgically return to Sparta and reunite with Menelaus, so that peace can once again prevail throughout both Troy and Greece. I could almost guarantee that King Priam and Agamemnon would each be satisfied with such a viable solution being implemented."

"Father, I've labored so hard in organizing the Danaans' armada of a thousand ships, and now you want to spoil my great enterprise by arranging a truce," Athene futilely argued. "As your omniscient mind already knows, I positively love the Greek cause, and my heart especially favors my splendid hero, Odysseus of Ithaca. If Troy is salvaged from destruction, and if the citadel in the future flourishes and prospers, then all of my industrious input in defense of the Argives will have been done in vain. Please don't spoil my great achievement!"

"The Trojans have always obediently and fearfully worshipped me," Zeus impatiently explained to his independent-minded daughter. "And their sincere sacrifices paying homage to me have been most respectful and satisfactory. At this juncture in time, I'm thinking about favoring Priam, Paris and Hector in their noble cause, and being objective, my mood is presently opposed to *your* spite for Paris pilfering Helen away from Sparta. However, precious daughter. I don't want to see a dangerous wedge materialize that would separate you from me. To reinforce our long-standing sentimental bond, I shall see that the in-progress war vacillates back and forth like mercury moving around a person's palm, as one manipulates his or her hand."

"Thank you, father," the fair goddess of wisdom professed. "Sparta, Argos and Mycenae are indeed my favorite cities, so if you decide to exercise your notorious wrath upon any of those places, I shall sadly endorse your wrongful decision. For I know that you'll stubbornly enact whatever whim enters your obstinate head, since you're the most potent and fickle-minded immortal up here on Mt. Olympus. In the end, I love and admire your omnipotent existence, and I maintain that you and I should not quarrel in a parallel manner that corresponds to what Greece and Troy are currently disputing and fighting. Do you agree with my general assessment?"

"Your devotion has encouraged me to endorse any stealthy trickery that your conniving loyalty to your hero Odysseus and the Danaans will engender. Go now Athena, and fly down to Earth and initiate any down to Earth policy that your sly mind can produce. For instance, if you desire for the Trojans to break the present truce, then my dear, you have my expressed permission to aggressively go for it!"

Pallas Athene gratefully thanked her dominant father for his vote of confidence, and in a matter of seconds, expeditiously zoomed-down from

Olympus, and soon zipped over to the plains of Troy in order to implement her new-found, devious strategy. The determined goddess's intended target was accessible Pandarus, a highly-skilled Trojan archer, who before the war, was an award-winning baker of delicious wheat and rye bread, and also, a producer of quality doughnuts, pies and bagels.

'Listen to me, Pandarus,' Athena's power of suggestion whispered into the famed archer's subconscious mind. 'This dream is of paramount importance to establish your high place in contemporary mythology. Now Pandarus, you can easily attain historic fame and fortune if you could deftly utilize your bow and arrow ability to instantly kill Menelaus of Sparta. Please recall that your trusty bow had been hewed from an ibex's four-foot-long horns, taken from the beast that you had hunted up in the Greek mountains. Now, audacious Pandarus; first off, you need to devoutly pray for imminent success to Phoebus Apollo, so that your' humble solicitation can obtain the courage for your name to go-down in the anals, er, I mean, the annals of history!'

'I could expertly shoot an arrow through a doughnut or a bagel with my incomparable bow and easily eliminate Menelaus without ever using-up any of my more lethal, poisonous arrows,' Pandarus's influenced brain creatively imagined.

After Pandarus made the recommended and appropriate sacrifice to Apollo, who incidentally favored the Trojan cause, in imitation of impish Cupid, the former baker-turned-archer drew back his bow and let the old arrow fly, straight toward the vulnerable navel of Menelaus. Using her natural guile inherited from Zeus himself, Athena surreptitiously guided and diverted the shot arrow into the targeted king's thick leather belt, with the sharp tip only slightly wounding Menelaus; the arrow's penetration merely gouging his abdominal flesh.

As Menelaus was lying upon the ground experiencing non-life-threatening-pain, vigilant King Agamemnon, witnessing the suspicious result of the surprise ambush, rushed to his brother's aid. "The tentative truce has been shattered, Menelaus. I'll bet you dollars-to-doughnuts that *that* villainous Pandarus has wounded you. Brother, I don't hardly understand how all of this happy horseshit has ever happened. Your intestines have been grazed and your damaged navel has sunken-inside your lower stomach. Now brother, here's the riddle that I can't completely comprehend," Agamemnon stated. "When shepherds graze their rams and lambs in a pasture, the sheep do not bleed from their grazing. How serious is your bleeding? I'll summon a herald to get our best surgeon, Machaon, to seal your wound."

"Don't worry a cunt hair, Agamemnon," Menelaus insisted. "A bagel or a sea gull shot from Pandarus's infamous bow would've created more bodily injury than that flimsy errant arrow had done! In the final analysis, I suppose that I have been most fortunate. No vital internal organs have been hit, not even my scrotum, my colon, or even my semi-colon!"

Feeling desperation and emotional panic, Agamemnon frenetically yelled to the Greek forces his patented *alarm:* "All to arms! All to arms!" the frustrated Greek leader reiterated. "Menelaus has almost been made into an invalid! But this invalid invalid lying superficially wounded upon the desert sand will quickly recover, rise to the occasion, and join us in battle! If we kill more than a thousand Trojans during this engagement, then King Menelaus will administer quality fellatio to each and every one of you!"

The two armies quickly assembled into their standard, customary ranks, and slowly advanced towards each other's straight (and gay) infantry lines. Soon, the roar of loud, hysterical shouting, along with delirious screaming, was discerned by human ears a full mile away as heavy metal swords clanked, and bronze shields experienced terrible continuous impacts. Warriors on both sides met their ultimate fates, and their released spirits were swiftly conducted-down to shadowy Hades.

Various soldiers attempted to claim the bodies of fallen comrades, but during their valiant pursuits, those brave troops also became indiscriminate victims in the ongoing dual massacres. A horrendous, macabre and hideous-looking site had evolved. The entire battlefield was terribly strewn with blood-soaked Trojan and Greek corpses.

During the massive imbroglio, the incomparable giant Ajax slayed brothers Antiphus and Antifa, both fucked-up bastard sons of King Priam. And then, intrepid Odysseus of Ithaca, showing plenty of 'spear-it', hurled his sharp projectile at Democoonis, son of Racoonis, with the javelin immediately striking-down the pusillanimous-but-bellicose son-of-a-bitch. Symbolically, during the raucous and clamorous military encounter, the Trojans were buoyed by interference from Apollo and Ares, and conversely, the Greeks were provided adequate encouragement, inspiration, and required stamina from sympathetic Pallas Athene.

Jay Dubya

Chapter 5
"DIOMEDES BECOMES AGGRESSIVE"

"May the unpredictable gods acknowledge my urgent plea. When I get my sweet revenge on that son-of-a-harlot Pandarus," infuriated Agamemnon promised his aching and bleeding brother who was lying upon the hot desert sand, "the perverted bastard will be breathing out of his ears, will be pissing out of his nostrils, and will be shitting out of his new-found Z-shaped dingle. And Menelaus, I'll have my personal medic rub a healing sea-bass against your gory wound, because the injury appears to be only a super*fish*ial gash!"

The Achaeans were gaining the initiative and pushed the Trojan forces back towards their towering citadel. Showing diversity in an ancient age of conformity, Athena soon chose for attaining glory Diomedes as her special hero of the day. Diomedes instantly embarked on a killing rampage, slaughtering high-ranking Trojan military personnel along with their contingent bodyguards. But then, the expert archer Pandarus spotted emboldened Diomedes riding in a chariot that was not on fire; the baker-turned archer took aim with his ibex bow, and the marksman shot an arrow that hit his enemy target's thick leather shoulder pad.

"Sthenelus, er, I'm sorry," Diomedes corrected himself. "Stenny; please pull-out that toxic arrow from my shoulder guard. "Then I'll elicit Athena's help in paying back that furtive Pandarus for mildly scratching the surface of my right shoulder. I'm gonna' make sure that *that* former dough-rolling, bagel-baker will never again be able to munch on any delectable female muffin!"

Pallas Athene heard Diomedes's beckoning and promised her new-found champion to grant the selected Greek warrior deserved revenge on Pandarus. "You'll be able to distinguish me from the remainder of the interfering gods, particularly my foremost rival, Aphrodite. But I caution you, Diomedes; avoid wounding any of the immortals with the exception of my main family opponent, namely Aphrodite, who Prince Paris had frivolously chosen over me as the winning contestant in a past beauty contest."

The surging attacks, led by chariot-riding Diomedes were ferocious, as the archer's accurate arrows downed several dozen additional Trojan lieutenants, among the group Astynous, Hypeiron, Hyperbolla, Xanthus, Thoon, Typhoon, Eurydamas, Euradumass, Chromius, Echemmon, and the always-overzealous Trojan officer who had a bad case of psoriasis, Itchentogo.

Aeneas, a spoiled sissy rumored to be a favorite of Trojan-biased Aphrodite, appealed to Pandarus in a non-sexual way. "Quick famed archer; say a fast prayer to Zeus and then aim your arrow at that insane bastard Diomedes, who is massacring a slew of our baby-faced infantry officers. Don't aim to please, but instead, aim to kill!"

"Some god or goddess, probably Pallas Athene, is apparently inspiring that son-of-a-bitch Diomedes to go berserk. I've already hit him once," Pandarus bitched, "but my dart seemed to change course on a windless day, veering from the scumbag's chest over to his shoulder guard. I won't be able to send the troublesome jerk-off down to Hades until I get a worthy chariot to best engage my fanatical foe; my imaginary chariot should have two stellar white horses that perfectly match Diomedes' black stallions."

"Pandarus, forget about piercing Diomedes in the breadbasket," Aeneas weirdly yelled back. "Here, now; stop loafing around; hop aboard my chariot that is pulled by my marvelous white horses that had been bred by Tros. If I had a third equine to hitch to my chariot, we could have a friggin' Tros-fecta going-on here!"

But observant Agamemnon alertly noticed Pandarus boarding the fantastic Trojan chariot with Aeneas being the driver, and the vengeful King of Mycenae simultaneously briefed Diomedes of the most-recent battlefield development. "Great warrior. I know my mythology inside and out. Here comes Pandarus as a passenger upon Anus's, er, I mean Aeneas's chariot. A popular myth has it that *that* youthful driver happens to be the son of the goddess of beauty, unrivaled Aphrodite!"

Diomedes clambered-aboard Agamemnon's stationary chariot. "If I get lucky and kill both Pandarus and Aeneas," Diomedes hollered-over to the King of Mycenae, also standing on *his* chariot's platform, "then hop-off and collar the two white horses that were bred in Sicily. I'd like for us plundering Greeks to possess and own that exotic pair of magnificent Italian stallions!"

Pandarus, whose wife had given birth to a baker's dozen bratty kids with another one already in the oven, came-up with one of his half-baked ideas. The Trojan archer was the first to draw his bow and shoot, but his on-target arrow penetrated the shield of Diomedes, and only scratched the Greek hero's right forearm. But then the Danaan warrior, selectively favored by

Athena, tossed his bronze spear at Pandarus. The lethal projectile pierced through the Trojan's helmet's facial flap, and the tip severely impacted his nostrils, brutally separating the victim's sinus cavities, as an immense amount blood and snot squirted-out of Pandarus's already deviated septum.

Aeneas, seeing Pandarus's blood-soaked corpse prone and motionless upon the desert plain, leaped from his stationary chariot and dashed toward Diomedes, who immediately lifted a nearby jagged boulder and flung the huge rock, as if it were a pebble, at Aeneas's vulnerable stomach. The Trojan prince buckled-over in pain; Aeneas's hip socket had been violently shattered, and the valiant warrior fell to his knees, incessantly groaning and moaning in excruciating pain.

Aeneas was about to succumb to death and have his spirit become the custody of King Hades and Queen Persephone down in the dank Kingdom of the Dead, but Aphrodite appeared upon the scene, and first protected Aeneas with a shielding mist, and then prepared to transport the wounded combatant to a place of safety where his broken hip could be administered advanced medical aid.

Not seeing Aphrodite rendering supernatural assistance to her wounded son, Diomedes flung a second spear at Aeneas to make certain that the valiant Trojan had truly perished. But amazingly, the Greek's toss hit invisible Aphrodite in the lower thigh, just above the right knee, and Ichor, the perfumed blood of the immortals, came squirting-out as if the goddess's punctured right leg were a fractured fountain. Aphrodite hobbled-off, holding her wounded knee.

"And then, with Aphrodite being injured, Apollo, another ally of King Priam and Troy, appeared on the battlefield to rescue ailing Aeneas, but maniacal Diomedes lunged his spear at the chariot/sun god, whose voice boomed at the Argive aggressor, "Back-off, you dumb-ass, puny mortal! Are you insane enough to actually think that your meager bronze spear can best an Olympus god at the fine art of death-struggle survival?"

Without any hesitation, Phoebus Apollo carried Aeneas off to the lofty heights of Pergamus, and there, Artemis, the famed goddess of hunting, volunteered to heal and reconstruct the afflicted Trojan's disintegrated hip.

Ares, nasty-tempered Greek god of war, showed-up and quickly aligned with Apollo. The duo combined their talents and caused an ominous gloom to settle over the dusty battlefield, and their collaboration also inspired Hector to lead a savage charge in the direction of the Achaean front lines.

While the wild assault led by Hector was occurring, Sthenelus was confiscating the resplendent white horses that had pulled Aeneas's chariot.

"Well done, Stenny," Diomedes sincerely commended his dependable comrade. "Yes, Stenny; well done in*steed!*"

Meanwhile, oddball Odysseus, accompanied by his five lieutenants, Eurshiddenme, Eurballsourout, Eurassisgras, Eurdicisin, along with Eurcockisnum, heinously slaughtered thirteen Trojan officers who were brandishing and wielding bronze swords in their immediate vicinity. "It's a good thing you dick is in," Odysseus said to exhausted Eurdicisin. "Or else, your erect wiener would never be able slide into a female bun, ever again! And also, Eurballsourout; you're lucky that your scrotum sac wasn't sacked, and that your tiny Greek meatballs weren't cruelly castrated! I mean, your annoying soprano voice right now is bad enough!"

Athena, appearing inside Zeus's marble temple situated atop Mt. Olympus, requested a favor from her sometimes more-than-tolerant father. "Great Lord of Thunder and Lightning; I'd like to enter the exciting fray on the Trojan plain and perform what I've always desired doing, kicking Ares' lard ass black and blue."

"Be my guest and pursue your pleasure, Daughter Athena," Zeus smiled and then laughed. "Kick his obnoxious ass good, but not with both feet at the same time! That quarrelsome war-monger has caused me more than a century's worth of accumulated grief and misery!"

In the interim, Hera, who like Athena, favored the Greeks over the Trojans, entered the combat zone. The wife of Zeus said to Diomedes, "Greek warrior: are you a wimpy coward, or what? You have retreated from the battle as relentless Hector attacks your inexperienced, baby-faced infantry."

"My sage intuition recognizes you as Hera, goddess wife of Great Zeus," replied Diomedes. "I do not shirk my military duty. I should not attack either Ares or Apollo, because Athena had instructed me that I should only aim my arrows at her bitter rival, Aphrodite, promiscuous wife of Hephaestus, the ugly, lame blacksmith god, who manufactures all of the bronze equipment for the fickle Olympus deities to utilize."

"Then if you have any virile sperm left in your testicles," Hera asserted to Diomedes, "you'll join me in a dual duel with Hector and my major nemesis, Ares! Now get your craven ass upon Aeneas's chariot, and in pursuit of liberated woman's equality, I'll do the damned driving!"

While Hera was erratically and wildly bumping along, holding the reins of the Trojan chariot, her partner, Pallas Athene, cloaked herself from Ares' scrutiny, and the goddess found the god of war stripping-away the armor and breastplate from a deceased Trojan general. Without any warning,

Athena thrust her spear into the gut of Ares, and Ichor oozed from the hollowed-out gash.

Instinctively, tattle-tale Ares flew-up to Olympus to register a verbal grievance against Athena, whom Zeus so often favored.

"Ares, you fucked-up, trouble-making crybaby," the king god austerely admonished. "All the fuck you ever do is make mortals quarrel and wage combat against one another. In short, you demented ignoramus, I have no degree of sympathy for your present physical suffering, or for your current emotional anguish. Court surgeon, come hither. I command you to heal this imbecile's wound so that this feckless asshole can go-down to Earth and promote additional dissension among the just-as-stupid humans!"

"Why do you favor Athena over me?" Ares insisted on knowing. "Do you prefer females over males? Are you' prejudiced against me? Are you some kind of weirdo heterosexual?"

"Listen to basic truth, Ares," Zeus demanded. "Even though we gods of Olympus are immortal, don't underestimate these cantankerous human vermin. The inferior race must always fear our power, and should never be able to challenge our authority. As you have just learned on the battlefield, you are *not* invincible, and can be injured. Whether a mortal can actually kill a god, well, that possibility remains to be seen. Nectar and ambrosia just make us immortal, but those ingredients cannot protect either you or me from being either wounded or assassinated! Much of our supremacy over mortals is assumed by both us and them."

Feeling relieved that Ares had been at least temporarily sidelined, Athena and Hera, relishing their recent battlefield accomplishments, returned to the comforts and luxuries of Mt. Olympus, leaving the rest of the day's impending events to the maneuvers of the fatigued Greek and Trojan armies.

Chapter 6
"HECTOR AND ANDROMACHE"

With Ares sulking and sobbing inside Zeus's Mt. Olympus temple, Diomedes led a military phalanx that pushed the Trojans back towards the gates of Troy, with the stench of rotting corpses permeating the air around their' strategic maneuver. Hector was worried that the gods were turning against his army, so Priam's son told his commander Helenus to first rally the troops, and then sprint into the city to instruct his mother Hecuba to make rich sacrifices to appease Athena, which might consequently stifle the coordinated Greek onslaught led by inspired Diomedes, who in reality, was imitating and substituting for absent Achilles.

"Intrepid Trojans!" Helenus shouted. "Show your strong mettle along with your heavy metal! Defend your city as if it were your girlfriend's hairy pink pussy hole!"

Carrying his armor and a small hammer, Hector dashed into Troy, and immediately, the renowned hero was swarmed by concerned women requesting news about the fates of husbands, uncles, cousins, brothers, sons, kindergarten kids, and great-great-grandfathers. Fleeing from the raucous mob of information seekers, Hector sped past King Priam's white castle's closed window, which had a large overhead painted sign, featuring hot dogs and hamburger images, that explicitly read: "War Is No Picnic!"

The enormous palace contained a variety of fifty-seven bedrooms for Priam's impotent sons and their respective wives, and across the expansive courtyard, there had been built thirteen "honeymoon honey-well bedchambers" for Priam and Hecuba's dozen promiscuous daughters and their sex-driven cheating husbands.

"My precious son, what brings you to the palace?" Hecuba cried. "Is it true that the insane Achaeans have mastered weather control and are about to storm the city walls? This is no time for sour grapes or for tart tarts! Let my servants find you some sweet wine to specially offer as a libation and tribute to Zeus!"

"Bring me no wine, mother, because the liquid would only soften and weaken my knees like blueberry buckle. And just observe how dusty and dirty I am from continuous fighting out yonder on the Troad Plain. Zeus and his family will be offended if I were to offer impure sacrifices with my skin and body being so unclean that not even the Greek white tornado giant Ajax cold cleanse my hide."

"When then, Hector. What assistance could I do to help you?" Queen Hecuba wondered and asked. "I'm too friggin' old, wrinkled and fat to perform a striptease inside the palace temple, or do a private-audience naked lap-dance to entertain Zeus, Ares, or Apollo!"

"Here's what you should do," problem-solving Hector stated. "First pray to Pallas Athene inside the palace temple. Then, have your most reliable servants sacrifice twelve hefty virgin heifers; that is, female cows, and not corpulent lard-ass teenagers, on the temple's recently-altered altar. Hopefully, your sincere act will give the Trojan army a respite from ruthless Diomedes and his barbarian minions."

Hecuba gathered her two finest scented robes and carried the garments to the palace temple, where she met the Old Ladies Civic Club of Troy members, and led the former hot prostitutes in prayers to Athena, which was followed by cremating the dozen hefty heifers to Athena in the temple's brick pizza oven. But unfortunately, for Hecuba, the goddess's heart was in harmony with the enemy Achaeans, and the well-intended sacrifices were completely ignored by the contemporary Mt. Olympus powers-that-be.

In the meantime, Hector made it his mission to visit his younger brother Paris's room, where the Trojan commander's initial impulse was to reprimand his cowardly sibling for embarrassing Troy in his recent, overmatched duel with incensed Menelaus.

"Paris; you hide and sob inside your room, grieving about your obvious incompetence, while your loyal peers are on the plain doing combat against the dastardly Danaans," Hector vehemently scolded. "You have humiliated your city, and your family, you craven, pusillanimous pussy! If you had a clitoris above your ass slit instead of your tiny dingle, I'll wager that Helen's clit would be much larger than yours! Even larger than both your diminutive testicles and your miniature pecker put together!"

Helen, curiously eavesdropping on the verbal harangue, entered the bedchamber and pleaded to Hector to cease browbeating Paris. "Stay inside the palace with Paris and me," the estranged wife of Menelaus begged. "You must be exhausted and weary. I don't blame you for despising and resenting me being here in Troy. If you want to learn the truth, I regret ever being born, and I wish that I could be thrown off the highest mountain peak, or be drowned in the deepest sea. But most of all, Hector, I wish that I could have both love and power, but with your brother Paris being a feckless wimp, I might as well shave my golden beaver and throw all of my precious gold coins, along with all of my soft blonde pubes, into the palace temple's flaming brick pizza oven!"

"War is hell, Helen," Hector heckled and hectored. "So, I must abandon my craven brother, and also you, his problematic hussy, and now my desire prefers reuniting with my faithful wife, Andromache."

Soon thereafter, Andromache affectionately greeted her militant husband, and showered the Trojan General with abundant hugs, kisses and crotch-grabs. "Oh, my wild and savage husband. Our son now sleeps inside his cradle, but before long, I dread that he will be fatherless, and that I will be spouseless! Oh, Hector! When you are gone forever, both I and your helpless infant son will have no one around to protect us!"

'My only hope is that baby Scamandrius will not turn-out to be a scam artist just like all of the other males on your side of the family," Hector angrily remarked. "It figures that you'd like me to stand on top of the city wall, above the large fig tree, where the Greeks have attacked three times, attempting to climb said fig tree, which is not a fake figment of my fig tree imagination. But please clarify certain relevant facts, Andromache. You and your name are of Greek origin, I believe, growing-up in Thebe, just below Troy."

"Yes, my strong, muscular husband. The city was founded by Hercules, and was named after the place where the Greek hero had been raised, the original Achaean city of Thebes. Because of my upbringing, I know quite a lot about Greek culture and history."

"You're shittin' me, aren't you Andromache?"

"No, Hector. I'm not shittin' you. As you should know, Eurshiddenme is a lieutenant under the command of the Greek champion, Odysseus of Ithaca! Oh, what the heck, Hector. I'll tell you everything you want to learn!"

"Well, wife; we are aware that the Greeks are here after Helen's gold, and that Menelaus is here after his wife's golden beaver, but kindly describe for me the hereafter in Greek religious belief."

"If you insist, Hector; here is what academic knowledge I can share. The ancient Greeks loved music as much as they loved adventure, lesbians, vacationing on the Isle of Lesbos, and wild unlimited sex orgies. When the famed Achaean musician Orpheus sang, trees would extend their boughs downward and shade the handsome lad from the sun, because the wandering minstrel was a damned albino with milk-white skin. The poison ivy' vines often reached-out their tendrils in response to Orpheus's majestic music, and everybody in the vicinity that already had venereal diseases didn't like the notion of doing additional skin scratching, so the worried area residents very discreetly stayed out of the forests, ponds, streams, marshes, marketplaces and swamps."

"So far, your revelations sound a lot like a shit-load of ethnocentric bull-crap!" Hector cynically criticized. "I hope that your rendition improves as your fragile explanation progresses."

"May I continue enlightening you?" Andromache politely rebutted. "When Orpheus sang and played his sensational tunes upon the lyre, rocks would rumble and tumble-down mountainsides, causing widespread devastation to nearby villages and outhouses. Wild beasts skulked-around low to the ground, because the dumb-ass creatures simply felt like continually pissing and shitting, and woodland gods would stop masturbating and screwing each other up the yazoo, just to benignly listen to the boy wonder's glorious, enchanting music."

"Those woodland creatures sound a lot similar to the fucked-up Greeks we're now fighting," Hector interrupted. "I trust that your lackluster story will get better as it evolves."

"Well, Hector. Orpheus *madly* loved a gorgeous girl named Eurydice, who had inspired the minstrel to go beyond 'madly', straight-on to 'insane', and then on to totally 'crazy' rap lyrics. The musician's creative powers to organize imaginative love songs had originated from *his* passionate longing to lose his disgusting virginity and pump the excessive poop out of Eurydice's eager beaver. All nature celebrated with the 'mythology period bard' on his wedding day, but unfortunately, Eurydice didn't want to get laid or have her swollen box munched, because the moody bitch was starting her own lousy bloody *period* cycle during the aforementioned 'mythology period'. What a lousy bummer!"

"The minstrel's girlfriend was having her menstrual cycle," Hector laughed. "Now your mediocre tale is most definitely getting somewhere!"

"Just listen to this next part," Andromache urged. "On the morning of the wedding ceremony, no pedophile priest arrived to officiate, because religion had not yet been invented in ancient Greece. Disappointed by no priest showing-up, and pissed-off because she was having her monthly period, Eurydice ambled-down to the riverside to have lesbian sex with her equally pissed-off bridal attendants. The despondent girls' gathered bunches of flowers to shove-down the throat of the first Greek priest to ever show-up, and then the bridesmaids were prepared to choke the sanctimonious son-of-a-bitch if and when the reputed pedophile should ever come around to their village after the eventual establishment of religion."

"So, what happened next?" Hector hypothesized and curiously asked. "Don't keep my fascination in suspense!"

"Unfortunately, Eurydice was suddenly bitten in the foot by a huge, poisonous snake, and her totally shocked maidens instantly became frightfully snake-bitten themselves, and then quickly serpentined their' exit the hell away from the river before the foul, venomous viper reloaded its fangs for a second more-lethal attack."

"Sounds like the bitches didn't enjoy playing with reptiles!" Hector stupidly joked. "The dumb-ass lesbian broads probably would also run-away from an erect fadorkenbender, too!"

"Allow me to tell you more," Andromache diplomatically objected. "Orpheus became quite despondent when the minstrel heard the bad news about Eurydice, and the horny adolescent was so extremely pissed-off that he couldn't get a hard-on with which to jerk-off, no matter how hard he tried. His somber songs were now very sad, and reflected *his* totally disconsolate disposition, and all of the wild male forest beasts got pissed-off too, because suddenly, they could no longer lick each other's long dicks, and also, the aroused creatures couldn't get laid either after vainly attempting to achieve even weak erections. 'Go to Hades you dumb stupid bastard!' the pissed-off animals all repeatedly yelled at Orpheus, no matter where he roamed."

"I'm getting pissed-off just listening to your fucked-up story," Hector butted-in. "But I've always believed that it's much better to be pissed-off than to be pissed-on! Ha, ha, ha!"

"Will you please let me resume my tale," Andromache somewhat-courteously retorted. "Now then; the rather-depressed Greek minstrel picked-up his lyre and made his way to the wide cave that led-down to eerie Hades; yes, the Greek underworld, where as you already might know, ancient gangsters and mobsters hung-out after the ill-tempered scoundrels had died. Orpheus believed that Eurydice's soul had already journeyed-down to bleak Hades, and the young lover theorized that *that* was where her *spirit* could ultimately be found. 'Who the hell wants to have sex with a damned thin, two-dimensional ghost?' Orpheus objectively conjectured. 'Eurydice no longer has a body, and her massive tits are probably now just hollow air bubbles; her ass is probably two noxious farts glued together, and her former hot-wet pussy is probably like a primitive air pump. Who needs this kind of fuckin' illogical shit in their already-troubled life?' Andromache asked."

"And I thought that my unenviable existence here in Troy was miserable," Hector commented to Andromache. "How could this character Orpheus ever screw a two-dimensional ghost, even if the lovestruck asshole ever was lucky enough to find her down there in dark Hades?"

"Anyway, Hector, the melancholy minstrel descended a vast vertical tunnel inside the diagonal cave, and successfully clambered-down a twelve-mile-long rocky subterranean cliff to finally reach the dreadful *River Styx,* which historically separated the land of the living from the morbid kingdom of the dead. Charon, the macabre, hooded, skeleton ferryman monotonously rowed his barge to shore to pick-up his next passenger for transportation across the stranger-than-fiction underground river to bleak and mysterious Hades."

"Did any conversation occur between Charon and Orpheus?" a now-fascinated Hector inquired. "Your tome is actually becoming quite intriguing! Please continue."

"Yes," Andromache tersely answered. 'Hey jerk, ya' gotta' be dead in order to get to the *other side,'* Charon chastised his still-living. mournful guest. 'Ya' just can't look dead, asshole! Ya' gotta' *be* fuckin' dead! Go back to Earth and get assassinated, murdered or eaten by a famished shark or lion. Have you ever fuckin' considered chugging-down either hemlock or arsenic?' Charon suggested."

"But my spirit is dead already, but not my body!" bitterly grieved and argued Orpheus. "So, what's an empty, pitiful mind and body to do?"

"Seeing her husband with his mouth agape, Andromache continued with her extraordinary myth. 'Just hand me a coin to pay for your toll of passage, and then simply commit suicide,' the ghastly, ghostly specter firmly recommended. 'Then you'll officially leave the *sticks,* and I'll take ya' across the *Styx* to some other part of the even more incomprehensible post mortem' *sticks*, ha, ha, ha,'!"

"What did the minstrel say in response?" Hector wanted to know. "Did he develop a case of instant laryngitis?"

Andromache proceeded with uttering her descriptive narrative. "Permanent death?" Orpheus exclaimed. "I'm not ready for that type of esoteric bullshit yet! I just gotta' find-out if I can get my rocks-off with my girlfriend's ghost, and that's all I wish to especially accomplish on this particular expedition."

"That's terrible," Hector concluded and mentioned. "The poor kid hasn't even gotten laid with Eurydice, and now the unlucky dumb-ass doesn't have a ghost of a chance of screwing her flitting two-dimensional specter!"

Smiling at her husband's fairly humorous response, Andromache proceeded with her most-excellent rhetoric. "The *dispirited* musician had to devise a fast solution to effectively remedy his present dilemma. So, the disenchanted minstrel went into his mystic, creative mode and sang a haunting love song that completely mesmerized the heartless barge-rower, Charon. The ferryman felt wonderful ecstasy for the first time in his eternally dismal life, so the skeletal figure voluntarily led Orpheus onto his barge, which would allow the saddened passenger to *barge-in* on the pathetic silent underworld. If the minstrel could enchant the fearful god Hades with his powerful, stirring lyrics, then the singer might be able to retrieve Eurydice's ghost and transport it back up to Earth where the dismal, itinerant spirit could be reunited with its no-longer-active 38-24-36 hourglass figure."

"It sounds as if Eurydice has run out of vital sand inside her temporal hourglass," jested Hector. "I need to hear this pathetic story simply to get my troubled mind away from the fucked-up Achaeans and that dangerous bastard Diomedes."

"Now then, Hector. Cerberus, the three-headed dog that growled ferociously and snapped its jaws and bared its fangs, was steadfastly guarding the narrow portal leading into Hades' interior. The fierce monster was so hypnotized by Orpheus's song that the awesome beast cowered-down like a puppy, and then the mutt was so thrilled by his newly-discovered blithe nature that Cerberus began wildly using all three heads to lick its erect dick, and then did the same to Charon's *boner*, giving the ferryman a pleasurable 'triple *head*er'."

"But what about the inconsolable minstrel," Hector wondered and asked. "Did the soprano punk suddenly become impotent with erectile dysfunction? Did Orpheus acquire a choir down there in Hades?"

"As Orpheus entered the dismal, dank, gloomy world of Hades, pale, spooky ghosts crowded and flitted-around the apprehensive hero, with all of the attracted shades being wholly captivated by his beautiful song. The visitor's extraordinary voice resounded throughout the myriad caverns and stagnant marshes, artificially giving the appearance of life to the formerly silent and ominous fucked-up place."

"Managing all of those deceased souls must have been a huge undertaking for Lord Hades and Queen Persephone to supervise," Hector contributed. "Your compelling story makes me glad to be alive and fighting the crazy Argives."

"The determined musician cautiously stepped into the well-manicured, flowered fields of Elysium. And all of the daffodils, the petunias, the dainty dahlias, and the 'creeping' myrtle that ordinarily gave everyone the creeps leaned towards the sound of the lad's marvelous voice," Andromache orally related. "The suddenly-happy dead danced and frolicked through the colorful floral meadows and shadowy dells, finally experiencing delight and pleasure as part of their' promised eternal reward. The jubilant ghosts held hands, and jumped and pranced around, inadvertently crushing all the beautiful flowers, and giggling incessantly, while acting like a billion ludicrous faggots and gay-spirited lesbians."

"Your depiction makes the spirits in Hades seem like the kin of the myriad whores and pimps that frequent the bordellos and brothels in downtown Troy," Hector realized and articulated.

"Then, my dear husband, Orpheus advanced through a shadowy cave and entered the spooky area of atonement where the pathetic, grieving ghosts of dead individuals were posthumously punished for violating the capricious Mt. Olympus gods' supreme laws. Even Sisyphus, who labors for all eternity pushing an enormous rock up a hill, only to have the boulder roll down the incline so that the process would have to be repeated over and over again; the punished fellow's sad spirit stopped his monotonous enterprise to appreciate and enjoy Orpheus's unique song. Sisyphus was so inspired by the marvelous melody that the ghost immediately organized his own underground rhythm band called 'The Rolling Stones and Pebbles', and instantly began mimicking Orpheus's fine example. Even the crackling flames that blazed and flourished in leaping fences of fire in that section of Hades danced around, and soon magically heated-up the whole damned area."

"Your fascinating tale, Andromache, is pretty interesting bullshit heaped on top of pretty interesting bullshit," Hector candidly commended. "I hope I don't ejaculate an explosive orgasm during its exciting climax!"

"Next, my dear husband. Orpheus and his music encroached upon thirsty and hungry Tantalus, who had been eternally punished by having to stand chained inside a pool that was filled chest-high with delicious, cold, fresh water. An abundance of fruits on tree limbs dangled above the hungry and thirsty man's head. When Tantalus was 'tantalized' to drink, the manacled figure would bend-over, and the cool water would rapidly drain out of the tank. When the penalized apparition would reach for a ripe peach, or for a savory apple, the fruit would either disappear or be blown away by a sudden wind gust. The unfortunate ghost was so enraptured and entranced by Orpheus's song that the brain-dead specter ceased performing his eternal sentence, and Tantalus's rejuvenated spirit fondly recalled what it was once like being alive."

"Holy Hades!" Hector exclaimed. "Tantalus, acting in a complete vegetable state, had to experience a totally fruitless posthumous existence!"

"Finally, husband. Orpheus arrived at the stone-cold, black-granite, pillared *Halls of Hades*. The ashen faces of past Greek heroes were sadly sitting at Hades' dark, ebony table. Even King Hades and his pallid-faced Queen Persephone showed rare animation, and began smiling in the direction of the young troubadour, dually acknowledging his wonderful music. The gods' cold hearts knew all misery, and cared not one iota about any of it, but amazingly, Hades and his pale, morbid wife were touched and moved by the magical rhapsody that their dull ears were then wondrously hearing."

"It's too bad that Orpheus wasn't accompanied by a full band of musicians; the minstrel could've orchestrated a wild rebellion down there in subterranean Hades!"

"You haven't lost your deranged sense of humor," admitted Andromache. "At length, Orpheus became fatigued from his difficult descent down into the underworld, and also, the musician had become exhausted from his extensive singing and meandering. The shades of the assembled, swirling ghosts mingled-in with the gentle winds, and at least temporarily, all nature in Hades was one and the same. Then, morbid King Hades frightfully addressed his latest visitor, and the awesome god's deep bass voice reverberated throughout *his* usually silent, cavernous, dark world."

"What did Hades say?" Hector wanted to know. "Did the scary god offer Orpheus an entertainment contract?"

"Hades emphatically said, 'Orpheus. Go back to the sunshine while my monsters are still under the spell of your hypnotic songs. Climb-up the steep vertical tunnel to the warmth of broad daylight, and I promise you, the spirit of Eurydice will follow your' ascent. But there is one caveat to this special arrangement,' Hades austerely warned. 'Whatever you do, don't turn around for verification of my words, and therefore, by doing so, doubting my promise. If you dare to turn around, Eurydice will return down here to the underworld, and your fond hopes will immediately vaporize into utter despair. If you learn to trust and believe my imperial decree, you can have living and breathing Eurydice back as your three-dimensional fiancee'!"

"Did Queen Persephone agree with King Hades' decree?" intrigued Hector asked Andromache. "The pair of deadbeats both sound like royal pain in the asses!"

"Yes, go back Orpheus," Queen Persephone implored from her dark ebony throne. "My crotch is getting wet for the first time in three centuries, and I actually feel like getting laid. Get the hell outa' here and give us some damned privacy! I'm as horny as Hades is right now, and I absolutely need to be pumped and humped like there's no tomorrow, right away!"

"Andromache, was Hades sexually aroused, too?"

"Yes, go back quickly," Hades anxiously concurred. "I'm getting a massive erection, and I think I know exactly what the fuck to do with it! Show me some pink Persephone! I'm headin' right toward the center of your hot juicy love tunnel!"

"Holy shit!" Hector exclaimed to his wife. "Hades and Persephone were ready to have some high-spirited sex!"

"Well, dear husband. Orpheus turned and retreated from the great *Hall of Hades,* and the teeming ghosts separated into two divisions, and made sufficient room for the wanderer to exit. The young minstrel desperately searched on both sides, and in front, for any sign of his lost Eurydice's spirit, but his eyes dared not look behind him in honor of Hades' stern edict. No sounds were discernible anywhere around him, as the talented musician advanced through the major dark rock mineral corridors, moving past Tantalus and Sisyphus, and then through the now-wilting flowers in the Elysian Fields. Soon, the sorrowed lover passed Cerberus's narrow portal, and then stepped assertively onto Charon's barge, which quickly sank-down two feet in reaction to *his* weight being onboard."

"I hope that Orpheus did not go overboard by violating Hades' specific instruction!" Hector gleefully concluded and shared. "I definitely prefer Greek comedies to Greek tragedies!"

"Is Eurydice behind me?" Orpheus asked macabre Charon. "I dare not look and violate Hades' weird prophecy."

"If Orpheus turned around," Hector remarked to his spouse, "then I think I'm going to lose my erection!"

Andromache disregarded her husband's semi-humorous comment and resumed her graphic exposition. "Behind every man, there is a woman!" Charon diplomatically and arcanely answered. "If you are *that* curious, you asinine asshole, why not turn your damned neck around and fuckin' see for yourself if Hades had been bullshitting you?"

"Oh, my Zeus!" Hector yelled. "This dumb-ass story is amazing! I promise not to interrupt you, dear wife. Please tell the remainder of your incredulous tale in its entirety!"

"No thanks!" Orpheus answered in response to a very magnetic temptation that he felt. "You must have virgin ears, Charon, because what woman in her right mind would want to suck on a piece of lousy cartilage dick for the remainder of eternity, or have sex with someone that looks exactly like the fuckin' Grim Reaper's twin brother?"

"Did you feel any additional weight shift the boat's equilibrium after you entered?" Charon replied with a question, enjoying his self-appointed role as an accomplished and sophisticated eternal ball breaker."

"No, but I must value Hades' promise in spite of your biased sarcasm; your pessimism, and your fucked-up cynicism," Orpheus proudly volleyed.

"Finally, the surreal ferry left Hades' bank, and slowly made it across the dreary *River Styx* to the shadowy opposite shore. The ascension to the upper-world of mortals was an arduous climb that was filled with strange shapes and alien forms floating around inside the tight, chimney-like cavity's tomb-like silence. Orpheus ceased his scaling to listen for any remote sign of his beloved Eurydice, but there was not a trace of a noise, or a hint of an echo of her soft voice. 'Maybe Charon was right and Hades was just bustin' my balls about Eurydice following my ass back up to Earth?' Orpheus suspiciously reckoned. 'I wonder if that miserable bastard is still getting it on with Queen Persephone? Both of those imperial, pallid-faced assholes looked like they needed ten blood transfusions each'."

"Orpheus feared that the God of the Dead had deceived him, and that *he* was alone and isolated between two worlds, but his soul had been belonging to neither one. 'What if I climb-up to the bright sunlight, turn around, and Eurydice is not there?' the adventurous minstrel skeptically considered. 'I had fascinated Charon, Cerberus, Sisyphus, Tantalus, Persephone and Hades once with my spellbinding music, but could I repeat those remarkable results with a second daring expedition into the underworld? Maybe I have lost Eurydice with my naïve eagerness to believe any and all bullshit from men and from gods?' the mirthless singer lamented. 'Gee; I wonder if Hades has enough blood to sustain an erection for a full century? I wonder if the diabolical prick has any blood at all'?"

"With every step upward, my dear husband, the befuddled hero took while carefully ascending the precarious precipices, Orpheus became more and more dubious of Hades' promise. The climber diligently labored-up the last treacherous stretch with his sad heart laden with doubt and despair. The darkness soon converted into a grayish mist, indicating that the weary minstrel had finally advanced close to the Earth's surface. The air was cleaner and more breathe-able, and as Orpheus inhaled the fresh oxygen, his brain realized that the entrance to the dreary, huge cavern was just ahead. Still, the musician's beleaguered mind questioned Hades' veracity."

"Now, Hector," Andromache continued her narrative. "Orpheus could not bear his heavy emotional burden any longer. Acting on impulse, in the ominous, nebulous light that belonged to neither the Land of the Living nor the Land of the Dead, the confused trekker veered-around, and his eyes beheld a thin misty shade at his rear, and quickly, the indistinct female specter with the beautiful face loudly cried, 'You really fucked yourself over this time, you stupid, dumb-dicked, virgin asshole'!"

"Orpheus frantically cried-out 'Eurydice!' But the faint female specter soon hazily crystallized, and then evaporated into nothingness. A slight echo of 'Farewell Orpheus' resonated throughout the deep, dark, vertical tunnel directly below his shaky feet."

"The disconsolate lover quickly gathered his sensibilities and hurried back-down the now-familiar, steep path which he had just laboriously ascended. The depressed lover's efforts were greatly thwarted by his extreme apathy, and by his overwhelming sorrow. This second time, Charon was deaf to the singer's prayerful voice, which lacked the innocence, and the romantic quality, of its first authentic presentation to the unhappy inhabitants of Hades."

"Stop trespassing where you aren't supposed to go," Charon warned in a bellicose tone of voice. "You must have a death wish, but if you want to achieve your fatal dream, you must honor tradition and go back to Earth and commit suicide like I had originally advised you to do."

"Shove your rotten oar all the way up your' stinkin' bony ass!" Orpheus angrily replied. "How in Hades do you manage to get into your house? With a goddamned skeleton key?"

"Fuck-off, you jerk-off mortal!" Charon vehemently yelled. "You should have more respect for the custodians of the dead!"

"Go home and work your skinny-dicked boner!" Orpheus screamed like a demented maniac. "Instead of white semen, you must shoot out pink marrow from your bony dick, if you aren't already impotent!"

"Finally, dear husband; Orpheus tried duplicating the original beauty of his song, but eventually acknowledged that his meaningless endeavor was a total failure. For a whole week, the glum singer sat upon the dismal banks of the bleak river, watching Charon transport doomed souls to their final resting places in Hades' black kingdom. The pathetic wailing of the morose *River Styx* canceled-out any cheerful love song that the depressed singer could muster. The swirling ghosts also ignored Orpheus's entreaties, and the frustrated musician finally realized that his sad intonations no longer had any tangible effect on his completely apathetic, inhospitable, now-alien, wretched environment."

"I guess I really pissed-away my one and only chance of reuniting with Eurydice," Orpheus sobbed and regretted. "I'm so dejected that I feel like slicing my balls off!"

"Disgusted and defeated, Orpheus rose from his sitting position and then trudged and stumbled up along the dark, steep path which he then knew so well. When the frustrated youth eventually arrived back to Earth, all bedraggled and begrimed, his lyrics and voice sounded both pitiful and hopeful. Orpheus could tolerate human company no longer, and the irate musician chased people away when the area natives came around to hear his exceptionally haunting melodies, along with sad love themes, that he kept *harping* on the lyre."

"In the end, the disillusioned lover met his ultimate demise. Women of Thrace were angered at Orpheus's refusal to play upbeat romantic melodies for them, so out of sheer contempt, the scornful bitches attacked, molested and attempted to rape the young man. And when he couldn't achieve an adequate erection, the crazy females choked and killed the unfortunate minstrel by shoving unsanitary sanitary napkins down his parched throat. Legends maintain that as the body of Orpheus smashed against jagged rocks in the *River Hebrus's* many rapids, the musician's waxen, dead lips faintly uttered 'Eurydice' all the way down to the *River Styx.*"

"Did Orpheus's spirit ever get to reunite with the ghost of Eurydice?" Hector asked Andromache.

"In the daffodil meadows of Elysium, Orpheus's specter met-up with the ghost of Eurydice, and since Orpheus no longer had a three-dimensional pecker, his shade used a daffodil stem as a vagina-insertion-device, which soon became known all throughout Hades as a 'daffy-dildo'! And where the main path in the complicated underworld network becomes particularly narrow, Orpheus's apparition goes first into the unexplored tunnel, and thereafter, his flat form admiringly looks back, and then beckons the spirit of its one true love, Eurydice."

"What a great myth!" Prince Hector enthusiastically congratulated Andromache. "It almost makes me wish that I was an Achaean!"

Just then, baby Scamandrius began crying in his cradle, which was hanging and suspended from a half-broken olive tree bough protruding through his bedroom window.

"I hope that that our little whimpering wiener doesn't grow-up to become a freakin' hot dog like his wimpy Uncle Paris!" Hector snickered. "I wouldn't relish such a grotesque development happening one iota!"

Andromache handed the screaming baby to Hector, and Scamandrius shrieked even louder at being transferred from parent to parent, obviously frightened by his father's war helmet.

"Don't be distressed by the symbolism of impending future calamity," Hector imperatively related. "No Greek enemy can kill me before fate determines that my time of demise has come. And Scamandrius must think that my bronze helmet must be one of those bizarre goo-goo or zombie dolls sold in the downtown marketplace."

At that moment, helmeted Paris came hustling into the upstairs palace living quarters, wearing his battle helmet and carrying his spear and shield. "Brother; am I too late or slow to resume participating in the battle? I feel rejuvenated and ready to engage in combat. Let's get our act together and make the scene!"

"Paris, you are a paris-site in both general appearance and demeanor," Hector intensely chided. "I can't find fault with the speed of your legs, but your Trojan will to fight and triumph are evidently lacking. It seems that you have the dream, but not the drive, in order to sufficiently survive vicious combat. The warriors in our camp often mention your condemned name in absolute contempt. It's up to your determination to salvage your reputation and to redeem our glorious family name. Let's now return to the all-too-familiar Troad battlefield, and dually experience what whimsical fate has in store for us!"

Chapter 7

"HECTOR AND AJAX DUEL"

Emboldened with a desire to cancel-out his cowardice while again dueling with Menelaus, Prince Paris killed the Achaean lieutenant Menesthius, while *his* older brother Hector killed Etonius, who did not have a severe case of meningitis like Menesthius, brother of Buenosthius, did. As the latest battle raged upon the Troad Non-Fruitive Plain, Athena, on her daily route to lofty Mt. Olympus, peered-down and noticed that the warfare was swaying in favor of the more-motivated Trojans. In her haste, the gliding goddess nearly collided in mid-air with Phoebus Apollo, whose perceptive eyes were also focusing upon the killings being administered and led by Hector and Paris.

"Are you arriving near Priam's city to help the Argives pursuit of destroying Troy?" Apollo asked rival Pallas Athene while both were hovering above an active volcano. "Listen to my infallible rhetoric, Daughter of Zeus. We both need a brief vacation from this dumb-shit war nonsense. Let's temporarily forget our separate allegiances and cooperate in stopping the conflict for today. We can each seek satisfying our daily boredom, and again enjoy maneuvering our Greek and Trojan pawns upon our gameboards tomorrow!"

"Very well, bachelor, hen-pecked, chicken god," Pallas Athene chided. "Are you planning first licking some succulent female breasts and thighs, and then screwing some unfortunate mortal beauty queen? In terms of abandoning your Trojan loyalty and responsibility for one mere day, do you desire to leave it to beaver, or what?" Athena asked. "But honestly, Apollo. I also need a twenty-four-hour requiem from this nerve-racking war bullshit. I mean, like yourself with the Greeks, I'm getting tired of breaking Trojan men's balls and deflating Trojan woman's tits! Now then, addled archer god; what duplicitous trick does your miniature mind cunningly propose?"

"Yes, immortal virgin chick," Apollo replied. "I'll casually zoom-down to the battlefield and whisper some suggestive instructions into Hector's infected left ear, pretending that I'm the idiot's wimpy brother, Paris. I just love implementing this oddball impersonation foolishness on the gullible Trojans, who have the bodies of muscular weightlifters, and the minds of little toddlers! The only pleasure *we* have in escaping eternal monotony is by causing friction and conflict in the lives of those totally fucked-up Greeks and Trojans!"

And so, being influenced by Apollo's imitation of Paris's staccato voice, Hector yelled for the Trojan forces to cease their deliberate advance and to heed *his* plausible suggestion, which was to be offered to both ready-to-fight armies.

"Listen to me, Achaeans and Trojans," Hector screamed from his chariot platform. "Zeus had arbitrarily decided to not allow our current truce to prevail. So, to avert thousands of more good warriors from being slain, I propose an alternative solution. I will fight any Achaean to the death, and whoever wins *that* struggle for personal glory, the victor will claim the armor of the deceased, and his fallen corpse will be properly prepared for burial by the loser's pedophile priest. Now, who amongst you weakling Danaans will come forward and challenge me, Prince Hector of Troy, to single combat?"

Silence reigned supreme among the shocked Achaean ranks. Worried Agamemnon commanded that the major Greek captains confer and figure-out which warrior would valorously confront Hector in the proposed imminent duel. While that important captains' consultation was occurring, Odysseus's five psychopath lieutenants were engaged exchanging irrelevant gibberish in their own dumb-ass sidebar conference.

"I'll bet that Ajax is just as strong as the legendary Hercules," Eurdicisin opined to his four knuckleheaded, psycho-case companions. "When Ajax finishes with Hector, that is if Ajax is selected to represent us Greeks and kicks the arrogant prince's rear end, the Trojan heir won't know his huge aching asshole from the volcanic crater on top of Mt. Etna!"

"Old Nestor told me yesterday that he had had several past adventures with mighty Hercules," Eurshiddenme confidentially disclosed to his four peers. "And then the old fart from Pylos described to me in detail the acclaimed Theban hero's fantastic Twelve Labors. Listen Eurdicisin; I'll now tell you about those Twelve Labors of yore."

"What the hell are you talking about?" Eurdicisin defensively challenged Eurshiddenme. *"My* Twelve Labors? I have no fuckin' Twelve Labors. Hercules is the one who had the twelve difficult tasks to perform."

"You stupid-fuck!" Eurshiddenme screamed at Eurdicisin, violently shaking his clenched fist. "By the Twelve Labors of *yore,* I did not mean *your* non-existent twelve labors! I had meant the damned, historic Twelve Labors of Hercules!"

"Forget slumbering on the night desert sand, Eurshiddenme! Instead, tonight go and fuckin' sleep on a gigantic, shriveled-up apri*cot!*" exasperated and neurotic Eurdicisin defiantly countered his prime nemesis.

Unfazed by Eurdicisin's insolent demeanor, Eurshiddenme attempted to educate his apathetic audience of four concerning the fabled Twelve Labors of Hercules.

"King Eurystheus of Mycenae had assigned Hercules the task of performing twelve super-arduous labors in order to atone for his alleged egregious misdeeds," Eurshiddenme prefaced his narrative. "In his initial assignment, Hercules' first choked to death the vicious Lion of Nemea, the carcass of which the legendary champion immediately returned to King Eurystheus to keep as a coveted souvenir."

"Eurshiddenme, you aren't lyin' one smidgeon about that ferocious lion," Eurassisgras eagerly confirmed. "That cowardly King Eurystheus could never develop courage if he wore a dozen lion's skins during a wicked blizzard. I've heard where the royal moron has two ovaries for testicles!"

"The second superhuman task was to travel to a place called Lerna to kill the nine-headed Hydra that terrorized anyone who accidentally came close to its native swamp," Eurshiddenme continued his dull depiction while ignoring Eurassisgras's general lunacy. "Whenever a head of the dangerous Hydra was chopped-off, another one would instantly grow back in its place. But then Hercules seared-off each of the nine necks with a burning brand, so that the heads eventually could not sprout-out again. It was a pretty ingenious solution for a brawny guy like Hercules to creatively solve such a challenging dilemma, ha, ha, ha! Hercules had invented the surgical art of cauterizing! Ha, ha, ha!"

"Wow!" Eurcockisnum exclaimed. "Hercules had branded his reputation by cleverly branding the nine-headed Hydra! I'll bet that old Herc used the poisonous blood oozing-out of the writhing beast's nine headless necks to invent hydra-chloric acid!"

Showing rare admirable intelligence, Eurdshiddenme also wisely ignored Eurcockisnum's faulty conjecture and proceeded with his fairly informative account. "The third obligation to be enacted by Hercules was capturing a wild stag that had been sacred to the hunting goddess Artemis."

"Was the hart on its way to a stag party?" Eurballsourout uttered and laughed, much to florid-faced Eurshiddenme's utter chagrin. "I'll bet that good old Hercules had to hang-on to those antlers for *deer* life!"

Eurshiddenme pretended that Eurballsourout's outrageous words had been spoken on another planet. "The fourth detail was for Hercules to kill a great boar, and the fifth command was to clean the filthy stables of Augeas that contained thousands of ill-tempered horses and cattle possessing very loose bowels. What a nasty, smelly mess *that* terrible environment must've been! Hercules imaginatively used his great strength to change the course of two rivers, making the separate diversions flood right through the stables as if the smelly barns were common sieves."

"That wild fierce boar sounds just as unstable as the temperamental horses and cattle that Hercules had evacuated from their confined enclosures," Eurassisgras contributed to the rather zany dialogue. "It also sounds like the stables of Augeas had been drastically influenced by the coincidental confluence of the two rivers!"

"And the sixth demanding labor was to chase away a flock of huge predatory, carnivorous birds using *his* trusty bow and arrow. Say, guys! These unique labors are not only funny, they're quite interesting, too!"

"I feel like breaking your two legs so that you can do sit-down comedy on stage at King Priam's Palace," Eurcockisnum replied to almost-livid Eurshiddenme, and then the fucked-up lieutenant loudly guffawed. "I'm really happy to learn that Hercules was able to get the flock out of there!"

"The seventh mandatory labor was that Hercules had to journey to Crete and capture King Minos's legendary monster, the gigantic sharp-horned Minotaur, and then put the wild beast on an immense boat and transport it to King Eurystheus' palace back in Mycenae, which is now Agamemnon's bailiwick."

"It sounds like King Eurystheus is the real cretin who belongs living with the other asshole Cretans on Crete," Eurballsourout zanily remarked, amusing his three other lieutenant colleagues. "But I'm happy that Hercules had utilized a con-Crete solution to trap and deliver the formidable Minotaur."

"The eighth labor of Hercules was to kill Eurystheus' principal enemy and to disperse *his* rival's hostile man-eating stallions out of their stables. And the ninth tough labor was to steal and bring back the girdle of the Amazon Queen, Hippolyta, which the very renowned Greek hero had scrupulously accomplished using both charm and guile."

"Did daring Hercules also steal Queen Hippolyta's bra, dildo, and sanitary napkins, too!" Eurcockisnum further harassed Eurshiddenme, testing the speaker's tolerance limit. "Did Hercules give naked Hippolyta to old fart Nestor, so that the former Amazon Queen could perform nude lap-dancing at hoary Nestor's world-famous whorehouse!"

Getting extraordinarily peeved, Eurshiddenme decided it was time to conclude his recollection of the Twelve Labors of Hercules as divulged to him by the gaseous old geezer, Nestor of Pylos. "Look, junior jerk-offs! I don't need any exacerbation to my exasperation by your nitwit collaboration and corroboration! These wonderful fantasy stories, or should I say, 'extraordinary myths' that I'm expertly relating, are indeed absolutely intriguing," Eurshiddenme maintained to his zestful, don't-give-a-shit fellow officers. "Ancient people probably were totally bored with the mundane difficulties of everyday life, so the creative mortals invented this crazy, outrageous fiction, making-up what we today call mythology, in order to entertain and inspire the happy campers around campfires."

"Hurry-up with the last three labors," Eurballsourout insisted. "I have to take a huge dump, and I feel like my throbbing asshole is pregnant with triplets!"

"Okay, Eurballsourout. Don't shit your exposed balls off while your asshole is blasting-out volumes of insufferable diarrhea! Now then, the tenth major job was for Hercules to bring back the cattle of Geryon, and in the process, the exceptional hero formed the Pillars of Hercules, now Gibraltar (then Calpe) in Southern Spain, and Abyla in Northern Africa, with the wine-dark Mediterranean Sea flowing between the two landmark rock masses directly into the Atlantic Ocean."

"We're glad to know that Hercules finally got into the flow of things by skillfully using his giant rocks," amused Eurcockisnum expressed and then chortled. "And with the cattle of Geryon, it was lucky that Hercules had possessed a certain herd mentality!"

"In Hercules' eleventh labor, the amazing hulk had to retrieve and bring back the Three Golden Apples of the Hesperides, and also briefly had to hold-up the sky for the very demanding Titan known as Atlas, who had volunteered to obtain the rare golden apples from the north African magic tree. That's why those famed mountains are called the Atlas Range."

"What?" Eurdicisin euphorically exclaimed. "Hercules was the first official bandit in history who had invented the crime of hold-up! Ha, ha, ha!"

Eurshiddenme was then fully pissed-off, but chose to finish what Nestor had recently told him. "Finally, you four dipshits; Hercules had courageously trekked-down to Hades for the purpose of releasing the champion Theseus from the Chair of Forgetfulness, and as part of his assignment, the hero next single-handedly captured and brought the savage three-headed dog Cerberus up from Hades, and then proudly carried the vicious cur directly to King Eurystheus in Mycenae."

Before Eurshiddenme could vigorously punch his four dumb-ass listeners in their hyperactive jaws, the conference that Agamemnon had organized with his captains came-up with a plausible method to answer Hector's challenge of man-to-man combat to save thousands of lives on both sides.

"This is quite a thrilling match-up; a lethal white tornado against a killer black monsoon!"Eurshiddenme announced. "I'll tell you four imbeciles this terrific wager idea of mine. If Ajax wins, I get to receive three blowjobs from each of you. But in Hector wins, I'm lick each of your smelly assholes twice, for five minutes each time!"

"Why don't you suggest the same fucked-up, non-nostalgic notion to King Odysseus?" Eurballsourout boldly answered Eurshiddenme. "Our mercurial-minded boss will make you fart your liver right out of *your shittin' me* asshole!"

Old fart Nestor inserted the various colored stone lots into King Agamemnon's helmet, shook them up inside, and the first one to exit was that of the Great Ajax.

"I'm anxious to eliminate Hector from this sacred soil!" Ajax shouted with his raised right hand. "Now all Achaean warriors on the non-fruitive desert plain should pray to Zeus for my swift victory. For the glory of Greece, I shall prevail! Achilles may be sulking inside his distant Bireme, but the Trojans will soon know that we have many equally-deadly soldiers within our ranks."

The pair of combat champions approached each other as their respective armies stood in separate lines at a short distance. Tension was mounting as the anxious spectators anticipated the upcoming brawl.

Meanwhile, the pair of combatants slowly encountered each other upon the sandy Troad Plain. "Hector, I will make your hemorrhoids wish that they were asteroids," Ajax bellowed above the massive cheering being yelled by both opposing armies. "When I get done with you, you won't know your ass from your little-boy kid knees! Ha, ha, ha!"

"Let's not bandy silly words!" Hector firmly screamed back. "Ready yourself, Ajax, to go-down like a five-pound turd during one of your easier dumps. I shall throw my spear at you to commence the contest!"

Ajax's massive shield had been made of seven thick bull's hides, and an eighth innermost layer had been composed of dense bronze. The giant's defense had miraculously stifled the penetration of Hector's toss, and then, the Trojan's dependable shield had absorbed Ajax's speedy javelin fling. Each combatant pried loose their opponent's spears from their own shields and together, the pair wildly charged at one another. During the loud collision, the Achaean's spear (really Hector's spear) drove through the top of the Trojan's shield, grazing the warrior's exposed neck.

With blood trickling from his neck onto his hairy chest, Hector reached-down, picked-up a large rock, and threw the object at Ajax's stomach, but the heavy item merely bounced-off the giant's muscular frame. But then, in imitation of his illustrious opponent, with one hand Ajax lifted a hundred-pound-rock from the desert floor and hurled the circular sphere into Hector's bronze breastplate, sending the injured Trojan Prince flying onto the arid Troad Plain.

Seeing the ferocity of the ongoing clash, heralds from both sides dashed between the two participants. Trojan old coot Idaeus, gasping for air, and also seriously afflicted with dementia, nervously offered one of his better ideas.

"Ajax and Hector; it is obvious that Almighty Zeus loves both of you along with your mutual courage and your shared integrity. It is advisable that, since dusk is rapidly descending, that fighting between you two killers should be suspended for at least a day."

"Idaeus's idea is right," the anonymous Greek herald concurred with the Trojan old codger emissary. "Put your swords and spears away, to live to fight another day!"

The two awesome army representatives agreed to a temporary truce as recommended by the mentally-deficient emissaries. As tokens of honor and dignity, Ajax and Hector, according to established tradition, exchanged appropriate gifts. Hector gave his capable foe his treasured silver-studded sword, and Ajax gifted Hector his purple-dyed, putrid-smelling, stinking, sweaty loin-guard.

Both armies brandished their raised swords and screamed approval of the battlefield bartering, and Agamemnon arranged a massive feast to celebrate Ajax's fighting ability, and a similar event was simultaneously sponsored by King Priam to praise Prince Hector's heroism.

At Ajax's banquet, Nestor rose and addressed the principal Greek military brass. "Fellow Achaeans. I propose a temporary truce for both sides to clear the battlefield of the hundreds of warriors whose stench-laden corpses are rotting upon the red-stained desert. Let us allow sufficient time for the Greeks and the Trojans to gather their dead for proper cremation on recently-assembled funeral pyres, for the hungry buzzards are swooping-down and scavenging human flesh, which horribly violates both Achaean and Trojan religious culture."

With Agamemnon's consent, Nestor was dispatched to the Trojan camp, and the stuttering courier presented the funeral pyre truce to Hector and Priam, but Paris instantly objected to one of the ancillary conditions.

"I endorse old fogey Nestor's truce idea to mutually bury our dead, but I oppose the provision that I must surrender both Helen's gold and Helen back to Menelaus. I mean, okay, I'm willing to value love over mammon, so let the Greeks have Helen's gold, but I must keep the most beautiful woman in the world as a much-warranted, acceptable compromise."

The two armies agreed on the burial proposition, so funeral personnel gathered rotting bodies from the blood-stained desert sand. However, most of the corpses were so mutilated and maimed that many Trojans were burned upon Greek pyres, and a plethora of Achaeans were cremated upon blazing Trojan funeral pyres.

During the night hours, with Odysseus's guidance and supervision, the conscientious Danaans assiduously labored and constructed a sturdy wall, and an accompanying trench, between *their* vulnerable beach encampment and the distant city of Troy. However, Zeus and Poseidon were displeased that Agamemnon had not asked for or gained *their* permission to commence the fantastic-in-scope building project.

"The invading fools never prayed or sacrificed animals and wine to acquire our blessing to construct yonder wall," aggrieved Poseidon mentioned to Zeus. "That new wall makes the one that Apollo and I had cooperatively designed and built around Troy look like a project conceived by infants and toddlers."

"Why complain your childish grievance to me," Zeus answered his sea-dwelling brother visiting Mt. Olympus. "You have the power to destroy that wall at your own personal discretion, any time you desire. And Lord Poseidon; even though I haven't eaten a morsel of food for simple pleasure in over a week, my bowels are currently in an uproar, just like yours! I think that we both should stop farting-around and polluting the entire atmosphere!"

The interaction among the two gods made Zeus so upset that the Earth-shaker filled the night sky with tremendous thunder and lightning, and the frightening spectacle lasted until dawn the following morning.

Chapter 8
"THE GODS DON'T PARTICIPATE"

"Why are we clandestinely meeting fifty-feet underground in the horizontal secret LBGTQRMSV meeting cavern?" Eurballsourout wondered and asked his main shipmate Eurshiddenme. "If King Odysseus finds out, he'll suspect that we're gay faggots and have us demoted to lowly infantry status. Then we'll liable to be executed at sunrise by either the Trojans or our own Greeks!"

"Because, brain-dead asshole; it's my theory that the gods are greedy bastards and bitches who have definitely implemented a conspiracy against mortals," Eurshiddenme explained to his four dunce-like colleagues. "Their sinister method is rather simple and rudimentary. If Zeus and his family fear that the human race has the potential to overthrow their control over Heaven and Earth", Eurshiddenme lectured, "just like the Olympus gods had overthrown Cronus and the Titans, their furtive scheme is to always have humans fighting amongst ourselves, as is now occurring with the Greeks waging war with the Trojans."

"Your logic seems to make sense," Eurassisgras agreed, stupidly nodding his head in the dark. "With us lieutenants surreptitiously meeting fifty-feet underground in pitch blackness, we won't be surveilled by either the fickle and capricious gods, by the fucked-up Trojans, or by Commander Odysseus."

"So, what the fuck are you going to tell us down here in this spooky dark tunnel?" Eurdicisin asked Eurshiddenme. "Are you preparing us for the eerie Area of Atonement down in shadowy Hades? I'd rather have death by chocolate!"

"No dipshit!" Eurshiddenme bluntly replied. "I'm now going to tell you all about how the devious gods operate, even though they're not medical surgeons. I'm going to thoroughly review for your education the story of Epimetheus and Prometheus."

"We know all about Prometheus being a Titan, and being banned from Olympus because the kind-hearted god had given men the gift of fire, but who the hell was Epimetheus?" Eurdicisin queried.

Eurshiddenme divulged to his uninformed comrades that in the beginning, only male humans were created to populate the Earth. Then,

Zeus requested that the blacksmith god Hephaestus sculpt a statue of what a female of the race should look like, and then magically, have the lame blacksmith god convert the statue into Pandora, the first lady, who, in the future, never lived in any White Cave. Zeus then presented the voluptuous new female with a trunk-full of glimmering amber that had a lid adorned with flowers and pomegranates, along with clusters of prickly porcupine quills. The amber chest had two polished semi-circular golden snakes that served as handles.

"So, what?" Eurcockisnum objected. "All women have boxes, hairy ones at that! You mean to say that you called this meeting fifty-feet underground just to tell us that women have boxes?"

Eurshiddenme, used to such stupid commentary from his unacademic, hedonistic peers, continued with his Epimetheus story. "Check her out," Zeus commanded his eminent Mt. Olympus family. "For this new woman we have created is really the cat's meow that can make any impotent man have an instant erection and blast messy sticky ejaculations all over the damned place! She is indeed endowed with heaven's most magnificent treasures," Zeus imperially prattled. "And I can't wait to take away her virginity and pump the poop out of her snatcheroo, so to speak! Of course, I'll have to swallow some pride and shrink-down from fifty-foot-tall to six-foot in height, and my penis will have to contract from three-foot-long to a mere twelve inches in length, but I can live with that compromise, for at least a half-hour of sublime pleasure!"

"What did the gods name the beautiful bitch?" Eurdicisin curiously asked, before short-tempered Eurshiddenme continued his lengthy narrative to his four lethargic-but-comical compatriots.

"Her name will be Pandora," Zeus attested, "which means 'All-Gifted', including doing anything from exotic couch-dancing to administering good professional blow-jobs. But Pandora is mortal and not fit to be a permanent mate for a *Mt. Olympus* stud like you, Apollo, or you Ares, or me. "

"Then why have you tempted and teased us with her abundant charms?" Lord Hermes challenged Zeus's ambiguous statement. "Why do you make me want and lust for what I can't have, namely this gorgeous bitch that Hephaestus has just artfully manufactured?"

"Because Shit-head!" Zeus thundered. "I intend to send Pandora down to Earth and wed Epimetheus, Prometheus's not so down-to-earth moronic brother, who can only see and understand things *after* they have happened, and then it is too late to do anything remedial about them," Zeus maintained. "In this way, *we* can get even with that traitor Prometheus by cursing Epimetheus, along with all mankind with the first woman. With the mortals preoccupied with sex and distrust, *Olympus* will now be safe from the challenge of human intelligence!"

"Way to go, Zeus Baby!" Apollo exclaimed to his fellow gods at the Mt. Olympus summit conference. "You're so shrewd and sly that you could even sell ancient grease to ancient Greece!"

"I get what you're implying," alert Eurballsourout piped-up in response to Eurshiddenme's recollection of mythology. "Prometheus had the gift of prophecy, knowing the future, and was fully aware that Zeus would punish him for compassionately giving mankind the gift of fire. But his twin brother, asshole Epimetheus, was in many ways like the five of us Greek dimwits. The poor idiot could not recognize evil danger until *after* it had been vividly shown and demonstrated!"

"Anyway," Eurshiddenme continued with his luminous account inside the dark LBGTQRMSV underground tunnel. "Zeus commanded Hermes, the official messenger god having wings on his sandals, and also upon *his* bronze helmet, to conduct Pandora to Epimetheus's gay village residence, which somehow had been spared being demolished by heterosexual Hephaestus's most recent violent sperm storm. "Tell the asshole degenerate Epimetheus," Zeus sternly instructed Hermes, "that the king of the gods extends *his* goodwill in the form of this enchanting bride, who is also an ultra-fine screwing machine, in addition to being a woman possessing a fantastic dowry being delivered by Hermes Express directly from *Mt. Olympus.*"

"So, how the hell was Pandora representative of women being evil as has always been believed?" Eurdicisin wanted to know. "Was she the first example of such a valid suspicion?"

Eurshiddenme gave Eurdicisin a dirty look inside the absolutely dark cave. "So, guys, Hermes delivered the first woman and dowry via *Olympus Hermes Express* to Arcadia, a pleasant northern region of ancient Greece, where the inhabitants' fun-loving and carefree descendants would eventually learn how to invent and play sophisticated pinball machine games. When the giant Epimetheus perceived what a knockout Pandora was, and soon learned that matrimony was her special assignment," Eurshiddenme emphasized, "the numbskull had three premature ejaculations during the day and four white dreams that night, completely obliterating seven innocent gay men's villages clear across the *Aegean Sea* and into Asia Minor."

"Even in the dark, I see your point, even tough points are for pinheads," Eurcockisnum contributed to the insane conversation. "Speak to us more irrelevant nomenclature!"

"Anyway," Eurshiddenme proceeded with his rather weird tale. "Prometheus's dumb-shit twin brother accepted his new bride along with her extensive dowry into his house, which was actually a primitive cave, because Epimetheus's dwelling had been destroyed by one of Hephaestus's catastrophic sperm storms originating from atop *Mt. Olympus*. Epimetheus soon wedded Pandora that day, without the services of any temple pedophile priest, and couldn't wait to get his noodle wet, so the demented ignoramus completely ignored Prometheus's prior warning about not receiving any possibly detrimental gift from conniving Zeus."

"What happened next?" intrigued Eurballsourout annoyingly asked. "Did Epimetheus get to pump the poop and sweet pussy juice out of Pandora?"

"According to geeky Greek mythology, as had already been alluded," Eurshiddenme explained, "Prometheus was clairvoyant and had the power of prophecy, but Epimetheus was a stubborn blockhead that couldn't see events until *after* they had happened. The following morning, the totally dense Earth inhabitant remembered *his* brother's statement about rejecting any gift from Zeus, but it was too late to repent about accepting the woman and about receiving the magnificent jewel-studded trunk. Epimetheus finally realized that the dowry Zeus had conferred upon Pandora had been designed to effectively break *his* balls and to sever *his* aching hemorrhoids. "Pandora, have you opened your box yet?" Epimetheus asked.

"Wow! I'm getting a boner just thinking about Pandora opening her box!" Eurdicisin vociferated to his four mates inside the dark cavern. "What the fuck happened next?"

"Of course, my dear husband," Pandora answered. "I opened my box eight times and you screwed the crap out of me eight times last night like a young stud in heat! I think you should change your name from Epimetheus to Big Dick-o-Pump!" Eurshiddenme told his four peers about the fucked-up myth. "Pandora, I had meant the amber casket Zeus had given you!" Epimetheus blushed. "Did you open *that* box?"

"Oh no, my dear, beloved spouse," Pandora responded. "I know right where it is, and am also eager to learn precisely what the unscrupulous *Mt. Olympus* immortals had placed inside it! I trust it's a wide array of new sex toys, along with a variety of pornographic drawings to stimulate *our* docile libidos!"

"Holy cow manure!" Eurassisgras hollered in the dark. "I think I just creamed my battle-loin guard and am about to crap my intestines into my already wet undergarment!"

Eurshiddenme ignored Eurassisgras's lunatic remark and resumed his lengthy exposition. "Pandora, please listen carefully to what the *Hades* I have to say!" Epimetheus emphatically indicated. "I have a suspicion that your chest contains some dangerous, evil secret that will haunt us and our accursed descendants throughout the decadent decades to come."

"I assure you, dear husband," Pandora idiotically replied. "*My chest* simply contains hard flesh and erect nipples for you to suck-on and fondle, and nothing else!"

"Damn it, Pandora! I meant *the chest* that Zeus had given you as a gift! Another word for a box is a chest! Learn the freakin' language, will ya'!" Epimetheus shouted at his beautiful, naïve and very gullible wife.

"Well, dear husband," Pandora defensively replied. "If *you* think that my box is my chest and that my chest is my box, then that's okay with me, as long as you keep licking and munching away at either! But when you decide to insert your erection inside my box," Pandora clarified, "make sure you don't try and shove it inside my sensitive chest!"

"Holy intercourse!" Eurcockisnum exclaimed. "I think that right now my tiny erection and my huge asshole are imitating Eurassisgras's dick and asshole!"

Aggravated Eurshiddenme decided it was time to conclude his interesting rendition of the Greek first lady who had been created by the very-cunning gods. "Pandora," Epimetheus stated. "As long as we keep that amber casket, or trunk, or whatever you want to call that box or chest that Zeus had given you, well wife, keep it shut and please, don't open the lid," the worried husband adamantly insisted. "Then the actual difference between a box and a chest really doesn't matter one fuckin' bit. Anyway, beautiful Pandora," Epimetheus continued his romantic discourse. "The hole in that amber box Zeus gave you is entirely too big and wide to screw. Not even *Atlas's* enormous fadorkenbender could fill-up that gargantuan cavity!"

"I promise you, dear husband, that I will never be overwhelmed by curiosity to ever open that amber trunk," Pandora pledged. "All I desire to do is to admire its magnificent external beauty!"

"Holy sperm cells!" Eurcockisnum bellowed in the dark. "I think I just ejaculated my balls and my epididymis right through my tiny penis hole!"

"Pandora was elated that her after-the-fact, dim-witty husband had permitted her to keep the amber chest, and the comely woman viewed it with pride the entire day. But after several centuries of staring at the dumbass amber container, Pandora wondered what its contents might be. The temptation to look inside the three-dimensional, rectangular chest had always been present, but Pandora was afraid that Epimetheus would become livid and *flip his lid* if she were to flip hers.""

"This sounds like some sort of Greek soap-less soap opera," Eurballsourout complained. "Why not tell us about Ajax's singular ability to deter gents? Especially, Trojan gents!"

"When Epimetheus was out of the house inspecting the heavens for the next possible nasty sperm storm raining-down from *Mt. Olympus*, the tantalizing amber box again inspired temptation to reign supreme in Pandora's curious mind. The first lady of Greece laid her avaricious hands upon the delicate surface, lifted the squeaky latch, and slowly and apprehensively raised the lid. To her chagrin, a swarm of teeming, winged spirits ascended, and then flew-out of the accursed amber trunk, swirling like a typhoon around the cave, and then vanishing outside into the atmosphere to plague mankind for the remainder of *his* tenure on this despicable planet."

"I see your impeccable logic," Eurdicisin complimented Eurshiddenme. "The gods are all ballbusters who want to distract us mortals with stupid-shit wars, chores, bores and whores!"

"Well anyway, fellow lieutenants, Pandora swiftly closed the box with a loud jolt, but her futile effort was far too late to attain any satisfactory results. Tears of guilt and disappointment filled her blurry eyes, for Pandora had released upon the world all of the grief, diseases, woes and miseries that have afflicted the human race from womb to tomb, ever since the very beginning of antiquity. The first lady of Greece had initiated widespread melancholy to flourish upon the Earth!"

"What happened next?" worm-brain Eurcockisnum wanted to know. "Did Pandora's swollen clit suddenly get numb like my dangling dingle?"

"Epimetheus entered the nondescript cave all covered with sticky *Olympus* sperm from another Hephaestus semen storm that had also recently destroyed a neighboring gay village five miles away. "Pandora, what have you done? I told you not to play with your box while I'm not around!" the brother of Prometheus strenuously objected.

"I'm sorry for opening *my box*," the penitent wife cried and grieved to accomplished idiot Epimetheus. "But you got me so confused that I thought

I was really opening *my chest* instead. At any rate, our unfortunate doomed descendants are going to be royally screwed by Zeus and his vindictive *Olympus* family for at least the next ten thousand years!"

"It's all partially my fault," Epimetheus reluctantly confessed as *he* wiped some excess sperm juice from his thin scalp and thick hair. "If only I could be like my brother Prometheus," the doltish fool reckoned. "Then, I could avoid divine orgasms and avert evil surprises *before* the fucked-up events happen!"

"Wow! This is some sensational story!" Eurdicisin commended Eurshiddenme. "Now that I've creamed my loin-guard a second time, please get to the anti-climax!"

"And finally, Epimetheus knew exactly what those unleashed evil spirits represented: death, famine, pestilence, disease, work, sickness, murder, theft, jealousy, envy, pride, war, constipation, diarrhea, and even nasty venereal warts. Thinking that all of the spirits had escaped the amber dowry box's interior, the sympathetic husband asked his upset-yet-obedient wife to cautiously lift the lid to closely examine the chest's presumably empty, mammoth compartment."

"Now guys; One timid weaker spirit still was occupying the interior, and the sprite seemed afraid to escape its singular confinement. But the remaining spirit was not a bottle of wine! As the last box occupant finally flapped its wings and fluttered upward, it then lamely ascended out of the most famous chest in history. Pandora and Epimetheus instinctively knew that the last spirit was abstract Hope, the only decent quality given by the gods for man to cope with all of the maladies and curses that had been packed inside the evil container."

"I hope you've finished with your exaggerated and very strange story," Eurballsourout indicated to Eurshiddenme. "I think that my ears can now see better than my eyes!"

"When Pandora noticed that Hope could not easily fly around the room and leave the cave like the malicious spirits had done, the wife of Epimetheus pitied the orphaned sprite, held it to her firm breasts, and nursed Hope to good health. Hope felt so content that *it* managed to eat right through Pandora's enviable nipples, and soon entered her warm heart, where inside women *it* has resided until this very day."

"That was a tremendous story!" Eurassisgras ecstatically told Eurshiddenme. "Now let's go up to ground level, kill a few stray cats, and enjoy eating some luscious pussy!"

* * * * * * * * * * * *

"Listen, my family," Zeus forcefully announced. "I'm ready to execute my dynamic plan into action. Let no god or mortal believe that he or she can oppose my indomitable will."

"We get the message," Hermes, the official Mt. Olympus courier replied. "Every vowel, consonant and syllable!"

"If any of you jealous idiots dare to plot rebellion against me, I'll cast you down to Tartarus where you can enjoy the shackled company of Cronus and his not-too-penitent Titan cronies. If all of you imbeciles held a separate length of my famed golden rope at one end, I could easily defeat your entire pulling force with a single, effortless tug."

"Father," Athena respectfully and anxiously stated. "Although some of us feel sympathy for Odysseus and the Argives, we promise to not directly intervene in the active Trojan War, but we'll only offer constructive advice to the intrepid, on-a-mission Danaans, but we'll provide no direct divine assistance."

"My child, I'll always value and try to satisfy your idealistic desires!" Zeus politely returned, and then the god of thunder and lightning promptly adjourned the brief parley, swiftly harnessed his team of white stallions, got onto his golden chariot, and rode his magnificent vehicle to the top of Mt. Gargaron where he would have an eagle-eye view of the Trojan Troad Plain.

Zeus held-up his golden scales of balance, with the Greek interest on the left and the Trojan perspective on the right-hand-side. Immediately, responding to the weight of Zeus's finger, the Achaean side tipped-down, indicating that the Trojans had been designated to win the ensuing battle. Several ear-shattering thunderclaps resounded and resonated throughout the Greek ranks, and the intimidated Danaans scurried in rapid retreat from the aggressive Trojan onslaught.

Diomedes halted his chariot and picked-up old and feeble Nestor, who had fallen to the ground when one of his chariot's horses had stumbled over a rock and had broken a leg.

"Zeus favors our avowed enemy today!" half-senile Nestor observed and related to Diomedes. "Let Hector brag and crow that he has scared your ass into abandoning the fight, and fleeing like a frightened mouse to your ship. Remember that tomorrow might see a reversal in fate, and that the widowed wives left behind in Greece could have some well-deserved vindication for the loss of their valiant spouses and louses."

Hector's speedy chariot pursued Diomedes and Nestor across the sandy plain, with the highly-focused Trojan prince yelling myriad expletives at his principal adversary, "Coward! Wimp! Jerk-off! Craven Faggot!"

The Achaean army had been trapped like corralled sheep inside the defensive wall that the Greek idiots had constructed the night before, and the fools were crushing each other in their futile stampede to escape the Trojans' fierce wrath.

Distraught King Agamemnon stood above the wall, shouting inaudible instructions that were indiscernible because of all the commotion occurring below: "Shame on you, Argives! You all claim and boast to be able to annihilate a hundred Trojans each, but now, you pussies wouldn't even be able to kill a colony of paralyzed chipmunks! Great Zeus!" Agamemnon hollered-up to the chief god. "I have offered to you superb burned animal flesh upon your altar! But I humbly apologize for sacrificing to you: ram, sheep and goat meat, so I guess you can call me a muttonhead. So, please don't scream-down from High Heaven, 'Where's the beef'. Oh, Mighty Zeus: if we Achaeans cannot savor victory today on the toad, er, I mean the Troad, then please grant my army a successful escape to the safety of their rotting, anchored Biremes!"

Amazingly, Zeus heard and fathomed Agamemnon's sincere prayer, so the king god dispatched a huge golden eagle, with a helpless fawn clutched to its powerful talons, and the baby deer was mercilessly dropped and deposited directly upon the Greeks' sacred altar to Zeus.

Seeing Zeus's encouragement being provided from above, the Achaeans, led by dauntless and relentless Diomedes, did a one-eighty about-face and sprinted towards the astonished Trojans in a brilliant surprise-move tactic. Diomedes smartly yelled several promises to his inspired captains: "If you kill your counterpart Trojan officers, we'll then flawlessly sack Troy, and you soldiers will be rewarded with fine horses, the best used chariots, and a dozen highly-versatile, kinky prostitutes to keep you warm and comfortable each night in bed."

Thinking of all the female muffins that the lieutenants could munch-on and screw, the Greek captains performed brilliantly, and easily massacred hundreds of Trojan warriors. But then, amusing himself, Zeus tipped his golden scales of injustice to the opposite side with his right index finger, and the tide of battle quickly switched to the decisive advantage of Hector and his crazed minions.

'I will not assist the invading Achaeans and pacify Athena and Hera's egos until belligerent Achilles wisely decides to resolves his differences with greedy Agamemnon and returns to again fight the Trojans,' Zeus contemplated. 'All is fair in love and war from the mortal perspective, but all could be completely unfair from mine!'

In two short hours, darkness had enveloped the battlefield, and Hector abandoned his goal of forcing the Greeks all the way to their anchored ships, and then in contempt, arrogantly torching the Biremes and instantly cremating all of the mariners aboard.

Hector ordered his specialized soldiers to construct watchtowers on the Trojan side of Troad Plain, and have surveillance teams spy and report on any unusual Greek maneuvers and activities. "Tomorrow, at dawn father," Hector promised King Priam, "we'll attack the somnolent Greek camp and see who will push back whom: Diomedes or myself!"

That star-laden night, the familiar constellations shined brightly in the firmament, and thousands of Trojan fires burned near the hundreds of sturdy watchtowers, absolutely frightening the feces out of the now scared-shitless Achaeans.

Chapter 9

"EMBASSY TO ACHILLES"

Seeing his forces getting their' rear-ends becoming black and blue, along with their testicles punctured and pulverized, King Agamemnon called an unscheduled military council meeting for his senior captains to develop a new crucial strategy in order to regain the essential services of Achilles and his Myrmidons to finally defeat the persistent Trojans.

"Captains, I see now that Zeus has betrayed me in favor of King Priam and Prince Hector," Agamemnon lamented and shared. "We'll never be able to sack the walls of Troy, because Almighty Zeus thinks that we're a bunch of sad-sack dirtbags. I propose that we should board our Biremes and sail for home in humiliation for unsuccessfully enduring our nine-year raid. We cannot fight against omnipotent Zeus, Ares, and Apollo, in addition to getting slaughtered by the ruthless Trojans, who I understand from our intelligence gathering, now intend to suffocate us with our heads, mouths, throats and nostrils smothered inside of tight-fitting, ribbed prophylactics."

Hearing the king's pessimistic lecture, Diomedes was disenchanted with Agamemnon's craven suggestion of abandoning the war after the Greeks had encountered so much adversity, and the young warrior was inspired to make a strong speech to contradict what he, the upstart, considered to be the Greek leader's unsound strategy.

"What the fuck's the matter with you, timid King of Mycenae? Do you have angry cow's disease?" Diomedes aggressively mocked Menelaus's brother. "Zeus may have given you dominion over men, but apparently, the Almighty Lord of Olympus did not allot you any emotional capital in the courage department. You may leave this struggle, King Agamemnon, like a small puppy dog with your tail between your legs, but I and thousands of determined Greeks will stay on task and plunder Troy; we'll capture Helen, and steal-back her immense treasure trove from Prince Paris. Even if everyone else in our contingent elects to follow your mortifying exit, Sthenelus, er, I mean my key man Stenny, and I, will remain until our last ounce of blood is drained from our Achaean arteries and veins!"

"Diomedes is positively right," Sthenelus declared in support of his immediate superior. "Many of the more-outspoken soldiers and army officers actually believe that you, King Agamemnon, are a silent, clandestine member of the non-macho Y.M.C.A."

"What the fuck's the Y.M.C.A.?" Agamemnon shrieked. "It sounds like some perverted Trojan propaganda nonsense to me!"

"It stands for 'Yahoo Masturbating Cowards Alliance," Sthenelus explained. "And I must admit, King Agamemnon, you definitely fit the faggot group's description rather perfectly."

Fearing dissension within the ranks gradually evolving into outright rebellion, old Nestor of Pylos spoke-up to add a degree of decorum and tradition to the escalating heated dialogue.

"Lord Agamemnon, let me add a new perspective to this fucked-up debate, for I wish to contribute an element of aged wisdom, mainly because I'm a wiz, and I certainly ain't dumb! You had been erroneous in judgment when you pissed-off Achilles by pilfering his cherished prize, the slave girl Briseis, which was the source of the dispute within our rank Greek ranks," Nestor articulated. "I recommend that you make adequate reparations to placate peeved Lord Achilles, to satisfy his distinguished honor, and to pacify his abnormal volatile temper. If you present to the son of Thetis some basic kingly gifts, I believe that Achilles will feel vindicated, will rejoin our crusade with a changed heart, and we will then easily be able to soundly trounce the devious Trojans, despite their notorious deployment of deadly prophylactics used as sinister suffocating weapons!"

Agamemnon bowed his head to acknowledge the elementary truth evident in old Nestor's words of experience, and the worried king confessed to his bevy of Argive captains that he had been wrong all along, and that the commander from Pylos was deemed correct in introducing a viable solution to the stalemate existing with stubborn Achilles.

"I'll gladly give Achilles seven chariot tripods; ten gold bars; three bars with accompanying restaurants; twenty copper cauldrons to distill rye whiskey; a dozen of my finest stallions in their 'hay day', not to mention the highly-coveted slave girl Briseis; and finally, I'll throw into the offer seven gorgeous lesbians imported from Lesbos, who naturally will teach Briseis all about female homosexuality, just to frustrate Lord Achilles's voracious and lustful heterosexual, virgin appetite."

"That's an excellent and admirable solution!" Ajax verified and commended Agamemnon. "If the gods permit us to sack and maraud Troy, Achilles, if he elects to lead us in our final hostile assault, will be able to sail for home with a cargo of jewels, gold, bronze, silver, and lesbian hussies, who don't have to worry about stupid bullshit such as reproductive freedom and dumb-fuck female slogans like 'my body, my choice'!"

"Do you have any other gifts to offer ill-tempered Achilles?" Nestor interrogated the Greek expedition leader. "How about some surgical equipment to creatively transform the seven voluptuous lesbian dolls into wage-earning, transgender, highly profitable male prostitutes?"

"Okay, Nestor," Agamemnon concurred. "Let's try this additional present I'm suggesting as an added bonus to give to Achilles. The Prince from Phthia will have the option to select one of my three ugly, obese daughters to marry, so that the mercurial-minded outlaw can become my principal heir and legitimate son-in-law, without any dowry being needed for Achilles to provide for me. All of this reward will be his, if only the obstinate idiot would relent and submit to my authority as high king of this sophisticated Greek invasion task force."

"Your shrewd solution with Achilles appears to be both rational and fair," Ajax complimented Agamemnon. "It sounds as Greek as the ideas of mother, gyros, and apple moussaka! Your obdurate Argive adversary will forget all about your quarrel with him over Briseis, and will soon be able to make a handsome profit by pimping the converted lesbians from Lesbos into money-making transgendered male hookers!"

Nestor was designated by Agamemnon to choose three other emissaries besides himself to approach Achilles's Bireme, which was anchored at the far end of the peninsula. Phoenix was selected for inclusion because the old codger had known Achilles as a boy, and had accompanied the lad out into the desert to catch and ignite on fire an indigenous bird into embers, just to see if the creature would reincarnate itself from the ashes to amazingly live another hundred years. Ajax was chosen next because the affable giant had once tossed Achilles to the top limb of a pine tree to prepare the teenager for future summit meetings, and Odysseus was the last representative of Agamemnon, since Achilles had always admired the King of Ithaca's skilled rhetoric and sagacious military strategies.

The four delegates left the Argives main camp and ambled two miles to the ships of the Myrmidons, the skilled soldiers of the affronted Achaean hero. The quartet, singing familiar Greco war anthems during their trek along the beach, found the disgruntled, leery champion idly playing his lyre, while dissonantly harping and carping off-key about being mistreated and bullied by cowardly King Agamemnon.

Achilles, with his main lieutenant, Patroclus, warmly greeted the "military truce entourage" into their modest officer's hut. A meal of meat and bread was hastily prepared, and the six acquainted men consumed their food and reminisced about past shared adventures and conquests. But then, sly and cunning old Nestor diplomatically changed the tone of the conversation to envelop the present dilemma involving the bitter debacle between aggrieved Achilles and tyrannical Agamemnon.

"Your noble father Peleus sent you off to war with the philosophy that power among mortals was the gods' discretion to give, but it was bestowed favorably only if humans respected the deities' whims, and controlled *their* fluctuating pride and arrogance," Nestor emphasized. "Now then, I encourage you, Achilles, to cease your ridiculous quarrel with Agamemnon and in so doing, master the art of courtesy to match your extensive knowledge of the science of war. I maintain that all of the Argives will admire your transformed desire to compromise with *our* Greek leader. I had heard your father often speak in public about the importance of utilizing words of tolerance. Have you forgotten *his* diplomatic genius?"

"Nestor is correct in his general assessment," Odysseus concurred with his revered elder. "Achilles, I now beg you; learn to become more moderate and conciliatory in handling your' oscillating emotions. Hector now has the Danaans with our backs against the sea, and his motivated forces might break through our vulnerable defenses tomorrow, and the Greeks might falter without your invaluable alliance and assistance. The Trojans will surely burn-up all of our ships as if we were helpless phoenixes out in the arid desert, and most of *your* comrades from various cities will perish and be incinerated while onboard. That horrible memory certainly will be ingrained inside your hassled brain until you arrive upon your deathbed. You'll be miserably haunted for the remainder of your days, Achilles of Phthia, by your tainted recollection of refusing to aid *our* joint and totally praiseworthy cause!"

Achilles was not-at-all impressed with Odysseus's summary of his relationship with the leader of the Greek invasion, claiming that Agamemnon was a slippery bastard who thinks one way, but maliciously behaves in an opposite manner. The aggrieved Greek warrior insisted that yellow-bellied Agamemnon had always treated cowards with the same regard as the egregious king rewarded his most loyal and audacious generals. The brave-but-egocentric hero argued to the four emissaries that he had successfully sacked and ransacked a dozen cities allied with Troy, and that after humbly presenting the treasures to Agamemnon, the king awarded Achilles a mere pittance of the booty, while keeping the bulk of the valuables all to himself. But when greedy Agamemnon deliberately stole Briseis away from Achilles's custody, then *that* very belittling embarrassment was more than the great warrior could either tolerate or accept.

"Agamemnon had raised a fantastic army of one thousand ships and fifty thousand soldiers, but for what purpose?" Achilles demanded hearing from his four guest ambassadors. "To retrieve Helen for the benefit of red-bearded Menelaus? Is Menelaus the only man who loves a woman? Didn't I love Briseis in a similar fashion? In my estimation, your King of Mycenae is a lying, conniving clown, and nothing more!"

"But the King has offered to you any of his three daughters in marriage?" Odysseus attempted to negotiate basic reason with Agamemnon's prime antagonist. "The King of Mycenae is indeed the richest royal personage in all of Greece? Are you going to pass-up *that* tremendous once-in-a-lifetime opportunity of being *his* main heir?"

"In truth Odysseus, I happen to value the abstraction known as love over the possession of physical treasure and property," quixotic Achilles idealistically answered. "And as far as the bastard king's three daughters are concerned, the trio of fat bitches all possess horrendous-in-appearance pachyderm skin. And also, two of the obese sluts look like female elephants lacking grotesque tusks, and the third hideous-looking, mammoth beast looks something like a pregnant hippopotamus that is about to deliver corpulent quadruplets!"

"Forget your incredible animosity towards Agamemnon for a moment," intelligently counseled wise Nestor. "For, Odysseus, Ajax, Phoenix's and my sake, won't you assist *our* Greek endeavor against Troy by joining our coordinated assault? In all honesty, Achilles; we four negotiators admit that we desperately need your indispensable allegiance!"

"If the gods in their mercy allow me to proudly return from here to my native Phthia, I'll easily find a good wife who could cook, sew, give good head, and screw like a rabbit. There are numerous, well-endowed, very pretty daughters of strong fathers living back home, and those stout yeomen staunchly guard the various towns and forts. I'll choose the one special woman whom I prefer best, and have her as my queen to help me rule over my father's kingdom."

"I deeply resent the way that you have nixed your mentor Phoenix," Nestor verbally lambasted Achilles. "But to cut to the chase, I am an avid student of child psychology, and I wish to learn the true reason for your unmitigated belligerence! Why are *you* so adamantly petulant toward the Greeks' arduous struggle against Troy and its allies?"

"My mother Thetis of the sea has told me of two separate destinies, depending on which decision or path I should pursue," Achilles almost-tearfully revealed. "First off, if I stay and fight here at Troy, I'll die in battle, but then, eternal fame and glory will be forever identified with my name. But secondly, if I return home from Troy to Phthia, my name will evaporate into nothing several generations later. But conversely, I will enjoy a long and happy life, adroitly reigning over my father's prosperous kingdom!"

"Are you saying that you value a long dull life over a short glorious one?" Odysseus challenged. "In my opinion, I would not make such a mediocre choice of destinies!"

"I believe that joy and love are more important in life than power and wealth!" Achilles austerely replied. "One cannot neither buy nor steal back honor and pride, which happen to be abstract qualities that Agamemnon has deceitfully pilfered from me. So, dear friends, my unsolicited advice to you noble men would be for you to voluntarily join me in sailing back empty-handed to our native lands with our mutual pride and our shared honor still intact!"

Phoenix then raised his right hand to his heart and solemnly pledged that Achilles was like his own flesh-and-blood son; the hundred-year-old geezer eloquently stated that the gods had cursed him to never have a child of his own; and then the neurotic curmudgeon declared that he would sleep the night inside Achilles's nondescript hut, and with his loyal troops, would set sail with the dissident fleet of Myrmidons in the morning.

"But before Odysseus, Ajax and Nestor leave these premises," hoary Phoenix commented, "I hope that you, Achilles, will learn to harness and control your haughtiness. I advise that you pray to Zeus and fear his many whims, so that the Greek cause can be salvaged without either you or I contributing to their ultimate victory. Everyone in the Greek camp is aware that Agamemnon had wronged you! And everyone in the camp admires your daring and skill more than *his* lack thereof. However, the King's generosity, regardless of his gutless character, is quite generous in nature, and Agamemnon has sent his cream-of-the-crop captains to represent his extraordinary concessions. I would prefer that you, Achilles, settle this complicated matter with grace and dignity, rather than with the childish temper-tantrum that you've so blatantly exhibited. If you make a minor yield, I'm certain that all of the Achaeans, with the exception of cowardly Agamemnon, will treat and honor you as a god of Olympus!"

"I have no particular regard or consideration for the petty Achaeans' negative opinion regarding my proud behavior," Achilles snapped back. "I don't trust that rogue Agamemnon one iota. When the bastard stole beautiful Briseis from me, that was the final hair than broke the giraffe's spine. I here and now warn you gentlemen that if you take Agamemnon's side in *our* personal dispute, then in so doing, you also oppose me, and will have then become my avowed enemies."

"Nestor and Odysseus, I now comprehend that Achilles cannot be swayed or convinced to ever accede to reason," Ajax assessed and related. "Our candid words are, in meaning, mute to his deaf ears and closed-mind."

"But Achilles, your colossal grudge will not budge an inch," Ajax insisted. "According to out ancient laws and traditions, even if a terrible murder has been committed, it is common practice for a brother, a father, an uncle, or an affected son to agree to accept blood money as a feasible compensation to settle a harsh wrangle with the murderer. But you, valiant warrior, have worked yourself into an implacable frenzy over one insignificant slave girl, even though Agamemnon, through our well-intentioned embassy, has offered you Briseis along with seven even-more-horny harlots besides. Why do you obstinately resist absolutely clear reason?"

"You speak the truth, big oaf Ajax. But when I reconsider and mull-over in my mind how that gutless son-of-a-bitch bastard had humiliated me in front of my peers, namely, the other Achaean captains, well, my blood still boils just thinking about the entire warped scenario."

Nestor, Ajax and Odysseus dejectedly paced back to the Achaean camp with the bad news that Achilles was beyond being unbearably obdurate. "The stubborn asshole evidently had been born with a stubbed-head," Odysseus evaluated and commented. "His noggin is harder than Hephaestus's solid metal anvil!"

"True," Ajax spontaneously confirmed. "Achilles's brains are more solid than rocks, and his dense skull is twice as thick as volcanic basalt!"

Chapter 10

"NIGHT-TIME FORAY"

"Eurshiddenme, why the hell are we again fifty-feet below ground in this fifty-foot-deep secret LBGTQRMSV tunnel that apparently isn't too secret if the four of us gabby lieutenants know about it," Eurballsourout asked his Argive friend. "I mean, we four nitwits are undoubtedly narrow-minded dolts! But are you now trying to give us a type of dumb-ass tunnel vision way down here in the dark?"

"Quiet idiot!" Eurshiddenme ordered, even though he was the same rank as Eurballsourout. "Down inside this horizontal hollow, even the shadows may have ears and mouths!"

"But why the hell are we down here?" Eurassisgras echoed Eurballsourout's inquiry. "Are you attempting to convert us into being condemned members of the gay, lesbian, transgender and tri-sexual community?"

'Listen assholes, and that includes you too, Eurdicisin and Eurcockisnum!" Eurshiddenme imperatively stated. "I finally figured-out how the gods, particularly Zeus and Hermes, operate when dealing with mortals who are humans, and with humans who are mortals. So that's why I specifically led you four insane asylum candidates down here to learn something relevant!"

"We could be in bed sleeping with our arms around our life-sized, straw prostitute dolls, so this better be worth our while!" Eurdicisin angrily complained. "Usually, Eurshiddenme; you don't know your ass from a hole in the ground, but now, quite apparently, you don't know a fuckin' huge dark tunnel from your damned diminutive asshole!"

"Hurry-up and tell us your loony bullshit story so that we can get back to having imaginary sex with our prostitute dolls, now that we're all half-awake! And your reason for being down here better be good, or else your butt will soon be poison ivy weeds!" Eurassisgras predicted.

"Well men, here's what I kind of finally figured-out," Eurshiddenme commenced with his wholly disheveled preface. "Although neither Zeus nor Hermes were down to Earth gods, the pair were having a serious conversation about how to evaluate humans down here on Earth."

"This is probably the last time I'll ever listen to one of your dumb-shit demands," Eurcockisnum grieved. "I'm always in the dark without ever before being down here inside this fucked-up, pitch-black tunnel!"

"We must show the crazy humans that we are essentially 'down-to-earth' guys once in a while," all-powerful Zeus reminded Hermes, the mischievous messenger god, as the two deities were ambling through a patch of forest in Phrygia. "I'm really fuckin' tired of watching those big-breasted Graces and Muses doing couch-dancing in my face. Now Hermes, let's try to act meek, meager and ordinary for a change, rather than hedonistic and fucked-up like we normally do! Sometimes, my dear Messenger, *we* must attempt setting a good example for those irascible assholes residing down here on Earth. The mentally-deficient numbskulls will hypnotically imitate our behavior as if they were ordinary mimicking monkeys."

"I fully concur My Lord," Hermes amiably agreed. "So, it's nice that once in a blue moon we disguise ourselves as mendicant suppliants, and rub shoulders with mortal riffraff, just to see if the rabble lowlife still worships us. And don't forget, almighty Zeus; we have to to shrink-down from fifty-foot-tall to *their* diminutive height before we fuckin' indiscriminately encounter any mortals; clever disguises or no damned clever disguises!"

"That's a great practical idea Hermes. You tend to have many pedestrian ideas when we walk together," Zeus commended and endorsed. "That way, as you have just so sagely suggested, our irritated and enlarged hemorrhoids will shrink-down, just like our fifty-foot-tall bodies!"

"This story better get better, or you might never again see the sunlight on the other side of the grass, er, I mean desert!" Eurdicisin threatened. 'Truthfully, Eurshiddenme. You need to go to primary storytelling school and earn a diploma!"

"Stop being so impetuous and presumptuous! Let me' finish with the introductory characters and setting descriptions," agitated Eurshiddenme angrily retorted. "Now then; Hermes was indeed the most cunning and creative of the great gods. The winged-footed deity had suggested to his superior Zeus that the two should show-up in Phrygia to investigate how receptive and hospitable the natives would be to *their* visiting-but-anonymous Olympus guests."

"You sound like a parrot constantly repeating yourself," Eurassisgras criticized the already-harassed speaker. "Pretty soon you'll be reiterating, 'My ass hurts! My ass hurts', hundreds of times, over and over again."

"Ya' know Hermes," Zeus indicated as the chief deity glanced at his pleasant peasant's garb that had instantly replaced his rich robe. "I want to see exactly how the mortals over here in Asia Minor are honoring my controversial Law of the Suppliants. If you recollect, all god-fearing mortals should…"

"Should give food, shelter and good cheer to traveling visitors, because luxurious lodges designated for travelers haven't been invented yet," Hermes interrupted his moody supreme boss. "According to *your* fine law, Master Zeus, all human itinerants must be treated with courtesy and dignity, even if they're wandering bandits, scoundrels, terrorists, or robbers; or else, the derelict homeowners not honoring your law will be visited by an earthquake, or perhaps a devastating tidal wave, or maybe wind-up having high-voltage lightning bolts flying up their targeted tender butt-holes."

"We'll wander through the pathetic land where other strange local gods compete for the humans' loyalties," Zeus summarized to his more jovial colleague. "Yes, dear Hermes. We'll knock on each door and request food and lodging, and if we don't get expected cooperation, then…,"

"Then Phrygia will be destroyed out of *your* arbitrary spite, and the land will be left to the other fuckin' obscure, indigenous gods to fuckin' worry about," the immortal courier finished.

"For your lucky benefit, your myth is getting a trifle better," Eurassisgras, out of character, complimented Eurshiddenme. "At this rate, you might just make it breathing and living until dawn appears tomorrow morning on the eastern horizon!"

"At every stop, the two nomadic guests were savagely cursed-out, treated with belligerent insolence, and greeted with hostile defiance, and *that* hostile rejection had occurred at least three-hundred-times, for the outlandish natives were pragmatic pagans, heathens, and cynical atheistic realists. The obnoxious Phrygians generally worshiped sex and perversion, much more than the natives honored impractical, arrogant, and egotistical foreign and local gods and goddesses, along with the Olympus gods' stupid and inflexible laws, decrees, and bullshit edicts."

"Almost completely frustrated, totally mortified, and virtually out of patience, the noble dual *Olympus* travelers decided to try one more home before taking-out their mutual wraths upon the barbaric Phrygian cave and shanty dwellers. Finally, Zeus and Hermes arrived at a remote shack situated all by itself in the countryside, because the already-scorned husband and wife occupants had been evicted and ostracized from the nearest city's numerous ghettoes and barrios."

"I would rather have my bouncing balls pieced by a Trojan spear than to hear any more of your dumb-fuck drivel," Eurcockisnum protested to Eurshiddenme. "I can never get a decent erection whenever listening to your fake bullshit!"

"After Zeus angrily knocked on the shack's splintery door, the pair were greeted by a cheerful male voice and courteously invited inside the raunchy, ramshackle abode. An elderly, thin gent with a long grizzly beard, instructed the wayfarers to sit-down upon the only hard 'bench', which was normally reserved for unethical area judges and magistrates that occasionally showed-up at the old man's door cold and lost, asking for directions to King Midas's ornate palace, or how to find the nearest Phrygian cemetery."

"Where are ya' odd-looking strangers from?" the aged man's old-looking wrinkled wife asked. "We haven't had any visitors in these parts for over fifty years. As you already can tell, kind sirs, my husband Philemon and I live way out here in the god-forsaken boondocks, far beyond this accursed country's damned hinterlands and dangerous cities."

"What's your name old woman?" the omniscient Zeus inquired just for the sake of polite conversation. "I'll have to enter it into my secret black date book!"

"It's Baucis," the old dame answered. "And my husband Philemon's two unfortunate brothers, Philharmonic and Philanthropic, were both philosophical philanderers that died from phlebitis over in Philadelphia, that ghetto town between here and Egypt. Now guys," Eurshiddenme continued. "Philemon's two idiot brothers always treated rare visitors to their homes with indignity and with violence. And consequently, both of Baucis's fucked-up brothers-in-law were punished by the gods with clogged arteries and with super-clogged sperm ducts. "Shit, kind sirs," Baucis elaborated to the weird-looking guests. "Philharmonic and Philanthropic were both glad that they were about to die from blood clots, and not from excruciating painful sperm clots inside their rotting-away crotches!"

"Baucis and I have always been cooperative with the gods' capricious laws, ever since the dreadful demise of Philharmonic and Philanthropic," Philemon added to his wife's testimony. "And neither of us want our assholes cauterized by some errant high-voltage lightning bolts, or by some lacerating liquid lava shooting and squirting-up our sensitive, withered anuses. That's why we so eagerly answered our door this afternoon," the old codger explained to shrunken-down guests Zeus and Hermes. "Ya' never know when a crazy pair of Greek *Olympus* wanderers will visit your humble dump for an unannounced, impromptu inspection, ha, ha, ha!"

"For the sake of our morale," Eurdicisin bitched to Eurshiddenme, "does this fucked-up story have a moral? Please proceed before my eyes close, and a number of zs start floating out of my mouth!"

"Do you two folks enjoy living way out here in abject poverty in the middle of nowhere?" Hermes curiously inquired. "If I had to live in a dirty shithouse like this one apparently is, I'd simultaneously contemplate blindness, insanity, starvation and a most-welcomed suicide."

"We are very poor as your keen eyes can determine," Philemon verified. "But Baucis and I have blithe spirits that rejoice whenever we recall and discuss the great sex life that we had shared six decadent decades ago. Our passion used to be hotter than the ashes and embers now-burning inside our modest fireplace," the decrepit husband explained. "Let me fan the flames on the hearth so that I may distribute more warmth for the four of us occupants to share. All I ever dream about, kind strangers, is growing and maintaining a nice stiff erection and planting the throbbing mother into a young Baucis's wet pink love tunnel. Those fond memories perpetually haunt my flagging spirit. But unfortunately," poor Philemon continued his sorrowful monologue, "her honey-well now is dryer than the barren Phrygian desert out there, and even more regrettably, I haven't popped a decent load in almost a non-fuckin', pussy-pumpin', fuckin' century!"

"Now, my fellow lieutenants, I have to mention that Baucis's water kettle was beginning to boil and steam. Soon, the wife poured the container's contents into a pot of common cabbage, which had been selected from the couple's sparse garden. *"Let' us* be good friends and eat this boiled cabbage when it soon will be ready to consume and digest," Baucis suggested to her fully-amused visitors. "I'll stir the pot with a piece of pork that's hanging-down from that termite-infested, decaying beam up there. I stare at that fabulous piece of pork every morning, wishing that it was a young Philemon's hard erection ready for some important bed action. But alas, gentle guests; my aged husband now has a tiny rat's dick that looks like it belongs on a friggin' chipmunk!"

"Then guys; Baucis methodically set the table with her gnarled arthritic hands that shook and exhibited an advanced case of Parkinson's disease, and next the afflicted woman used a broken plate as a shim under one of the shorter bench legs, because the attached picnic table had contracted a nasty case of polio in its youth. And finally, the old domesticated dame set some olives, carrots, and turnips upon the rickety old table, along with several eggs that she had been saving for hungry area 'poachers'. Appalled Zeus and Hermes were then invited to sample the horrible food, and to flourish in the poor couple's genuine hospitality inside the dilapidated framed home that itself would have served a better purpose as winter kindling wood."

"Get to the essential theme and plot," Eurballsourout objected to Eurshiddenme. "I had seriously studied advanced literature in kindergarten, and your lackluster story is about as interesting as me committing suicide twice. And honestly, Eurshiddenme; your wholly mediocre unholy tale is akin to someone saying that sour dough tastes better than dildo!"

"Please accept this wine in wooden bowls. I apologize that its foul flavor tastes like sour vinegar," Philemon offered his incognito-but-neato distinguished guests. "I wish I had better vintage to offer you two weird vagabond travelers, and I hope my dirt-clogged ears do not hear any sour grapes originating from the lips of either of you two strange-looking freeloaders. I sincerely trust that you two peculiar-looking gentlemen are enjoying our heartfelt hospitality."

"This is the best damned fuckin' wine I've ever tasted, either being sober or drunk," Zeus commended his poverty-stricken hosts. "And may Dionysus bless your rural asses with a productive grape harvest in years to come. In fact, I believe that this rancid shit will kill every radical germ and bacteria thriving inside my whole friggin' body. And if it makes me piss vinegar," the king-god remarked, "then I'll definitely urinate into a decanter and celebrate you Philemon, and your wrinkled-faced wife, as both of you being real pissers!"

"Baucis and Philemon stared incredulously at each other when the pair noticed that no matter how much their' thirsty visitors and they drank, that the wine bottle incredibly remained full and undiminished in liquid volume. Then, the toothless host and the incontinent hostess stared at each other in utter astonishment, fully realizing that their gregarious guests were indeed visiting immortals of the highest magnitude. Both mortals dropped to their knees in adoration of the two traveling *Olympus* itinerants, apparently masquerading as common wayfaring bums."

"Kind sirs," Philemon timidly stated as the host's astonished eyes squinted and finally observed Hermes's shrunken winged sandals. "Baucis and I have a goose stashed-away that my wife would gladly prepare for you. I'll attempt to catch it if you would like to observe and be humored by my awkward frivolity. I mean, My Lords," Philemon stuttered and paused. "My whole pathetic life has been one vast wild-goose-chase in pursuit of wealth, pleasure, decent and indecent pornography, and other idiotic, sinful, earthly nonsense that you gods matter-of-factly enjoy all the fuckin' time."

"That's perfectly all right, old man," Hermes indulgently laughed. "We don't want to sit here all night and watch your quack wife suck-on your skinny bird. Just the thought of such a gross sight makes me want to split my gut while laughing my ass off before vomiting my guts out! Geriatric sex would be too much raucous entertainment for my weak heart to ever endure," the great messenger god confided. "I might then become the first fuckin' giddy immortal to ever die laughing, and wind-up going to that very notorious University of the Dead, *Hades Hall*. Ha, ha, ha, ha!"

"It sounds like Philemon's aged dick is as big as Eurcockisnum's shriveled pecker!" Eurdicisin said and then laughed. "Call the army medical patrol because Eurcockisnum needs a stretcher, right now! This whole scenario is entirely too rich to tolerate! Ha, ha, ha!"

Ignoring Eurdicisin's mocking of Eurcockisnum's miniature manhood, Eurshiddenme proceeded with his wholly insane narrative. "Zeus then said, you two mediocre and ridiculous senior citizens, who already look like walking zombies, have been wonderfully generous hosts to me and to my dear companion Hermes," the chief god sincerely declared with a thankful smile. "I shall prodigiously reward you two hapless adult dolts for your wonderful acceptance of a pair of wayward travelers into your pathetic abode, that doesn't even have an outhouse in which to take a freakin' healthy dump."

"What do you intend to do to the remainder of sinful Phrygia, Lord Zeus?" Baucis curiously asked. "Do I have to go through damned menopause again with the other males and females? What a lot of bloody bullshit that messy business was!"

"The wicked inhabitants of your bizarre country shall be severely and *amply* punished for their blatant violation of my sacred laws, and also for their audacious mistreatment of Hermes and me," Zeus promised the elderly couple. "Those antagonistic and repulsive assholes will be deluged with the biggest catastrophe of their fucked-up lives."

"*Amp*ly punished usually means Lord Zeus administering high-voltage electric lightning volts up the old asshole," Hermes reminded his flabbergasted mortal listeners. "Your aberrant Phrygian countrymen back in the city and town ghettoes and barrios will then think that they've become ancient Ass-Searians! Ha, ha, ha, ha!"

"Look over there at yonder fireplace!" Hermes pointed his index finger and directed the quivering old couple. "Your goose is cooked! Ha, ha, ha!"

"This story better be getting to its dead end, or you will be, too!" Eurballsourout said to Eurshiddenme, even though the lieutenant's balls were out, but couldn't be observed by his three companions inside the dark tunnel.

"Zeus opened the shack's squeaky door, brushed some active termites from his hands, and escorted the other three occupants outside. Amazingly, the king-god and Hermes instantly shot-up to their normal fifty-foot-tall height. Baucis and Philemon trembled to their knees in sheer supplication of the show-off Olympus deities. And when the elderly couple stared in all directions, the two penitent paupers frightfully observed that a gigantic flood had just devastated Phrygia in all four directions of the knoll upon which their' deteriorating house had been crudely constructed eighty years before. The visibly distraught pair wept for their' old age, and cried-out loud utterances, vehemently protesting to the majestic, radiant gods that the elderly couple had not also been drowned in the terrible calamity that Zeus had maliciously and vindictively caused upon baneful Phrygia."

"And as the bleary-eyed old duo perceived their hands, feet and each other's faces, all of their ugly wrinkles had miraculously disappeared, and Baucis's visage was once again young and beautiful, and her rejuvenated slit hole was now a bright pink and sporting well-lubricated walls; and finally, her crotch again looked like a decent healthy brown bush."

"Now your obnoxious tale is finally reaching its climax," Eurassisgras commented with a sigh of relief. "Honestly Eurshiddenme; I hope that Philemon's body explodes into flesh fragments from having his erect pecker erupt in a wild, volcanic-type sperm orgasm!"

"Philemon looked-down and was delighted to see a large bulge sticking-out from his newly acquired, rich-looking, embroidered tunic. The two old farts immediately passionately embraced, lowered their newly-acquired young bodies to the wet ground, and wildly screwed like horny lions in heat for three consecutive hours. And while the two were euphorically humping and pumping and changing positions like there was no tomorrow, their decrepit old shack magically transformed into a splendid marble mansion, featuring a magnificent golden roof, with a large quacking, non-edible, silver goose at its summit.

"Good fucked-up people. I have sympathetically provided you with youth and with a fine home, simply because you have shown noteworthy respect for us, the disguised omnipotent gods," Zeus, the accomplished voyeur, related as he and Hermes ascended into the sky. "And I shall now form a shrine with large marble pillars, and send the two of you off to a distant future place called *Temple University* to study and learn to be my official priest and priestess in this fucked-up land of Phrygia, or what's left of Phrygia. And please remember, humble hosts," the supreme deity emphasized while partially hidden behind several cottony clouds. "All future incantations and chants to Hermes and me must be played and sung exclusively in the key of Asia Minor. Now, do you two raunchy, incompetent, lucky imbeciles have any further requests before my immortal, illustrious companion and I zoom back-up to eternal *Mt. Olympus?"*

"Why indeed yes!" Philemon affirmatively answered and yelled-up with his hands forming a sort of megaphone in front of his now-vernal mouth. "I don't want to live forever and then have to be thoroughly bored to death like you two pedestrian immortal assholes obviously are! With that remarkable remark being truthfully said, I would prefer that once Baucis and I enjoy each other's company and our new-found prosperity on our second splendid chance at married life," Philemon solemnly indicated to Zeus and Hermes, "please grant that we may both die and be united as one soul immediately after the next miserable millennium commences."

"Zeus enthusiastically acceded and quickly and benignly granted the old gent's unusual request. Not one pilgrim, lost or otherwise, ever accidentally or purposefully visited the sensational white marble temple and accompanying pillared mansion during the next hundred years. After an eighty-year-tenure as appointed custodians of the recently formed temple, which was conveniently situated next to the exquisite white marble mansion, the second-time-around, the old odd couple finally, mutually and sadly, died locked in a tender embrace."

"Until death descended, the dumb-fucks did depart together," Eurballsourout concluded, breathing a sigh of satisfaction. "But I was hoping that Zeus and Hermes somehow die and not those freaky mortals Philemon and Baucis."

"But instead of turning into gruesome bony skeletons, Baucis and Philemon had an unusual bark miraculously form around their human remains, and Philemon's body became an oak tree, and Baucis's corpse coincidentally transformed into a linden, that remarkably their symbiosis grew from the exact same entwined roots, because Zeus and Hermes were still *rooting* for the pair up on *Mt. Olympus.*"

"So, what does that fucked-up, bullshit story of yours actually in essence symbolically mean?" dumbfounded and befuddled Eurcockisnum asked Eurshiddenme. "It all sounds like a crock of phony-baloney religious propaganda to me!"

"It simply means that the great gods of Olympus are extremely fickle and unpredictable, but sometimes, the omnipotent nutcases may enter into your life unexpectedly, and in so doing, fortuitously confer upon you your deepest wishes and desires; that is, if you had faithfully and religiously worshipped and revered them in your prayers and in your sacrifices!"

* * * * * * * * * * * *

That night, Menelaus noticed Agamemnon standing atop the wall that the Greeks had constructed for the purpose of thwarting a direct, massive enemy assault on their campfires.

"What besides your two legs has you standing up there?" Menelaus asked Agamemnon. "Are you trying to get closer to the gods in Heaven?"

"I'm so damned depressed about the possibility that the reprehensible Trojans are about to raid and conquer our various camps, that the very thought of such a major catastrophe has me climbing the walls!"

"What should we do?" Menelaus asked his older brother. "Build the ten-foot-high wall ten-feet higher?"

"No, but my troubled mind has conceived a certain viable plan," Agamemnon shared his design with his red-bearded brother. "Immediately contact the army captains, and we'll have an important conference where I shall divulge my latest brainstorm to my key officers."

At the hastily-arranged meeting, Agamemnon addressed his already-dubious unhappy campers. "I'm worried that Hector and his fanatical Trojans are going to push our defenses back to the sea, and then set our anchored Biremes ablaze," the dejected King confidentially told him grim-faced captains. "We should strive to cut the Trojans' feet off at the ankles, because I'm extremely concerned that they're about to kick our asses right off of our friggin' anatomies!"

"Yes, my sagacious King," Nestor agreed, nodding his aged head. "The enemy has become smug and complacent, and Hector and his lunatic minions need to have an element of terror instilled into their psyches. What particular action do you propose?"

"From what I can observe and rationally decipher, my dear officers, Zeus now favors Hector and Paris over us," Menelaus interrupted and added to the discussion in a melancholy tone of voice. "What sort of counter-stratagem does your' demonic character have in mind?" the King of Sparta asked the King of Mycenae, inadvertently reiterating Nestor's prior entreaty.

"I hereby command that I will select two of you subordinates to venture into the fringe of the Trojan camp and conduct a surprise foray upon the unwary enemy troops," the expedition leader ordered. "Now all of you dimwits raise your right hands, and I'll randomly chose one from amongst you as the raid's reconnaissance commander."

"I'll gladly volunteer for this crucial commando mission, and I would like to choose brave Odysseus as my trustful accomplice," Diomedes clearly declared. "The incomparable King of Ithaca is demonstrably shrewd in difficult battle situations, and my trustworthy comrade is always cool as a squash, er, I meant to say 'cool as an encumbered-cucumber'. And besides," Diomedes added. "Odysseus has the support and protection of Pallas Athene, and quite possibly, I might be shielded by her awesome powers, also! I would, without question or doubt, follow Odysseus through towering fences of fire, desperately searching for some old flames of ours!"

"No need for flattery and other associated phony bullshit," Odysseus chided Diomedes. "The evening is two-thirds expired, so let's get started on initiating our surprise foray."

The pair of spy-scouts stealthily set-out to the east on foot, and in an hour, reached the perimeter of the Trojan encampment. Every Achaean captain waited impatiently for news of what the enemy was planning to enact. Then, feeble Nestor, who had a severe hearing impairment, heard the galloping of horses approaching from the east.

"Is that sound my ears perceive Diomedes and Odysseus triumphantly coming, or is it the sound of Trojan chariots encroaching onto our beachhead?"

The two courageous scouts soon came into the view of the Greek's blazing torches, and the pair were immediately recognized by the jubilant, cheering Achaean captains.

"Where did you get such beautiful white stallions attached to this fabulous jewel-studded chariot?" Agamemnon marveled and asked his valiant spies. "Did they belong to Paris or Pandarus?"

"No!" Odysseus answered from his high position upon the chariot's platform. "These phenomenal steeds had just arrived from Trace, an enemy ally of Troy. Diomedes and I had confiscated them after entering a brief conflict with several inebriated Tracian guards."

"We killed a dozen of the intoxicated bastards along with their disoriented drunken king," Diomedes added as the murderer threw a guard's severed head upon the desert sand.

"And two heads are better than one!" Odysseus exclaimed as the Ithacan champion tossed a second guard's decapitated head at the sandaled feet of King Agamemnon.

Chapter 11
"THE GREEKS FACE DISASTER"

Eris, who had intentionally rolled the golden apple on the marble floor at Peleus and Thetis's wedding, which had initiated the famous beauty contest between Aphrodite, Athena and Hera, was again active in inspiring the Achaeans with new-found courage, and with using her great power of suggestion, compelled the vulnerable-minded Danaans to forget all about voyaging-back to their native lands. Motivated by Eris, also known as 'Strife' or 'Discord', the following morning the rejuvenated Greeks, led by compulsive Agamemnon, marched forward to battle the Trojans upon the Troad Non-Fruitive Plain.

Imitating his principal Achaean foe, namely Achilles, Agamemnon had organized the current charge against the enemy front lines, riding upon his stately chariot that was being pulled by two powerful gray horses. Stimulated by a massive adrenaline rush, the insane Greek leader had managed to execute a wicked assault that had successfully infiltrated the Trojan front line, killing and trampling several dozen disposable opponents who had been obstructing his soldiers' advance, dying with *their* failed efforts at defending a makeshift wooden barrier.

But during the incursion, Almighty Zeus, keenly examining the ongoing action upon his magical gameboard, dispatched the fleet-footed Rainbow Goddess, Iris, with a message specifically earmarked for Hector's ear. "Stay back, Hector while Agamemnon slaughters all unfortunate Trojans in front of you. Yell for your men to keep-on battling, and their horses to keep-on dancing and a-prancing. But according to Zeus's command," Iris softly whispered, "if and when the God of Thunder decides that Agamemnon should be injured, and subsequently speeds back to his lines in his jeweled chariot, then Hector, you should swiftly advance forward and drive the insidious invaders back to their anchored sleek black ships."

"Agamemnon managed to callously kill several lieutenants among the recently-arrived Trojan ranks originating from Thrace, but in so doing, the obsessed king received a hard spear thrust to his curiass, which to curious asses reading this chronicle, is located in front of the warrior's plated loin-guard. And although minorly wounded near his crotch, crotchety Agamemnon, pretending that he was Achilles, also suffered a second blow that had punctured the skin below his right elbow. With one quick swoop of his bronze sword, the Greek leader deftly decapitated the enemy soldier Iphidamas, brother of Givadamis, who as a result of losing his head, could no longer neck with either his wife or his slutty girlfriend, nor lose his head over any other whoring piece of ass.

Feeling dizzy from the extreme loss of blood, Agamemnon commanded Odysseus to continue the battle, as the possessed and injured king drove his gray horses and chariot back to the Achaean lines. Immediately, Hector, remembering Iris's message from Zeus, spontaneously swung into the fray, ferociously killing a dozen Greek warriors in his path.

During the frenzied melee, Odysseus's five zany lieutenants developed a unique survival plan where Eurshiddenme, Eurballsourout, Eurassisgras, Eurdicisin, and Eurcockisnum formed an irregular circle and began slamming and smashing their bronze swords against each other's raised shields, pretending to be frenetically parrying heavy blows against attacking Trojans.

"Hand me your knife," Eurballsourout demanded to Eurassisgras, "so that I can scrape its dull blade against my left wrist and create a minor gash. Then, I'll make another small cut above my right thigh."

"I'll do the same thin slashes to myself," Eusassisgras nervously answered his nutcase colleague. "These superficial cuts will be our scarlet badges of cowardice, er, I meant to say, 'of courage'."

"Let me have your blade after you're through harmlessly penetrating your epidermises," Eurdicisin requested of Eurcockisnum and of Eurassisgras. "But I gotta' make sure I don't sever any artery or vein!"

*"Suit your*self if you happen to slice through your thin skin too deeply!" Eurdicisin inadvertently punned. "I'm no damned surgeon, so don't expect me to sew your gashes back together! I mean, my mother had amnesia and never taught me how to knit-one, purl two! And quite frankly, I only know how to stitch together my flimsy loin cloth, but I never mastered how to mend a fractured femur or a fountain-like, hemorrhaging asshole with exploding hemorrhoids!"

"I think you four worthless dumb-dicks are totally daft!" Eurshiddenme assessed and exclaimed above the clamor erupting all around them. "You' stupid, weirdo shits must take hour-long meteor showers every damned friggin' morning!"

Diomedes and Odysseus, fully engaged in real combat, were unaware of the ridiculous ruse being perpetrated by the Ithacan king's nearby five stooge-like lieutenants, and the dueling dual Greek dynamos were dynamic killing machines mowing-down Trojans with their trusty blades as if the enemy soldiers were thin blades of grass. But then Paris shot an arrow at Diomedes that grazed the Achaean hero's foot, which compelled the aggressor to challenge the Trojan prince to man-to-man combat.

But Odysseus's five dumb-dick lieutenants, still feigning dueling with imaginary Trojan warriors, stumbled atop a hill, and rolled and tumbled down the steep embankment, hitting into both Diomedes and Paris; the double collisions had knocked the prospective duelers plopping onto the desert sand. Becoming lost in the general frenzy and fog of war, Diomedes could not discover Paris's location, and vice versa, Paris had lost track of incensed Diomedes.

However, during the myriad in-progress altercations, Odysseus had been superficially wounded above the groin, immediately suffering a 'my groin' headache, as blood rushed from the champion's head down-toward his abdomen, thus making the Ithacan king very groggy and disoriented. "Which way is China?" delirious Odysseus loudly yelled to bewildered Menelaus. "I only wish that my five valiant lieutenants were here to rescue my embattled ass from the Chinese antagonists!"

Menelaus, demonstrating a degree of humanity and compassion, carried unconscious Odysseus to his chariot, but then Ajax, fiercely crippling Trojan after Trojan, grudgingly retreated back in the direction and relative safety of the Achaean camp. The colossal giant was soon joined by Odysseus's five conniving lieutenants, whom Ajax instinctively praised, after noting that the five mischievous scoundrels were bleeding from their wrists, arms and thighs.

"Did you brave fellows kill many Trojans today?" Ajax innocently inquired. "We need to steal a couple of their head-covering, suffocating prophylactics, and then figure-out the precise materials from which those bizarre smothering weapons are manufactured!"

"Too many victims to count on a common, unsophisticated abacus!" Eurshiddenme fibbed and alertly replied in regard to his slaughtering prowess. "Maybe tomorrow, our inimitable captain King Odysseus, will provide us with a competent statistician to keep an accurate record of our' combined total number of brutal slayings!"

"You men need to get a good night's sleep," Ajax boomed to the five inane, lying lieutenants. "Tomorrow you'll have to go into battle and get rolling again!" the massive giant inadvertently and coincidentally stated to Odysseus's main officers. 'I predict that tomorrow, our crucial battle will finally be downhill!"

Jay Dubya

* * * * * * * * * * * *

While the intense conflict was reaching its crescendo, Achilles was astutely watching the battle's termination from the stern of his anchored Bireme, all the while observing the Troad Plain with his personal bodyguard, Patroclus from Iolcus. "Look over to your right!" Achilles verbally indicated and pointed. "That apparently-wounded old coot looks like my elderly friend Machaon, riding in one of Nestor's chariots on fire. Go and see if my eyes are correct in their suspect visual acuity!"

Five minutes later, Nestor was preoccupied in his tent conversing with Machaon, with both Generals sitting inside the Pylos king's flimsy enclosure, drinking potent wine to restore their already-expended energy. "Welcome long-lost Patroclus!" Nestor politely greeted the new arrival. "Come into my humble headquarters and share some delicious vino with us! Let us merrily reminisce our past convivial camaraderie!"

"I cannot stay too long bullshitting with you two old farts," Patroclus unpatriotically apologized to doddering and dementia-stricken, feeble Nestor and Machaon. "Achilles has dispatched me to see if you, Machaon, had been near-fatally injured. Now that I've comprehensively evaluated the obvious situation, I believe that I should immediately return to my superior's headquarters, where Achilles and I are scheduled to receive from kinky-sluts quality head in his headquarters. What I mean, Nestor, is that our privates will no longer be private!"

"I don't understand the thinking of your fucked-up General Achilles," Nestor confided to the unexpected visitor. "Hundreds of his countrymen have been seriously maimed and wounded today; Odysseus, Diomedes and Agamemnon, to name just a few. Yet your boss Achilles is solely concerned with my healer friend Machaon, who has not been injured as badly as the others have!" Nestor maintained. "What the hell is your comrade waiting for? Is your superior waiting for our ships being all in flame with their crews inside being cremated and incinerated? Does Achilles wish to see our entire army being decimated and obliterated? If only I were a young stud again," Nestor genuinely confided. "I would first show the troops a tent full of naked whores; promise them to be rewarded with any kind of hot sex that they might desire, and then lead the ready-and-willing assholes into the center of the glorious fight!"

"Nestor is perfectly right in his thinking!" Machaon logically confirmed. "As an unorthodox doctor, I can verify that sex, either straight or gay, is usually the best motivational medicine! And also," Machaon eloquently elaborated. "I'm frantically afraid that the enemy soldiers are getting stronger and more muscular, and that we wimpy Greeks are becoming weaker in both strength and size. I believe that we should re-examine our consumption of meat, fruit, vegetables, milk, and grain, because in my professional opinion, in regard to dietary matters, my regiment needs a new nutritional regimen."

"Patroclus, do you recollect the morning when Odysseus and I came to your city to recruit your ass into this fucked-up war?" Nestor asked his fellow Greek. "We had promised you a toy sex doll to sleep with at night, and it has been generously provided to you. Now then; your mentor Achilles is half immortal, with his mother being the sea-goddess Thetis, and he was his mother's cherished fetus after being her precious embryo. But you, Patroclus, are a few years older than your arrogant commander, and hopefully, a few years wiser, too."

"What are you driving at, even though your obsolete chariot is parked outside?" Patroclus irately questioned aged Nestor. "Now then, old fart! When you were a much younger stud and were about to have hot sex, did you then also beat around the bush as you do now? Get to the fuckin' point, you wrinkly old pinhead!"

"I think that if Achilles stays stubborn and refuses to lead the Myrmidons into the fray, then you should step-up and do so, because I believe that you, noble Patroclus, are equally qualified in terms of courage and ability. If your master conveniently lent you his armor, then the apprehensive Trojans, thinking that you were your invincible commander, would stick corks up their asses to stop their diarrhea discharges, and automatically start dashing the other way!"

"Consider heeding Nestor's impeccable words," Machaon cleverly advised. "Knuckle-down, Patroclus, and put your finger on the basic problem! Our in-jeopardy lives are now solely in *your* hands, and not in those treasonous palms of your unscrupulous commander, your seditious, pithy Achilles of Phthia!"

After ambling out of Nestor's headquarters in a rather-confused and addled state of mind, Patroclus encountered and addressed an old trusted acquaintance. "Eurypylus, you old goat. Is this the day that Hector trounces and defeats the Danaans? Are the Greeks doomed to imminent disaster? Will future generations be reading about the Argives' impending demise in their various library Archives? Will Pallas Athene lose her coveted virginity to her acknowledged hero, Odysseus of Ithaca?"

"There's no salvation, Patroclus, neither in this despicable war nor in our fucked-up religion!" Eurypylus tersely and succinctly answered. "But if you can render us even a tiny bit of marginal aid, without engaging in actual fighting, then your' welcomed assistance would be vastly appreciated. Confidentially, most of our best surgeons have recently been somewhat mauled and mutilated on the Troad," Eurypylus disclosed. "And I understand from hearsay, and it behooves me to say, that you possess certain healing ability that had been acquired from the reputable drug experimenter, Chiron the Centaur, who never horsed-around when it came to administering medicine and dispensing both legal and illegal drugs!"

"Friend, Eurypylus; you've somewhat appealed to my sense of national pride, so if no direct fighting is involved, out of sheer empathy for my fellow Achaeans, I shall accede to your benign request and help bandage the fallen wounded, and also as a bonus, I'll perform rudimentary surgery on several of your officers!"

While Patroclus was skillfully practicing his physician skills, the Trojans were attacking the Greek front line with tremendous ferocity. The Achaeans desperately fought-back out of survival necessity, but the dedicated enemy used ladders to clamber-up the long wall that the Achaeans had crudely constructed, and then tossed spears and small rocks at the targeted Argive troops.

Ajax, after drinking three gallons of potent wine that had been 'deported' from Sicily, met and slayed his rival match, the giant Sarpedon, who had earlier drunk six gallons of 'deported' Sicilian wine. And so, the ensuing conflict reached its culmination, with neither side establishing any observable advantage.

Being inspired by Zeus, Hector lifted-up a five-hundred-pound boulder and flung the huge stone at the central gate inside the Achaean wall, and the enormous rock crashed through the wooden portal, with hundreds of screaming Trojans soon quickly rushing through the opening to confront the startled Greeks, who, including Eurassisgras, each soldier fearing that *his* tender ass was about to be grass.

Chapter 12

"BATTLE AT THE BARRICADE"

"Okay, junior jerk-offs. I have one more plume in my helmet than any of you deranged nutcases have, and that single feather makes me higher in rank than you four non-Cretan cretins," Eurshiddenme redressed his apathetic lieutenant peers. "This additional red plume is irrefutable evidence that you retards have to listen to me."

"So, why the hell are we again meeting down here in the forbidden gay, lesbian, trans-gender, tri-sexual dark tunnel?" Eurballsourout requested knowing. "Are we finally gonna' be initiated and indoctrinated into the LBGTQRMSV community? I'm not thoroughly-convinced that I want to go down that perverted-sex avenue!"

"No asshole! I'll venture to guess that even Eurassisgras knows more about Greek culture and about our peculiar religion than you do. We're gathered down here this hallowed evening because I have to tell you that King Odysseus's Cunt Tree Shrine is not the only smelly, stench-laden cunt tree in Greece."

"Well then, where are the others?" Eurdicisin wondered and asked. "I could spend an entire day climbing its limbs and branches, just randomly fuckin' around! When this fucked-up war is over, if I'm still alive, I'll take an advanced course in tree-climbing at the Ithacan Arbor University!"

"Yeah! Good idea!" equally moronic Eurcockisnum piped-up. "If I could find one of those cunt trees out in the country, I might be able to overcome my erectile dysfunction and get my first hard-on since I entered puberty."

"All right, you mentally deficient dunces," Eurshiddenme evaluated and stated. "I'm going to tie the four of you' assholes together down here in the dark, because it seems that you four nutjobs have already spent your whole freakin' lives in the friggin' dark. Then, I'll stuff four separate gags into your individual mouths, so that I don't have to listen to your perverted prattle interrupting my scholarly mythological presentation. Now, if you four numbskulls keep quiet and cooperate, then I promise that I'll hire four highly-skilled prostitutes to give you extremely satisfying blowjobs that will blow-away any other blowjobs that you've ever received at any state-sponsored bordello or brothel."

The empty-brained, ludicrous, sex-starved lieutenants quickly considered Eurshiddenme's intriguing proposition, and simultaneously agreed to be tethered together, and mutually gagged, to again mentally suffer through another obscure, dumb-ass myth lecture, in order to later be rewarded by four registered government hookers administering four professionally administered blowjobs.

"Okay men, I'll now commence with my little informative symposium," Eurshiddenme began his academic myth seminar.

So, *this* tale that follows is the contrived, convoluted myth that Eurshiddenme recounted and related to his gagged and tied-up peers.

"Oedipus did not have eight, strange-looking arms like his deformed ugly older brother Octopus had grown. Octopus had been violently discarded and hurled into the sea, where he and his descendants have been dangerous denizens, molesters and on-the-prowl predators ever since. Oedipus was the great-great grandson of a cad named Cadmus, who was a great-great pain-in-the-ass, who was so fucked-up that the gods decided that all of his degenerate future generations, including Oedipus, should be doomed to suffer great hardship and adversity to make them even more fucked-up than they already were."

"King Laius of Thebes, who liked to get laid but had a bisexual wife that inexplicably had cement formed inside her atrophied vagina, was the third ruler of that dysfunctional ancient Greek city after Cadmus had reigned in Thebes. According to his regal family's fucked-up tradition, the royal pain-in-the-ass King Laius had married a distant cousin named Jocastra. Soon, Oedipus came under the influence of Apollo's Oracle at Delphi, which was far worse than being under the influence of drugs, tobacco, and alcohol. The Oracle actually fucked-up Oedipus even more than his fucked-up genetics had biologically fucked-up both his older brother Octopus and himself."

"Apollo was the renowned Greek god of music, medicine, legal and illegal drugs, and of truth or consequences. The indecisive deity communicated with humans through his famous Oracle at Delphi, a lesbian priestess with a clitoris bigger than all five of her tits put together. Hearing a rumor about free sex, Laius had gone to the Oracle of Delphi to get laid, but when the pussy-hungry king discovered that the priestess was a practicing lesbian nymphomaniac with a clit bigger than his erection, the dipshit monarch reluctantly asked the Oracle to tell him his future instead engaging in regular sex."

"Laius, you will die at the hands of your younger son after you throw Octopus into the sea for good riddance," the totally gay, demented priestess predicted. "And you gotta' admit; throwing Octopus into the sea is much better than pissing into a strong wind!"

"How could that be?" Laius incredulously challenged the Oracle's omniscient prophecy. "Octopus is more likely to kill me with eight arms, and my human-in-appearance younger son Oedipus has only two hands. How then am I to die at the hands of Oedipus? I mean, I could just cut his damned hands off by creating a new 'Hands-off edict' in my totally bizarre kingdom of Thebes!"

"Apollo says that it's your fuckin' problem to solve, Asshole!" the faggot lady Oracle told Laius, who was now doubly disappointed because he couldn't get laid with his gay wife, who had mysteriously formed cement in her collapsed crotch, and now the livid king had learned that his younger son was, in the future, going to murder his deserving ass right-off the friggin' planet."

"When King Laius had tossed Octopus into the sea one October morning, Oedipus was only an infant, but still not old enough to join the Theban infantry. Laius realized that close genetics indeed did have certain physical and psychological repercussions, and that the famous Greek maxim 'Incest is best!' might actually be a blatant fallacy."

"The Theban King soon began to worry. 'Octopus was genetically defective and looked like an absolute miniature monster,' Laius lamented while glancing into his favorite mirror. 'And now Oedipus looks all right physically, but the rambunctious child might be a fuckin' crazy lunatic. I gotta' dispose of the insane little bastard before the future assassin eliminates my happy, privileged existence from this deplorable Earth! My mother had always warned me to stay away from gloom and doom fortunetellers! Sometimes, I wish I weren't such a stupid, asinine jerk-off'!"

"Laius handed to a faithful servant the complex baby Oedipus to carry-off to a secluded high crag that was so distant that area mountain goats had not yet even discovered it. The obedient servant tied the infant's feet together, but did not have the heart to leave Laius's second son on the lonely precipice to die."

'I can socially engineer my future better than that homosexual dyke Oracle's predictions can,' Laius thought. 'By Zeus, her goddamned clitoris was twice as large as my biggest erection! That freakin' gay Oracle was more of a freakin' freak than my ugly son by incest Octopus was!'

"Twenty years later, King Laius arrived at a very important crossroads in his life. The Theban monarch and his traveling entourage of bisexual bodyguards got into an argument with a young punk' hooligan over the right-of-way at an intersection that was devoid of any "Stop Sign". The pugnacious hooligan leaped-out of his souped-up chariot, accosted Laius and his four intoxicated bodyguards, and after a vitriolic argument ensued, the punk whippersnapper first beat the shit out of, and then allegedly slaughtered the five adults with his birthday-gift bronze sword. The young thug murderer happened to be Oedipus, and by slaying his father, he had fulfilled Apollo's pathetic prophecy that had been forecast by the lesbian' Oracle at Delphi."

"A false rumor circulated around Thebes that an army from the city of Athens had slaughtered Laius and his loyal bodyguards. The heavy gossip thus glorified the former despicable, wimpy Theban king as a warrior and a martyr. However, one of the bodyguards had not died and had only been critically wounded. A traveling fruit and vegetable huckster had stopped his oxcart at the intersection, picked-up the sole survivor, and transported the lucky asshole to the crowded marketplace stalls in Thebes."

"Now, no one in Thebes, not even the king's wife Jocastra, gave a flying shit about Laius's cruel death, because the city was then being besieged by a very great threat. A monster that was known as 'the Sphinx' had been terrorizing and killing any Thebans that dared venture outside the city's southern gates. The Sphinx had a lion's body, eagle wings, a woman's face, a female elephant's tits and ass, and a gigantic clitoris even bigger than the one the Oracle at Delphi had."

"The venomous creature clandestinely hid in waiting and halted any traveler it confronted by surprise on his or her way to Thebes. The Sphinx presented the apprehended trekker with a ridiculous riddle, and when the unfortunate traveler could not give the correct response under great duress in a one-minute time period, the horrible creature ferociously devoured man after man alive, first sucking and then eating their throbbing dicks, and then chewing-up and swallowing the remainder of their predestined, doomed bodies, flesh, blood, sweat, tears, piss, shit and all."

"After Laius's funeral and burial had occurred, the seven great gates that allowed entrance, to and exit from Thebes, were permanently closed, and the citizens began suffering from severe famine and pestilence. Worse yet; the horrid Sphinx had devoured most of the Theban men, and consequently, Jocastra and the other promiscuous ladies of the accursed city became even bigger lesbians in the absence of eligible males than the fucked-up Oracle at Delphi ever was."

"Soon, a total stranger with exaggerated physical features similar to those of the deceased King Laius arrived at Thebes. The newcomer knocked-down one of the wooden gates and egotistically entered the isolated city. The intruder was intelligent, intrepid, obnoxious, arrogant and audacious. The brazen adolescent introduced himself' to the usually apathetic Theban citizens as Oedipus the Fifteenth from Corinth, son of entrepreneurial King Polybus, who owned several fleets of chariot and oxcart taxi cabs."

"I am in self-exile," Oedipus told his biological mother Jocastra outside the regal palace. "The Oracle at Delphi had told me that I was destined to kill my father, which oftentimes is not a bad idea for acne-faced teenagers like myself to consider."

"So, why have you come to Thebes, young stranger?" Jocastra asked her itinerant son Oedipus, whom she never recognized. "Aren't you afraid that the voracious Sphinx will consume you? She has a fuckin' edible complex about men, ya' know!"

"I didn't want to kill my father Polybus," Oedipus lied to his biological mother, "because I am a strict practicing heterosexual, and it is a myth in Corinth that Polybus eats from a magical cunt tree out in the country. If I was to savagely kill my father Polybus, then I could not ever learn exactly where this magical cunt tree out in the country actually is located!"

"I have planted a similar tree in the center of my palace bedroom," Jocastra confided and informed Oedipus, presuming that her son was dead. "But only my lady friends and I are allowed to eat the delicious fruit of the womb from my own fabulous cunt tree, which is most-certainly not out in the country!"

"Oedipus set-out on foot to walk from Thebes to Corinth to locate King Polybus's famed mythical cunt tree out in the country. On his wayward escapade, the tragic hero encountered the wicked detestable Sphinx, who then presented her singular riddle for the itinerant wanderer to solve in one minute's time."

"What creature walks on four legs in the morning, two at noon, and three appendages in the evening?" the monster nefariously asked the hero. 'You have *one minute* to provide the correct answer, or you will be reduced to rice grains!"

"That's a rather easy riddle, Bitch!" Oedipus confidently replied. "The answer obviously is 'a man'. As an infant, the child creeps and crawls on all fours, all over the fuckin' place; in manhood, the adult male walks erect, with or without an erection; and in old age, an elderly coot walks with his staff, and if he is poor and doesn't have any goddamned secretaries, the codger walks alone with his fuckin' cane without his fuckin' staff. What do ya' Sphinx about *that* extraordinary bullshit, you dumb fuckin' cocksuckin', riddling man-eater!"

"Oedipus had amazingly delivered the correct response to the monster's cryptic conundrum. The Sphinx was so pissed-off that she killed herself by biting-off her giant, swollen clitoris, and subsequently, bleeding to death, and finally plunging off of her cliff."

"Thanks to Oedipus's exceptional mental dynamics, the Thebans had become miraculously saved from their wretched nemesis. The jubilant numbskulls transported their new-found champion into the city and gave Oedipus an outstanding hero's welcome. The happy revelers roasted the disgusting dead creature in ancient grease, meticulously carved-up the Sphinx's scaly corpse, and ate a sumptuous supper at a splendid barbecue and hot wings feast."

"At the merry All-Meat Banquet Buffet, the grateful citizens quickly elected Oedipus as their king, and Jocastra was pissed-off that she had to marry a young stud with a big dick, because it violated her avowed lesbianism, and also because his thrusting pecker would naturally force the concrete in her vagina all the way up to her windpipe when she would have to engage in straight incestual sex with her royal son. It seemed to Jocastra that Apollo's prophecy delivered by the Oracle at Delphi had been false, since Oedipus the Fifteenth was believed to be the son of King Polybus of Corinth, who claimed that he had secretly gotten a vasectomy at the age of six."

"Jocastra reluctantly allowed Oedipus to screw and sodomize her, and that's exactly how Oedipus became the biggest ball-breaking, and vagina breaking, mother-fucker in all history. That sinful, incest behavior inadvertently brought a terrible plague to Thebes, especially provided by Almighty Zeus. Men died from venereal diseases all over the place, and it didn't matter whether the fools were screwing their wives, their girlfriends, or sodomizing sheep, or ramming rams during that fucked-up time of widespread peril."

"Herds of animals and orchards of fruit also inexplicably died during that terrible time period. It was even rumored that King Polybus of Corinth and Queen Jocastra of Thebes' dual cunt trees had dried-up, had shriveled, and then had regrettably expired. And those unlucky mortals that didn't die from sex diseases, or who weren't eliminated in the next locust invasion, were then also plagued by an atrocious famine. Oedipus felt guilty for ever living anywhere on the damned Earth, and possibly causing the devastating 'damnations' all over his damned nation."

"Oedipus was developing a mental complex about all of the disasters that were occurring in and around Thebes. The new king dispatched his Uncle Creon, Jocastra's older brother who still liked scribbling inside coloring books, to the notoriously gay Oracle at Delphi to learn how the abominable plague and the formidable famine could be permanently eliminated."

"Creon returned to Thebes with meritorious news. The infallible Oracle, whose heart, as was already known, had only one auricle, publicly revealed that Apollo would lift the wicked curses only on one relevant stipulation. "Whoever had killed King Laius at the crossroads must be severely punished," Creon wrote with his favorite coal' crayon for all to see on a scroll of papyrus, and then the message soon appeared as distasteful graffiti all over the city's walls."

"I'm relieved, and I haven't even taken a decent shit!" young King Oedipus told Creon. "Surely, by virtue of the Oracle's sacred words, the men, or the individual, who had killed King Laius, must still be alive and can be captured and brought to justice. Then, Oedipus spoke to his disgruntled, pissed-off people from the palace balcony."

"Citizens and Assholes of Thebes: Let none of you *harbor* the killer of Laius since Thebes is not located anywhere near an ocean, or anywhere near the sea. Don't give the anonymous murderer of Laius any shelter, including tax annuity shelters, animal shelters, or fuckin' fallout shelters. You are hereby officially directed to bar the anonymous shit-head from your homes and businesses. You must solemnly commit to bar the unknown asshole from your taverns. And most importantly, you must bar him from your pubs, saloons, and bars, and also from all your asshole bar associations."

"Laius's murderer is a villain that must be condemned, mocked, scorned, tortured and perpetually whipped and punished. And I, Oedipus, sincerely pray that the gutless, cut-throated bastard-assassin's dick rots-off, and that his balls should also become polluted, infected, and contaminated, requiring immediate castration."

"Oedipus then sent for Teresias, the hoary blind prophet, and at the time, the most revered of the three remaining decrepit Theban men. The soothsayer had once blindsided teenaged Oedipus while the prophet was trying to drive a runaway chariot along a narrow alleyway. According to ancient oral chronicles, Teresias's Theban mom was the very popular Mother Teresias."

"Hey Teresias, you old, dumb, blind fuck," Oedipus gregariously greeted. "Use your gift of prophecy to tell me the identity of the men, or man, that had evilly killed King Laius at the infamous crossroads."

"If I ever told you'," the very shrewd, old, blind savant cautioned Oedipus, "you'd be mighty pissed-off. You might first be inclined to beat the shit out of me, or maybe even go into a blind rage! The city residents don't call you Oedipus wrecks for nothin', ya' know!"

"For the love and mercy of vindictive, emotionally-unstable Zeus," Oedipus continued his query. "Who the fuck killed Laius? Tell me now, or I'll dig-up Mother Teresias, and have you screw her, you old, blind, soft-dicked mother-fucker!"

"Fools!" Teresias cleverly and enigmatically answered. "Idiotic fools disposed of the former king. Only Laius's smelly asshole has remained from the scene of massacre, and as you know, his anus has been on display at the Theban Proctological Colon Museum."

"I suspect that you were one of Laius's murderers," Oedipus impetuously accused the sightless prophet. "And I believe that you', old man, were having an affair with Queen Jocastra, and that you had violated the sacred moral precepts of your Mother Teresias by teaching my wife the secret formula for making cement."

"Those ugly words had greatly angered the aged soothsayer, who then communicated a certain grotesque truth to the adolescent King. "How's this for some concrete thinking, young Oedipus? It is *you* that are the murderer whom you seek! It takes a no-good-bastard to murder another no-good-bastard!"

"Oedipus thought that the elderly prophet had gone bizarrely insane, so the teenaged king ordered the mentally-deranged old fart out of the palace. "Disappear old man," Oedipus screamed. "And never come inside this palace again until you get your next hard-on, which hopefully, will be fuckin' never!"

"Jocastra had been eavesdropping on the loud conversation from behind a curtain, and the Queen had heard the old man's startling testimony to her young husband, and regarded 'the drivel' as absolute bullshit. "Prophets and oracles have limited knowledge just like we other mortals do," the disbelieving queen later ineffectively argued to her despondent husband/son/king. "And prophets and oracles are mere mortals, the same as we are, and twice as fucked-up, too!"

"Stop speaking in preposterous, absurd riddles, Jocastra," the youthful King warned. "You're beginning to sound like the insane maniacal Sphinx.

I made her commit suicide, and I'll make you do the same thing if you persist in bustin' my goddamned balls!"

"Oedipus, there's something salient I must now disclose," Queen Jocastra articulated. "The stupid priestess at Delphi prophesied that Laius would die at the hands of his son, so my deceased husband and I saw to it that you, our son, should be left alone upon a distant mountain peak to peacefully die with a dumb-ass yo-yo while playing rock the cradle. Then, my husband Laius was later murdered near the busy convenience bizarre-bazaar store, not far from 'Three Points', where the triple dirt roads intersect."

"When the fuck did that tragedy happen?" the young King asked his matronly-looking wife. "I hope I was not yet born!"

"Just a few days before you had arrived in Thebes!" Jocastra instantly answered. "There are too many coincidences to ignore!"

"How many assassins had performed the vile deed at the crossroads?" Oedipus interrogated his mother/wife/queen."

"Rumor has it that there were four felons in all," Jocastra replied. "All were killed but one. The surviving highway thief was picked-up by a traveling hawker, tossed onto the back of the huckster's fruit and vegetable oxcart, and then conveyed into the city."

"I must see and question that lone survivor, for only he knows the truth as to what had really transpired on that auspicious day," Oedipus forcefully demanded. "Send for the dirty old prick right now!"

"I shall summon the survivor," Jocastra promised her impulsive husband/son/king. "But what is the truth regarding this series of events from your perspective? I mean, I'm your damned wife, and I hardly know a thing about your past prior to your coming to Thebes. What do you think is actually your real friggin' ancestry?"

"I shall honestly tell you all that I know about my past," Oedipus contritely stated. "I had traveled to Delphi to consult Apollo's Oracle. A nobleman back in Corinth had divulged to me that I was not the biological son of King Polybus. I was totally pissed-off, because I thought that I would never inherit his fleet of chariot and oxcart taxis, and as a result, would never possess his mythical cunt tree somewhere out in the country. Anyway," the newly elected Theban King pontificated. "I was not about to apologize to Apollo for anything. The psychotic priestess at Delphi then told me a most horrible thing."

"That you had herpes, psoriasis, syphilis and gonorrhea?" Jocastra sarcastically and un-elegantly asked."

"The fucked-up Oracle foretold that I would kill my father, marry my mother, and would have children uglier than someone named Octopus, and even uglier than the lousy, hideous-looking Sphinx. I didn't want to kill eminent Polybus, so I left Corinth and journeyed here to Thebes."

"But you could've been a pillar of the community back in that other city," Jocastra theorized and then communicated. "You could have been a Corinthian column in that famous city!"

"Anyway, you dumb lesbian slut," Oedipus elaborated his narrative. "On my way from Delphi to Thebes, I came upon a man and his bodyguards at a crossroads."

"Near the busy bizarre-bazaar convenience store at Three Points?" his wife asked in amazement. "There's a gay and lesbian house of prostitution upstairs!"

"Yes," Oedipus reluctantly admitted as a former patron. "We got into an intense argument as to which one of us had the right of way. There was no 'Yield' or 'Stop' sign at the congested Three Points dirt trail crossroads."

"So, you became cross at the crossroads!" Jocastra criticized. "Like biological father, like biological son really happens to be a very true moral axiom! Some punk delinquent teen vandals must've stolen the damned traffic sign," Jocastra hypothesized and related."

"Anyway," Oedipus impulsively interrupted his mother/wife/queen. "The short-tempered man riding on the chariot platform struck me with his whip, and being a young whippersnapper myself', I killed the dumb cock-sucker, along with his goddamned pathetically weak attendants."

"Holy shit Oedipus! The one man that had survived the ordeal returned critically wounded to the city on the back of a huckster's oxcart," Jocastra informed her astonished-but-attentive son. "He reported that Laius had been assassinated by bandits attempting to get away with highway robbery. And I then wept for another five minutes, because my son reportedly had died upon a distant mountain peak, and now my bullheaded husband, King Laius, was also dead."

"Did you feel guilty about the murders? Had the fear of possibly killing your father drive you from Corinth?" Jocastra asked."

"No; it was my black horses and my chariot that drove me from Corinth, and then to Delphi, and then to Three Points near the busy bizarre-bazaar convenience store," Oedipus stupidly divulged. "The murder didn't drive me anywhere."

At that moment, an excited courier from Corinth coincidentally arrived at the Theban palace to deliver an important message. "King Polybus has died," the messenger solemnly informed Jocastra and Oedipus. "He died of a parched tongue, dry mouth, and arid throat while eating some dried-up fruit of the womb that had been growing on his remarkable cunt tree out in the Corinthian country."

"I'm relieved that Polypus died a peculiar natural death rather than being killed by me!" Oedipus vociferously exclaimed. "My false guilt has now been eradicated. I now believe that I'm vindicated from being accused of committing the alleged vile sin of murdering my father!"

"Polybus was not your biological father," the Corinthian King's servant attested. "The King had raised you from childhood as if you shared his fucked-up genetics, but you were definitely not the son of King Polybus and his promiscuous wife Queen Omnibus."

"Well then, exactly how did I get into the King's hands?" Oedipus insisted on knowing. "Where and how did you, or anyone else, get to deliver me to the King of Corinth?"

"I know nothing of your true biological parents," the out-of-breath messenger from Corinth acknowledged. "But a wandering shepherd had found you freezing to death upon a mountainside while toying with a yo-yo in your rocking cradle, and then the merciful herdsman presented you to me. I soon donated you to King Polybus and Queen Omnibus," the loyal servant/courier indicated. "Dear Oedipus; I'm afraid to disclose that you are a mere red-blooded commoner; the son of impoverished mountain peasants, and an impostor to blue-blooded royalty everywhere."

"What kind of fuckin' bullshit is this story you have told?" Oedipus yelled in a fit of rage. "You' falsely say fake news that I have been discarded by mountain peasant scumbag parents? I'll have you slain right this minute!"

"Jocastra's countenance turned whiter than a lily. Absolute horror radiated from her face. "Oedipus, don't pay any attention to this old senile Corinthian fuck. He's even more fucked-up than Teresias, and the asshole's dead matriarch, Mother Teresias. Everything this moron from Corinth has just told us has been imaginatively fabricated, except possibly the fact that King Polybus is dead!"

"Jocastra, you are claiming that my birth origin doesn't fuckin' matter?" Oedipus impetuously yelled. "You're a bigger bitch than the pernicious Sphinx ever was!"

"Say no more, you demented ignoramus," Jocastra admonished her son/husband/king. "My agony and my misery are now complete non-ecstasy! I must replenish myself and my damaged ego at my cunt tree in the center of my private garden!"

"The blind prophet Teresias then accidentally stumbled into the palace throne chamber, thinking that he had entered a public rest room to take a half-hour leak. The messenger from Corinth instantly recognized the chief Theban prophet."

"Oh, noble King Oedipus; that's the old fuck shepherd that gave you to me," the courier from Corinth stated. "He was a blind young fuck shepherd, though, at the time!"

"Hold your sacrilegious tongue!" Teresias balked as the revered soothsayer recognized the voice of his past acquaintance and distant cousin from Corinth."

"Teresias, did you bring me from Thebes to Corinth and place me on top of the cold mountain?" the shocked Oedipus asked his chief-religious counselor. "If I were a woman cow herder, I could've been a frozen dairy queen!"

"I must confess the truth and get the whole fuckin' mess off my about-to-die conscience," the old blind prophet explained. "Your wife Jocastra is also your mother. She and Laius gave you to me. I didn't have the heart to leave you abandoned up on the frigid mountain, so I presented you to my distant cousin, who then orphaned you to King Polybus and Queen Omnibus."

"I made my father into dead meat. I made him into road kill!" Oedipus sobbed. "And today, I am also most-grieved upon learning of King Polybus's passing. But worst of all," Oedipus somberly concluded. "The good people of Thebes have been right on the money every time they call me a dirty mother-fucker! Indeed, I have been cursed by that son-of-a-bitchin' Apollo, and his deranged lesbian priestess, who had slyly tricked me into marrying my dyke mother!"

"The priestess's prophecy has been verified," Teresias confirmed. "You have murdered your biological father, and you have married your biological mother, who has turned from a bisexual into a practicing lesbian with a solid concrete love tunnel. You, Oedipus, have been adequately cursed by Lord Phoebus Apollo, and as a result, have been completely fucked-up your whole damned life!"

"Oedipus left the Theban throne chamber in a wild, raging state of mind. The young king searched the entire palace until he eventually found his mother/wife/queen lying dead in her private garden. "She's choked to death eating fruit of the womb from her cunt tree! Her throat is fuckin' clogged with black, brown, blonde and red pubic hair!" the teenaged monarch sorrowfully realized and muttered."

"Then, Oedipus's perplexed mind evaluated his entire life. 'I hate viewing and reviewing what fate has repugnantly presented me,' the Boy King regretted in despair. 'I'm going to blind myself and become a disciple of eminent Teresias. It is better to live life blind to its evils rather than see contemptible events happening before my very eyes every fuckin' day. What a lot of bullshit both eyesight and human life really are!' Oedipus mourned to his mirror-reflection in Jocastra's private garden water-pond, situated next to the deceased queen's now lethal cunt tree."

"So morally speaking," Eurshiddenme announced and concluded to his disgruntled and sleeping four gagged and tied-up, peeved listeners. "We foolhardy soldiers should piously pay homage to the gods of Olympus, and just as importantly, we should get our damned mendacious minds off of sex, which will only further destroy our already fucked-up characters. Instead, be celibate, my fellow lieutenants, and concentrate your vital energies on maintaining abstinence, and also on obeying Lord Odysseus. And while doing so, enjoy killing as many diabolical Trojans as we possibly can. We must religiously implement these vital moral lessons represented in the story of Oedipus to ensure the essential continuation of the human race throughout Greece."

* * * * * * * * * * * *

The Trojans again assailed the Greek barrier wall, but were repelled by the Achaean forces out of a desperation for surviving the escalating battle. The Danaans' recently-dug trench before the wall had effectively kept-out Trojan chariots, and every wounded enemy soldier, before the victim died in the deep ditch, was given mud inside his mouth, thus automatically contracting and dying from trench-mouth. Ajax fought like a berserk killer from atop the wall, spearing Trojans as if the attackers were trapped fish in a barrel.

The great giant Sarpedon, Jr. got into an urgent wrestling scrimmage with his Greek counterpart, Ajax, who astonishingly elevated the Trojan weightlifter upon his broad soldiers, put the enemy grappler in a dizzying propeller spin, and then tossed the hulking behemoth off the recently constructed wall onto three quickly-clobbered foes who had been busily fighting with several Danaan warriors below.

"Nice going Ajax!" the giant's partner and comrade Teucer commended. "You threw Sarpedon, Jr. down to the desert floor as if he were a scrawny rag doll! The fearsome behemoth will be immobile for quite some time. He's still lying upon the hot sand down there, and I don't think there's any crap left in his intestines with all of that brown-feces surrounding his abdomen and asshole! My eyes don't deceive me. The stationary ogre even has crap and sand inside his sandals!"

Hector became infuriated at witnessing the celebrated champion Sarpedon, Jr. being so methodically knocked unconscious, so the Trojan prince lifted a second immense boulder, thrust it at high speed, and crashed the mammoth rock through the still partially-standing second gate in the Greek defensive wall.

"Almighty Zeus! Hector shouted-up to the clear blue sky. "Thank you for making me stronger and bolder, with me easily hoisting-up and forcefully tossing this second five-hundred-pound boulder!"

Chapter 13

"TROJANS ATTACK THE SHIPS"

Zeus was satisfied that his strategy of allowing the Trojans to take the battlefield advantage was being successfully implemented, so the chief god was certain that no other residents of Mt. Olympus would dare to interfere with his plan to appease Thetis, in deference to her sulking son, Achilles. But as soon as Zeus sped-off to (nearby-Troy) Mt. Ida's high peak in his golden chariot, Poseidon, who had been surveilling his sky-brother's recent activities, used his supernatural influence, and rallied the crestfallen Achaeans, affording the newly-inspired warriors' divine strength to take the battlefront initiative.

Hector, who had been savagely slaughtering and decapitating dozens of Argive soldiers daring to raise their bronze swords, was suddenly stymied by the trio of Ajax, Odysseus and Diomedes, and although the three heroes were mildly injured, the Greek fighters were exceptionally motivated to contribute their combined talents in thwarting the Trojan prince's ambitious assault. The clamorous combat was fought within tight quadrants, so at times, Trojans were wildly stabbing Trojans, and Greeks were accidentally slashing Greeks.

Thirteen heroes on both sides were killed in the grueling battle, and many soldiers were incidentally maimed by their own comrades. Hearing the loud clanging and banging of swords and shields, Nestor left aching Machaon inside *his* tent and exited to investigate how the war zone was rapidly changing from one side to the other. The King of Pylos located Agamemnon taking an extended dump outside his tent, and the two plotters decided to visit Odysseus to see if the military guru could concoct some suitable battle scenario to advantageously stifle Hector and his minions.

The two vigilant kings found Odysseus sitting inside his modest tent conferring with his five zany lieutenants, who had that same afternoon been showered with praise by Ajax for "cleverly rolling down the hill" and knocking Prince Paris off his feet.

"I must commend you five stout-hearted men for your noteworthy bravery," Odysseus cited with a rare smile. "Keep-up the good work, and who the hell knows? Perhaps you'll all earn the privilege of being promoted to the rank of captain."

"Sorry to interrupt your impromptu conference," Agamemnon said to Odysseus upon entering the Ithacan king's tent. "The Trojans are beating our ranks back toward our black Biremes, and the wall that you suggested is not confining the enemy groups to their original positions. We must tax our brains and develop a new dynamic plan. Do you', brilliant savant Odysseus, have any novel ideas besides authoring a fiction book once writing and alphabets are developed?"

"The well has run dry," downtrodden Odysseus confessed. "Perhaps my creative-minded lieutenants could describe a viable solution to our current dilemma," the Ithacan king stated, passing the buck to his subordinate five nincompoops. "What say you', Lieutenant Eurshiddenme? Give us a constructive plan of attack!"

"I say that we utilize this amazing flammable black substance my fellow officers have discovered that's spewing-up from below the Earth's surface," Eurshiddenme offered. "The substance burns very easily, and the men call it 'petroleum', or smelly, common oil. We've managed to collect several hundred barrels of the black liquid to run our bonfires, which are burning near our rudely-constructed watchtowers."

"And we could muster and have a hundred naked slave girls and a hundred nude, muscular infantrymen stand in front of the bug-eyed Trojan troops," Eurballsourout suavely recommended. "The heterosexual Trojans will chase after the hundred voluptuous naked dolls, and the homosexual gay jerk-offs will instantly pursue the nude and muscular, tanned, Adonis-like faggots."

"Won't the hundred Achaean vivacious chicks and the hundred nude gay guys dash into the surf and possibly drown?" Odysseus skeptically asked. "The two hundred nude sprinters better know how to swim like sharks!"

"No, my king," Eurassisgras disagreed. "We'll artistically draw in the sand two similar-in-dimension rectangles, five-hundred-feet long, and two-hundred-feet wide. The two identical rectangles will be parallel to each other, and situated a hundred feet apart."

"How the hell are two rectangles going to stop the crazed Trojans from chasing after the hundred gorgeous girls and the hundred gay Adonis imitators?" Agamemnon challenged the five stooge lieutenants. "There better be more elaborate details to your dumb-fuck plan."

"The hundred barrels of oil will be spread around the entire perimeter of the twin drawn rectangles," Eurdicisin added to the oddball discussion. "And after the hundred naked chicks and the hundred nude studs run through the drawn rectangles, the hundreds of Trojan pursuers will enter the drawn-out areas. Then, our most-skilled soldiers will torch the surrounding oil, and the horny Trojans will be trapped inside the dual conflagrations with no possible escape from the rising fences of fire!"

"That's absolutely right," Eurcockisnum remarked and endorsed. "The tricked, sexually-aroused Trojans will be promptly barbecued, and their scorched flesh will be gratefully consumed by the numerous vultures and buzzards patrolling the late afternoon skies."

"If your ingenious plan, being converted from theory to practice, is a success," Agamemnon enthusiastically declared, "then you five stellar strategists will be swiftly promoted to the rank of captain."

The hundred naked bitches and the hundred gay, nude bastards quickly gained the attention of the sex-starved Trojans, who reflexively scampered after their two-hundred lures with great speed and dexterity. Upon reaching the designated rectangular traps, the two-hundred Trojans, sporting stiff erections, were instantly roasted by the blazing shafts of fire.

'You five saviors are like god-sent messiahs who have salvaged our already-battered Biremes," King Agamemnon happily congratulated Odysseus's sagacious new captains. "It's too bad that Hector wasn't involved in the spectacular chaos, or else, the hot-to-trot prince would've been incinerated into embers just like his pathetic comrades had been broiled and fried."

"That plan you've fabricated was absolutely incredible!" Odysseus lauded his five new captains. "The Trojans fond Sex Wish had transformed into the idiots' very fatal Death Wish! Ha, ha, ha! Remember this very important maxim, men; always think with your brains and not with you erect fadorkenbenders!"

* * * * * * * * * * *

Hera had perceptively noticed that Poseidon had been engaged in enacting certain mischief against Zeus's supreme will when the Achaeans had taken to the offensive, and the alert wife also observed that her moody spouse was idly resting and basking in the sun atop nearby Mount Ida. Hera then considered paying a visit to Aphrodite's luxurious suite atop glorious Mt. Olympus to have a much-needed summit conference.

"Spellbinding Goddess of Love and Beauty," Hera politely addressed her goddess counterpart, who obviously favored the Trojan cause. Brother and sister Oceanus and Tethys have been quarreling about trifles for some time now, and I absolutely loathe conflict and estrangement. Please lend me your wondrous Girdle of Desire, so that I may soften the pair's contentious relationship, and have harmony and tranquility again prevail amongst our extended family. The feuding twosome must be reconciled," Hera convincingly insisted, "and with your cooperation, *that* peaceful end to hostilities between the bickering siblings can and will be achieved."

"You speak and seek a noble goal, even though you and I are on opposite sides of the mortals' dumb-shit war," Aphrodite replied. "Now Hera, if your unusual request has nothing to do with promoting the Achaean cause, I shall lend you my coveted Girdle of Desire."

Feeling guileful, Hera zoomed-off to the Isle of Lemnos with Aphrodite's Girdle of Desire to communicate with Sleep, the snoozing and slumbering brother of Death. "Sweet Sleep. Sorry to awaken you from your loud snoring. But I must ask a favor of you, which is designed to guarantee peace among the immortals. As you are aware, my husband Zeus has chronic insomnia, and never fully receives the therapeutic benefit of enjoying deep sleep," Hera insisted, feigning both alarm and concern. "If you assist me in accomplishing my endeavor, I'll make sure that my blacksmith son Hephaestus builds you a magnificent golden throne equal to the one that Zeus sits his chubby ass upon."

"Listen, Hera. I once before tried that sleep antic with Zeus at your behest, and if it weren't for my mother Night descending and saving my butt from Zeus's wrath, I might have been condemned to the Black Pit of Tartarus on a non-reversible, non-rehabilitation sentence."

'Hurry-up and grant me my wish,' Hera impatiently thought. 'This tight girdle I have borrowed from svelte Aphrodite is chaffing the clit right off of my sensitive slit hole, and the friction is quite irritating. The friggin' too-small girdle that I'm uncomfortably wearing doesn't seem to be producing satisfactory results!'

Then, all-too-cunning Hera remained on task and resumed her cordial conversation with gullible Sleep. "Oh yes. I do remember now. But that situation you've recollected involving Zeus was much different than the current dilemma I wish to resolve. If I recall, Zeus groggily awoke from your influential sleeping spell, and his blurry eyes perceived Hercules shipwrecked on the Isle of Kos. Thank goodness your mother Night saved your ass from major harassment. But you didn't have your hemorrhoids explode as you had originally feared, and not one minor lightning bolt from my husband ever penetrated-up your vulnerable asshole!"

"Do you have any other gift besides the Golden Throne offer?" Sleep curiously asked. "I already have seven Golden Thrones situated in separate spots all over this remote island."

"I promise I will give you one of the beautiful Graces to have as your private valet, and also as your personal mistress, whom you could screw day and night in fabulous pleasure all the way to High Heaven! You'll no longer have to pop a white dream load into that magical inflatable doll of yours, and then have to clean-up the sticky mess every time."

"Yes, Hera," Sleep amenably concurred. "I've always desired to marry and have both conversational and sexual intercourse with lovely Pasithee, and now you present me with my strongest desire as a wonderful gift. Quite frankly, my fidgety fingers can't wait to explore Pasithee's passionate pink pussy-pit. Yes Hera; I shall gladly accompany you to Mt. Ida to send Almighty Zeus upon a marvelous fantasy adventure to visit old, reliable Mr. Sandman."

When Zeus saw Hera appear in his midst atop the mountain overlooking Troy, the chief deity became sexually aroused, and as the Thunder and Lightning god shoved and thrust his incredibly lengthy godhood deep into Hera's wet-pink love tunnel, magical Sleep induced Dreamland onto Zeus's subconscious libido, simultaneously saving goddess Hera from experiencing a painful, ruptured esophagus.

"Thank you for saving my partially-pulverized ass, and also my aching love tunnel from experiencing total destruction," Hera said to Sleep. 'Ah yes,' the goddess imagined. 'Zeus is now sound asleep and quite distracted from his involvement in pacifying Achilles's interest and ego regarding the dumb-shit Trojan War! Thetis's intercession has been neutralized!'

"Have no anxiety over your in-progress request," Sleep happily assured Hera. "Soon, your vindictive husband will be all relaxed, imagining in his calm trance either him chopping a hundred cords of wood, or him watching several thousand sheep slowly jumping over a high fence, one by one!"

* * * * * * * * * * * *

While Zeus soundly slept, and his impressive godhood had shrunk-down to three-feet in length, back on the Troad Plain, Hector and Ajax were duking it out near the Achaean ships, even though both combatants were princes and not dukes. The Greeks were pushing their disarrayed enemy back onto the Trojan side of the Argives' wall, throwing many of the resisters off the elevated platform and into the recently-excavated nearby trench, also referred to as "the moat".

Hector was the incensed aggressor, partially hitting Ajax in the chest with his sharp spear, but the thick leather cross-bands inside the Achaean's shield had deflected the impact of the sharp weapon's deadly tip. Then, responding to Zeus being fast asleep and unable to aid Hector's initiative, Ajax seized a large boulder and flung the heavy object at his main rival, striking Hector in his sternum, and sending the livid Trojan prince (stem-to-sternum) spinning in circles like a gay pole dancer on meth.

The Achaeans surged forward, simulating a colossal tidal wave, hurling spears, javelins, and a plethora of insults at the retreating Trojans, who had out of necessity, closed their ranks, forming a defensive circle around fallen Hector, whose body was lifted and carried to a nearby chariot that was not on fire. The Trojan price had cold water from the Xanthus River splashed upon his face and body, and the son of Priam began coughing-up and vomiting large amounts of dark blood from his mouth and lungs, and also was heavily hemorrhaging through his nostrils.

"He's gone unconscious," the shocked commander of the rescue troops uttered. "His eyes are dull and his vision is growing dim. What we are witnessing must be what the local shamans say is a near-death-experience," one voice heard above the rest attested. "This is the first time I've ever seen Hector in a comatose and immobile state, lying prone in *this* terrible situation. I mean," the astonished warrior finished his remark. "Hector certainly battles like a maniacal wild cyclone, but that fuckin' behemoth Ajax violently fights like a fanatical white tornado."

Chapter 14
"THE BURNING OF THE BIREMES"

Zeus awoke from his abbreviated slumber that had been induced by Sleep, and immediately, the chief deity observed in the dusty plain off in the distance that Hector had been severely injured, and that Poseidon had probably intervened during *his* brief siesta, and had mischievously aided and abetted the Greek forces. Hera had also been napping on the Mt. Ida summit, and Zeus suspected right away that his conniving spouse had been involved in a secret pro-Achaean alliance with roguish Poseidon.

"Disobedient wife!" Zeus thundered and boomed. "Do you recall the last time you defied my orders? In anger, I hung you from the sky with anvils attached to your ankles? The other gods appeared on the scene and tried to rescue you from my experiment in learning about gravity, which I had incidentally and accidentally created centuries ago! But their efforts were futile. My addled mind tells me that I should viciously strike you down as if you were a tall timber, that is, if you weren't such a good piece of ass!"

"I swear by my entire heart and soul that I have never engaged in any conspiracy with Poseidon against you regarding the mortals' Trojan War," Hera uttered and then cried. 'It is Athena, Lord Zeus, who is the Argives' biggest non-athletic supporter!'

"Now begone with you, distrustful wife!" Zeus bellowed. "Go and find Iris and Apollo, whom I wish to consult in caucus. Thetis is also bothering me with her dumb-fuck favor requests, and it's about time that her crybaby son Achilles stops his persistent pouting and sulking, and returns to his participation in the war, which is now starting to bore me all-the-way to High Olympus!"

Several hours later, Zeus ordered Iris to locate Poseidon and direct the sea god to abandon his assumed allegiance to the Greeks, and to then thereafter, find Apollo, and state that Zeus commands that the archer god must assist Hector in regaining consciousness, and after attaining full cerebral and physical normalcy, promptly resume *his* mental obsession of devoutly defending Troy.

"Prince Hector, I have replenished your quivering quiver with a fresh supply of toxic-tipped arrows," Apollo, disguised as a vague vision, communicated to a still rather-dazed Hector. "Now, get your ass in gear and find some barbaric Greeks to maim and slaughter."

"Who the hell are you?" Hector interrogated the purple-hazed image. "Are you a rock-and-roll minstrel? I'm no fuckin' amateur meteorologist, but just a few minutes ago, I was almost perilously killed by Ajax behaving like a swirling white tornado."

"Sit-up now, Trojan prince!" the nebulous-in-appearance purple image sternly urged. "Your protector, Phoebus Apollo, will allow your acclaimed chariot to pass through the battered Greek wall!"

Hector rose-up from his knees, and stood above the baking-hot ground; the Trojan hero sprinted like a cheetah to his damaged chariot, and to the astonishment of his wide-eyed captains, sped forward to massacre any doomed Danaan who confronted his advance. With the assistance of Apollo aiding Hector, the Greeks instantly became intimidated, and the invaders hastily raced to the nearest outhouses to empty their smelly bowels. Apollo then collapsed the frail wall and its interior moat, thus allowing the Trojan chariots to easily chase the freshly-arrived Greeks to retreat and defend their anchored Biremes, because those new troops weren't among the panic-stricken Argives that were frantically scampering-back toward their stench-laden outhouses.

As the battle of the Argive ships ensued, Agamemnon took a moment to pray to Olympus, hoping that merciful Zeus would not permit Hector and his minions to overwhelm the moored vessels, and thus, emerge victorious in the nine-year-conflict. And during the culmination of the conflict, Odysseus's five newly-appointed captains, by virtue of their new-found high rank, were compelled to strenuously stay and fight in the escalating battle.

"This shit is nerve-racking," Eurshiddenme yelled above the active fray's noise. "I'd rather get my dick licked by Medusa the Gorgon than get my balls castrated by some berserk Trojan!"

"Fighting these swarming bastards is worse than receiving a bad blowjob from a homo Trojan having razor-sharp teeth!" Eurballsourout screamed above the ongoing sound of heavy metal against heavier metal. "If I survive this fucked-up war, I'll gladly get castrated and become a transgender priestess serving the fucked-up Oracle at Delphi!"

"I don't know which essential organ I'm going to lose first!" Eurassisgras's voice hollered above the surrounding clamor of bronze swords and shields banging and clanging. "I hope it's neither my precious scrotum sac, nor my cherished epididymis!"

Eurdicisin was the next captain to shriek-out a ludicrous comment during the intense melee. "Listen guys! I'd rather screw Queen Persephone's frozen-cold, icy sex tunnel down in dark Hades than die an insignificant death here upon this contemptible Troad battlefield."

"I refuse to die before I get my first erection," forty-two-year-old Eurcockisnum bellowed as he parried with a boy Trojan. "When the fuck am I going to ever experience the joys of puberty?" the fearful, disenchanted captain yelled above the disturbing noise and awesome clanking. "My pathetic limp dick has remained numb for over four lousy decades!" Eurcockisnum complained to his four disinterested and preoccupied colleagues. "If I'm ever lucky enough to survive this reprehensible war, I think I'm going right to the nearest butcher clinic and be transformed into a goddamned transsexual S and M instructor! I'd rather have two limp legs than a flaccid, limp pecker!"

* * * * * * * * * * * *

King Priam's army was gaining the upper hand, and the weary Greeks were emotionally drained and physically exhausted. Agamemnon was becoming increasingly irritated that a mere several thousand Trojans could thwart fifty thousand supposedly superior Greeks upon the Troad battlefield. Only the king's huge animosity toward Achilles was greater than Agamemnon's mounting disdain for Prince Hector.

While the sounds and cries of carnage were discernible from far away, Patroclus was assiduously bandaging his old friend Eurypylus's wounds in a medical ward tent situated inside the Archaean main camp. But at the Bireme fleet that was moored along the beach, standing upon the stern, fleet-footed Ajax was defending his favorite vessel and jabbing at Trojans with his heavy, twelve-cubit-long pike, which was inflicting major stomach and abdomen wounds upon encroaching Trojan aggressors.

Hector was afraid that the Greeks would strip-away and confiscate as coveted trophies the armor of high-ranking Trojan brass, and then display the obtained prizes as special souvenirs from the masts of their anchored ships. The intensifying struggle near the Greek vessels raged-on, with every second revealing an eye for an eye, a tooth for a tooth, and a penis for a penis scenario. Although severely hindered by the devastating loss of life, both sides fought like male lions in heat, seeking dominance and possession of the ready-for-sex females in their pride.

"If your ship is burned and destroyed as is about to certainly happen," Hector screamed-up to the giant Ajax, "will you awkwardly walk across the deep wine-dark sea and arrive home on foot twenty years later? Zeus favors the Trojans in this wicked game of mortal death struggle! Your' end is near, Argives! Prepare to shake hands with your doom! I had always suspected that you were a piker, Ajax, and now, looking at your chosen weapon, I know for sure that you are!"

"Use your blazing torches to cauterize and seal the Trojans' assholes!" Odysseus loudly commanded his five new captains. "The enemy will wish that their butt apertures had been struck by Zeus's electrifying lightning bolts instead! Onward and upward, or some silly shit like that! Singe their' hairy assholes, I say!"

"You know Eurballsourout," Eurshiddenme said as the head captain scraped grimy sweat and blood from his right wrist. "We were better-off as inconspicuous lieutenants when we could easily hide and avoid battle and injury. Now that we're bona fide captains," Eurshiddenme regretted, "we're always expected to be constantly visible, getting our tender asses kicked in view of the perceptive eyes of Agamemnon, Diomedes and Odysseus!"

"I should've listened to my mother and committed suicide twenty years ago," Eurballsourout ruefully remarked. "She said to me: 'Eurballsourout! Your ugly, pimpled dick is out, too'!"

"Woe is me! Why the hell couldn't I be All-Powerful Zeus rather than being puny fucked-up Eurshiddenme!" the head captain disgustedly bitched to his four hapless-but-compatible subordinates.

Chapter 15
"THE DEATH OF PATROCLUS"

Drama was beginning to permeate throughout the camp of Achilles and his world-famous Myrmidons. Many among the ranks resented the fact that their eminent commander was openly denying them participation on the battlefield, simply because their illustrious general was involved in a picayune dispute with King Agamemnon over possession of a single captured slave girl.

"Patroclus, why are you crying?" Achilles asked his close friend and confidante who had just returned from the Achaeans' camp to his master's Bireme. "Are you magically turning into a fuckin' weeping willow tree, or what? Honestly; you're acting like a spoiled toddler who wants his doting mommy to pick-up his soft ass and carry his pouting mouth to his bedroom in order to be breast fed! Now then, I happen to have a rather erudite idea to convey to you, Patroclus. Why don't you take a long walk off a high cliff and evaluate your pedestrian ideas!"

"Brave Achilles, I am grievously sobbing for my Achaean friends who have been either wounded or killed in battle," Patroclus sorrowfully declared. "Odysseus, Diomedes, Agamemnon, Eurypylus, brother of Eurapylon, have all been seriously injured, all happening because you're a selfish dunce in continuing your petty squabble with Agamemnon over an unimportant slave girl's tiny tits and shaved pussy. From my perspective, that is also shared by a majority of your troops, you evidently lack basic pity and loyalty!"

"What the hell are you saying?" Achilles questioned and objected. "Don't you have any loyalty to me, your very competent commander? Haven't I brought you military discipline, honor and praise in the past?"

"You fear the oracle's announced prophecy, much to the detriment of *our* wounded and dying countrymen!" Patroclus accused his stubborn superior. "Kindly lend me your gleaming armor so that I can lead the caged-up Myrmidons into the heart of the heated conflict. Our troops are fresh, and being fresh, the irate soldiers even curse each other out quite frequently! I predict that the Trojans will flee like scared pigeons when their eyes see me wearing your armor, and the idiots will think that I am you!"

"You speak of past prophecy that has been spoken by weak and scared-shitless prophets," skeptical Achilles verbally parried. "Those feckless priests, priestesses, and oracles adroitly use religion as a mechanism to control the illiterate masses, and thus, make the public afraid of curses and plagues! Basically, religion is a form of cultural propaganda! Now dear Patroclus; I stay isolated here inside my camp solely for the purpose of punishing Agamemnon. It all boils-down to a matter of will grappling! My singular intent is to show the dirty bastard that he cannot defeat Hector and his maniacal Trojans without me and my valiant soldiers directly involved in the middle of the fray," the son of Thetis elaborated. "I'll concede to your general argument this one salient point: you Patroclus, should put-on my armor, but I caution your present boldness: once you've pushed the enemy back away from the moored Greek ships, cease your aggression so that you do not diminish my glory and sully my earned reputation among the Argives!"

"Will you ever again join the Argives in their nine-year assault on Troy?" Patroclus asked Achilles. "Or are you a shivering, petrified chicken as the popular rumor around camp claims that A-pollo is!"

"If and when the enemy approaches my beachhead and their encroachment jeopardizes my Biremes and my troops, then, and only then, will I feel compelled to fight for Greece. Now, my eyes see smoke rising in the distance. Several ships have already been set ablaze! Put on my invincible armor while I assemble the Myrmidons to prepare for combat. Patroclus, this is your shining moment of personal growth as a commander!"

The two-thousand-five-hundred muscular Myrmidons were quickly assembled and organized into five distinct marching groups, with five-hundred virulent troops within each designated division. Achilles stood high above the stern of his Bireme and firmly addressed his soldiers.

"Bold and audacious Myrmidons. You have been like hungry lions caged-up and ready to show the enemy how you are similar to the fierce carnivores. Follow Captain Patroclus into battle, and then slaughter as many Trojans as you possibly can. Don't return until you have your opponents' blood upon your spears and swords! And if you come across any food, steal it fast, even though I despise fast food!"

After the Myrmidons led by Patroclus marched in cadence from the aforementioned Greco-held beachhead in the direction of Troy, Achilles removed a solid gold cup from an inlaid chest that Thetis had especially given to her son to deal with any emerging crisis situation. Immediately, the renowned hero poured and offered libations to Zeus, and then drank seven lucky gulps of smooth-tasting wine from the chalice.

"Almighty Zeus. Protect my dear friend Patroclus as the inexperienced fool leads my veteran Myrmidons into the crux of the fight. My naïve captain has an abundance of valor thriving in his heart, and seeks glory and prestige under the protection of your invincible aegis. After honoring my trusty captain with victory, have Patroclus and my troops return safely back here, so that we may together savor his magnificent triumph."

The fresh Myrmidon warriors eagerly joined the battle, and buzzed around the Troad Plain like a frenzied colony of agitated hornets, swarming and making annoying bee sounds in their heightened mania.

"Just look at that teeming enemy activity!" Hector incredulously yelled to his loyal lieutenants. "There's Achilles over to our left, who has just entered the fight! And those fanatical swarming and buzzing wasps make me wonder why those fucked-up Achaean Myrmidons don't *beehive* like ordinary soldiers!"

Thinking that Patroclus, riding upon his commander's chariot, had been awesome Achilles, Hector became more-than-apprehensive, and immediately retreated back towards the city gates of Troy. Other commanders followed Hector's prudent example, but their heavy chariots and galloping horses could not climb the dug-out ditch's soft inclines, so many of the speeding teams toppled-over and could not safely make their active retreat back to Troy. Showing tremendous audacity, Patroclus and his vanguard violently killed a dozen Trojan officers as the unfortunate victims were clambering-up the steep banks of the recently excavated trench.

Seeing the bizarre confrontation unfolding, Great Zeus feared that his favored Trojan son Sarpedon would soon be smitten by Patroclus's lance, so the chief god informed Hera that he wished to whisk his bastard son away to Lycia before the highly-motivated Greek warrior would send Sarpedon's spirit swirling and spiraling-down to Hades.

"Husband, what the hell are you saying!" Hera chided her louse of a spouse.

"This mortal man, Sarpedon, although half-divine, like other petty humans, has been born, only to eventually die. It doesn't really mean a rat's ass whether Sarpedon perishes now, or a mere century from now! If you save his ass from being annihilated, every god and goddess who has a dog in the hunt, so to speak, will desire doing the same for their favorite mortal champion. Let your valued child Sarpedon bleed to death from a sharp spear's penetration," Hera boldly suggested. "And besides, who the hell care's whether or not your half-god's tiny dingle ever penetrates any mortal whore's wet love tunnel!"

After Sarpedon's chest had been severely punctured by inspired Patroclus, Almighty Zeus, viewing the tragic event from on high, was greatly saddened, and the king of Olympus mystically blackened the sky over the Troad Plain at high noon, as the sound of clashing spears, swords and axes resounded across the neighboring plains and valleys, and soon loudly echoed throughout the nearby hills and mountains.

Still feeling disconsolate, Zeus assigned Apollo to dispatch brothers Sleep and Death to place Sarpedon's corpse upon a sturdy stretcher, and fly the hero's body back to his homeland for proper burial.

Soon thereafter, Apollo judiciously decided to enter the evolving fray and found ambitious Patroclus ascending an outer wall of Troy, after climbing-up a high olive tree and latching onto the high rampart's ledge. "Back-off arrogant Achaean!" the awesome archer god frightfully yelled. "I shall first break-off the limbs of your olive tree, and then I will break your fuckin' limbs and pull them off your deceased body as one would pull the legs off of a dead crab or spider!"

Being traumatized by Apollo's appearance and the archer god's numerous threats, Patroclus clumsily fell from the high olive tree branch and plummeted twenty-feet onto the hard ground below. Achilles's captain's unprotected behind was then wounded from behind by a well-thrown Trojan javelin, and then keen-eyed Hector confidently approached the writhing downed Achaean, and enthusiastically plunged his sharp-bladed spear directly into Patroclus's vulnerable mid-section.

"This is your moment of glory, Hector," the dying Argive captain hoarsely uttered. "With the help of Zeus and Apollo, you have temporarily triumphed, and I stress, only temporarily triumphed. A certain prophecy, however, will soon be fulfilled. Your remaining time on this planet is short-lived!"

"Just like your fucked-up superior, General Achilles," Hector answered and evilly laughed. "I too am a man of war and have no particular use for frivolous prophecies spoken by craven and feeble priests, by virgin-pussy priestesses, and by gutless, knee-knocking, pusillanimous oracles! The world is full of blood-sucking impostors, and prophets, priests, priestesses and oracles are the most successful bloodsuckers prospering on this fucked-up planet!"

Hearing the bad news about Hector killing Patroclus, Ajax stampeded into Agamemnon's tent to be the first messenger to tell the Achaean leader.

"Great Agamemnon! Brave Patroclus has been killed. All four auricles in his heart have been punctured!"

"Ajax, you pathetic asshole!" Agamemnon bellowed. "Do you think that I'm a stupid shit like you are! It's impossible for anyone to have four oracles in their fuckin' heart!"

Chapter 16

"THE FIGHT FOR THE BODY OF PATROCLUS"

"Listen guys, now that we're no longer lieutenants, I believe that rank has its privileges," Eurshiddenme haughtily lectured his four fellow captains. "I now have a spacious tent to hold meetings, so we don't have to worry about being caught conferring down in the gay, lesbian, transgender and tri-sexual horizontal dark tunnel."

"Okay about that!" Eurballsourout agreed and admitted. "But don't tell us any more cornball moral mythology lectures. I happen to enjoy committing mortal and venial sins as much as anyone else!"

"I'll level with you four dunderheads!" Eurshiddenme exclaimed. "I was once in the cemetery, er, I meant to say 'seminary', studying to be a priest of Apollo, and I know exactly how the archer god thinks and acts. And I see a definite parallel between an Apollo story and the recent demise of Patroclus!"

"Do you mean to tell us that you called this so-called military meeting to explain some immaterial mythology bullshit!" Eurassisgras strongly protested. "I suppose that the next thing you'll tell us is that the world is round and not flat! Flattery will get you nowhere, ha, ha, ha!"

"You dimwit! Your mind is as closed as a virgin's untouched pussy!" Eurshiddenme countered. "On the other hand, to you four nitwits, an open mind contains no brains inside."

"Do we again have to keep silent during your horse manure oration!" Eurdicisin wanted to know. 'Your softest words are like hard turds deposited inside my earlobes!"

"Well, the more dumb-ass questions you ask, the longer the meeting will be," Eurshiddenme answered. "If you want to get back to your daily masturbation sessions, I suggest that you four dipshits remain quiet while I educate you about important moral and religious issues!"

"I see merit in your illogical rhetoric!" Eurcockisnum assessed and replied. "Hurry-up, Eurshiddenme, and get your fucked-up, sanctimonious presentation over with! Your holier-than-thou attitude leaves much sex to be desired!"

"Okay, garrulous dolts; here is my pertinent lesson for today. In the far-off land of Ethiopia, a punk teenager named Phaethon impatiently listened to his mother Clymene brag that *his* father was Phoebus Apollo, the Greek god of music, medicine, masturbation and the sun. According to exaggerated ancient renditions, every morning Apollo would mount his magnificent golden chariot and would commandeer four white stallions that flew across the sky from east to west, obviously dragging the sun on its daily celestial path from the eastern to the western horizon."

"A schoolboy friend that pretended to be a son of Zeus scoffed at Phaethon's claim that *he* was a bona fide offspring of Lord Apollo. Naturally, Clymene's son became incensed at his pal's malicious ridiculing."

"Look, asshole," the other boy scornfully hollered. "I am a son of Zeus, and my daddy can kick your daddy's stupid ass any fuckin' day of the whole fuckin' year. How do ya' like them fuckin' apples?"

"But my mother," Phaethon said, paused and then reiterated. "But my mother has told me this truth that I am indeed Apollo's son, and that someday I might be able to perform comedy routines and revival music acts at one of my father's many theaters. As you know, Greek heroes like Hercules are born after a god of Olympus has sex with a mortal woman."

"Get a fuckin' life!" the other wise-ass punk suggested. "Phaethon, your mother is nothin' more than a goddamned kinky whore-turned-prostitute, and you're *her* illegitimate son! This lyin' story she's giving you is a lot of stinkin' *Mt. Olympus* bullshit! I know, because my mother's also a goddamned hooker, too! And I ain't no goddamned son of Zeus! And you ain't no goddamned son of Phoebus Apollo, either! That's all a bunch of speculative, self-serving horse manure!"

"Phaethon sadly walked home from nursery school for lunch in a mighty depressed state of mind. "Mom, tell me the truth," the boy requested. "Are you a goddamned whore or prostitute? Or is this weirdo story that I am indeed the son of Apollo actually true?"

"Son, you are indeed of heavenly birth," Clymene swore. "And if I speak falsely, may the gods punish my arrogance and make my hyperactive vagina atrophy. I strongly suggest that *you* journey to the eastern horizon and visit the temple of my handsome husband Apollo. Ask *him* about *your* divine origin if you don't believe me."

"Okay Mom, pack my lunch, and I'll go and check it out. How do I get to India? I was never too good in geography and failed the damned subject last semester in toddler town nursery school!" the all-too-curious, slow-learner teenager asked. "I hear that India is the exact place where Dad's new marvelous marble temple is located."

"Just keep walking east for about a century," Clymene informed her impulsive son. "And hurry-up and get the hell out of here, because I have a wealthy client arriving in about fifteen minutes, and I need to wash my stinky crotch and freshen up a bit!"

"Apollo's Indian sun palace had columns of pure gold and glittering jewels that magically glistened and twinkled in the morning sunlight. The walls were made of rich platinum ore, and the ceiling of gleaming ivory. Murals of Earth, sky, sea and *Mt. Olympus* had been painted upon the walls of every chamber inside the splendid, colossal temple. Hephaestus had erected the fantastic edifice in tribute to Lord Apollo, who didn't know or care a shit about anything except music, medicine, masturbation, screwing beautiful mortal women, and tugging the hot sun across the sky the four separate seasons of each and every monotonous year."

"Phaethon cautiously entered Apollo's charmed sanctuary seeking confirmation of *his* true identity. The determined kid approached the radiant god imperially sitting upon his glimmering golden and jeweled throne, and the impetuous know-it-all punk soon had to cover his eyes for protection from the intense dazzling glare. The sun god was wearing a fabulous diamond-studded purple robe to complement his overall supernatural appearance."

"Oh Apollo, lord of the sun and custodian of its daily trek across the sky; I request of your excellence," Phaethon bullshitted, "that you please provide me some proof that I am indeed your mortal son."

"Who is your whoring mother?" the sun god thundered in a booming voice that shook the entire throne room, pillars and all. "I have screwed so many gorgeous mortals that I really can't remember all of *their* unimportant names."

"My mother is 'Tigress' Clymene, the finest prostitute in all of Ethiopia with the firmest set of knockers this side of the *Euphrates River*," Phaethon boldly stated. "Do you remember her?"

"Wow, yes!" Apollo exclaimed. "How could I ever forget those fantastic tits she possesses? They were absolutely incredible, even for a little sucker like yourself! In fact, I'm getting a major hard-on just thinking about them!"

"Then *you* really are my father!" Phaethon eagerly screamed-out while thinking: 'Why you dirty mother-fucker'! That asshole son of Zeus ought to have his balls busted and ground into dog meat! The lying shithead!' Phaethon's diminutive brain internalized."

"Apollo beckoned for his bastard son to approach *his* stately-shimmering throne, so that the father could better admire the boy's strength and audacity. "You are indeed my son," Apollo informed Phaethon. "And *you* shall enjoy my genetics for the remainder of your years, and you'll have the stamina to screw at least sixty mature females a day, which comes to about three pussies an hour, if you don't sleep and decide to go non-stop. And to show you my appreciation of your surprise visit," the sun god continued in a booming voice, "I shall grant you any wish your little fart, er, I mean 'little heart' desires."

"Phaethon contemplated Apollo's promise for a full minute, and without giving the matter sufficient consideration, the dumb, overly-ambitious, proud kid blurted-out, "Please father, I beg of you; allow me to drive *your* exotic sun chariot across the sky for just one day to demonstrate to the world *my* true *Olympus* ancestry."

"But Phaethon, you don't even have a chariot driver's license yet!" Apollo objected. "You don't even have a goddamned learner's permit! I beg you my son, do not attempt to surpass your limited bounds," the sun/archer god sincerely pleaded. "You're a mere aspiring mortal, and might suffer a mere mortal's fate unless you wise-up and make a more reasonable request! Not even Zeus could steer the flaming chariot without a week's worth of intensive lessons and flight training!"

"But Phaethon was adamant in his persistence, so Apollo had no alternative except to honor *his* promise to *his* and Clymene's son, and permit the impulsive idiot to attempt the impossible. "Never lose your grip control of the four powerful white horses," Apollo imperatively cautioned Phaethon. "And don't be distracted or lose your grasp on the reins when you get hit in the face by stenchy flying horseshit exploding out of the horses' smelly assholes. And whatever you do," Apollo continued, "never look down to Earth because that will make you as fuckin' dizzy as drunken *Lord Dionysus.* And my son, the horses' lungs are also full of fire, and if the animals turn their heads toward you, be careful, for the flames from their nostrils can singe the hair right off of your balls, and the flares might even set your hairy asshole on fire!"

"Apollo looked into Phaethon's eyes, which were bloodshot from the long trek to India from Ethiopia via a detour through, Russia, and then through ancient Palestine. Immediately, the divine father understood all was futile, and that persuasion was a useless tool to implement against the cocky teenager's obstinate insistence. "I hope you've already gotten laid many times, because otherwise, you're going to die a fucked-up virgin!" the sun god declared to his haughty, naughty, adventurous, over-zealous offspring."

"The scrupulous sun god accompanied his stubborn kid out the temple's platinum back door, where the fabulous golden chariot had already been hitched to the four immortal white stallions. "You still have time to change your mind," Apollo recommended, "because pretty soon, you won't have time to change your shit-streaked underwear! What do you have to say about it?"

"That's okay Pop," Phaethon reflexively replied. "I don't wear underwear!"

"The glorious sun god then applied some protective oil called 'suntan lotion' to *his* son's rosy face, so that *his* nose and chin would not be seared from the fiery sun's heat, or from the horses' hot breaths. "Take the shortest route across the sky, and whatever you do," Apollo cautioned the oblivious punk-dunce Phaethon, "don't deviate from *my* daily course. If *you* allow the horses to take charge of your responsibility, then you might as well commit suicide right now, because otherwise, you're as good as fuckin' dead!"

"Phaethon leaped upon the rider's narrow ledge of the heavenly golden chariot, and anxiously grasped and held the reins. The nervous white stallions snorted fire, and then stomped their hoofs in anticipation of their daily flight across the majestic sky. The chariot zoomed-off toward the western horizon, and after a minute of careful flying, the four imposing horses realized that the highly-skilled and experienced sun god was not at the helm piloting their present excursion."

"The chariot's intense speed was soon unbearable, and the task too overwhelming for any mere mortal to ever endure. Soon, the sun god's vehicle began to sway and vacillate as it meandered between constellations, planets, and the Earth and the moon, and then Phaethon became quite fearful, regretting that he had ever pleaded with his divine father to drive the sun chariot alone from horizon to horizon."

"The fire-breathing horses soon wildly ascended and erratically descended in abnormal flight patterns and zany oscillations across the morning sky, the magnificent steeds taking full control of the chariot from the alarmed and suddenly-frightened asshole teenager trying to do a god's job without proper training or practice."

'This excessive heat is intolerable!' Phaethon thought, 'and this hot horseshit smacking me in the face is far worse than any bullshit I have ever heard, or ever seen, or ever smelled! Alas, I'm being justly punished for being so fuckin' arrogant and so fuckin' stupid'!"

"As the fiery chariot swiveled, rocked, vacillated and then plunged toward the Earth, Phaethon frantically and desperately tugged and manipulated the reins. Finally, out of sheer fear of dying, the young rookie charioteer made a last-ditch effort to save himself from ultimate destruction."

"Amazingly, the beleaguered youth regained control of the seemingly-doomed chariot as *he* miraculously managed to reverse his *crash course* in sun pulling. The chariot astoundingly righted itself on a steady route, and the four white horses obediently responded to the courageous lad's loud commands. Apollo's impressive golden vehicle rose-up to a safer altitude, and eventually out of harm's way. Catastrophe had been temporarily averted."

"Then, just as Phaethon finally regained his cocky confidence and demonstrated admirable dexterity while vigorously piloting the heavenly, weaving, and bobbing chariot, an unexpected obstacle suddenly appeared before him. "Who the fuck is that idiotic asshole?" the stunned son of Apollo exclaimed as the confused lad crashed into Lord Hermes, zooming across the sky on an important errand for Zeus. In an instant, Phaethon blew-off of Apollo's flaming sun chariot, and crashed-down upon the Earth, deader than Patroclus!"

"That was a great story," thrilled Eurballsourout lavishly commended Eurshiddenme. "I'm almost-glad I listened to most of it."

"I agree," Eurassisgras concurred. "Even though it sounded like utter horse crap, the lesson taught is that we must obey those in authority, or else face the consequences of destroying ourselves!"

"When Phaethon ignored Apollo's advice, the kid placed his life in jeopardy on the wheel of fortune! What an asshole!" Eurdicisin added to the inane conversation.

"I suppose that the moral of the story is that we should never question the knowledge or wisdom of our superiors, just like Patroclus had violated the advice of veteran warrior Achilles!" Eurcockisnum concluded and shared.

"I hope you mini-minds enjoyed my little myth's moral," Eurshiddenme stated. "Meeting is dismissed!"

* * * * * * * * * * * *

Menelaus spotted Patroclus's body lying upon the hot sand, so the King of Mycenae wildly steered his chariot around in the direction of the corpse, in order to defend Achilles's armor from the avaricious Trojan officers who desired to possess the treasured item as a meritorious war trophy. Several Trojans approached the slain Achaean, but realizing that Menelaus had the reputation of being a superior killer, the timid armor robbers cravenly retreated to fight in a safer battlefield environment.

But not willing to make any concessions to Menelaus, Phoebus Apollo inspired Hector to consider pilfering Achilles's armor from Patroclus's chest as a powerful symbol of Trojan war supremacy. 'I'll proudly wear the gear of Achilles, and then both the Argives and the Trojans will fear my formidable existence. The breastplate formerly belonged to Peleus,' Achilles's father,' Hector considered. 'So, maybe after this fucked-up war is over, I can pretend to be Achilles's father, find the sea nymph Thetis, and screw the hell out of her salt-flavored love tunnel!'

Almighty Zeus, knowing from Fate that Hector's remaining time as a Trojan warrior was quite short, made Achilles's armor fit comfortably upon the haughty prince's shoulders. King Priam's older son then stood erect and addressed his silent vanguard, most of whom were from various cities allied with Troy.

"Listen to me, you parasitic vultures. The people of Troy have sacrificed greatly just to feed your hungry mouths during a time of horrible famine, as a result of this ass-backwards war!" Hector yelled. "Our horny women have also given you clumsy assholes quality sex, even during their monthly periods! Help me' force Ajax and his comrades back to the Argive ships so that I can then capture Patroclus's body as a trophy to exhibit with Achilles's purloined armor at the Trojan Museum of Unnatural History."

The two armies, in a struggle to possess Patroclus's corpse, battered each other with tremendous ferocity. To make matters even worse, Zeus imaginatively cloaked the escalating clash with a mystifying mist that was so thick that Trojans were killing both Achaeans and Trojans, and Argives were slaughtering other Danaans as well as enemy Trojans.

Meanwhile, Achilles was not aware of Patroclus's terrible fate, since the dense mist that had been generated by Zeus had clouded the stubborn warrior's view of the noisy Troad Plain. Agamemnon shouted an instruction to his brother Menelaus that the King of Sparta should send a speedy runner to inform Achilles that his "gay lover" Patroclus had been mortally wounded.

"Antilochus! Become anti-walking and dash to Achilles and tell the obstinate prick of Patroclus's demise, and also, that Hector has stolen his father Peleus's sacred breastplate!" Menelaus commanded. "Sprint quickly now Antilochus, before you get the runs, and shit your already wet loin cloth right off your skinny ass!"

Chapter 17

"ACHILLES'S ARMOR"

'What the hell's going on out there on the Troad?' Achilles wondered. 'It looks like a friggin' swirling dust bowl. And why are the Argives running out of the haze like scared rabbits? I have a dreadful premonition about all of this havoc; my mother Thetis had once told me that the best of the Myrmidons would be killed in battle! Dear Zeus; I hope that her prediction turns-out *not* to be true, and that Patroclus will be spared from Hector's sword.'

Antilochus sprinted from the inclement Troad toward Achilles's hut and then gasped and panted, "I have terrible news to convey. Patroclus has been killed by that ruthless bastard Hector, who has also greedily stolen your armor off of your Captain's dead body."

"Oh no!" Achilles moaned, falling to the ground and lying and sobbing face-up with his eyes shut; the Myrmidon commander's mind swimming in a totally hysterical, emotional state. Immediately after Antilochus had sped-off to tell other officers of the bad tidings, Ifavagina, a horny slave hostage, ran-over to the weeping and delirious General, raised-up her tunic, squatted-down, and positively enjoyed having the closed-eyed, whimpering Achilles licking and lapping her aroused clit and eager beaver.

'Different strokes for different folks!' Ifavagina gleefully imagined as the savvy sex kitten gyrated up and down upon Achilles' long-hard nose, which was rubbing against her ever-pumping engorged clit, and the sobbing General's foot-long tongue was massaging and licking the girl's crazily riveting genitals that were moving like a primitive piston. And then, Ifavagina reached the biggest multiple-orgasm of her whole whoring life. After the kinky slut's eighth pleasurable climax, completely exhausted, the promiscuous harlot arose to her feet and groggily wobbled and stumbled back to her slave-girls' tent.

Several minutes later, Achilles opened his eyes from his trance-like state, started gagging incessantly, and suddenly experienced a lengthy choking fit. The encumbered General reached his fingers down his throat, and was able to remove several hundred brown pubic hairs from his swollen larynx. 'This is all I need! A lousy hairy situation after learning the bad news about Patroclus being brutally killed by that scumbag Hector!' the confused General reckoned, as dumbfounded Achilles again examined the several hundred dark-brown pubic hairs in his palm.

Meanwhile, deep under the sea, immortal Thetis telepathically became cognizant of her son's overwhelming grief, so the sea goddess assembled her companion sisters, the Nereids, beautiful nymphs all, to share her grieving misery. 'Oh, my faithful Nereids. I'm so inconsolable. My son Achilles had sailed off to Troy, where the young adventurer was destined by prophecy to perish in battle after his friend Patroclus would die. Soon, my dear son will also have his demise, and his troubled soul, according to the prophet's words, will swiftly travel-down to Hades, where the mysterious god of darkness and Queen Persephone will have indisputable custody of my audacious Achilles forever!"

The Nereids, notorious denizens of the deep, accompanied Thetis through the tumultuous underwater sea currents, swimming like graceful dolphins until they and she parted company at the sandy shores of Troy. Thetis then employed her supernatural powers and located Achilles, who she found sitting-upon the ground and sniffing and obsessively smelling the palm of his right hand.

"My psychologically disturbed child!" Thetis whispered into Achilles's ear. "Always look at the brighter side of the storm. Zeus has granted your wish that the Trojans are winning the war, and that Agamemnon realizes that he has no chance of victory without your cooperation in bringing your brutal Myrmidons into the ever-vacillating combat zone. Why are you so distressed? You're too big and old to suck on your baby pacifier!"

"The Trojan prince Hector has slain my dearest friend, Patroclus, who is also my significant other," Achilles related to his sea goddess mother. "And to top-off that horrendous catastrophe, the obnoxious Trojan prince now wears my father's armor, which was given to your husband Peleus by Hephaestus when you two had married. Now, I wish that my father had taken home a mortal woman as his bride, instead of you, you conniving immortal bitch!"

"Oh, my Zeus!" Thetis exclaimed. "It had been prophesied by an anonymous oracle that once Patroclus would die, your fatal end would soon follow! If only Discord could be banished from terrorizing and plaguing mortals, then happiness could abound among humans."

"If only Hector could have murdered Discord instead of killing pure-hearted Patroclus!" Achilles hypothesized and declared. "Now Mother, I intend to go and hunt-down Hector and make the Trojan women weep as those in my camp are presently now doing over Patroclus's death. And don't try and stop me, no matter what the fucked-up pedophile priests and prophets predict, along with what the insane lesbian oracles think and say!"

"My son, Hector now has your armor, and without it, you cannot challenge the fierce Trojan and win any match in a death struggle. Stay calm and vigilant. I'll visit the blacksmith god Hephaestus, whom I know very well. He owes me a few sexual favors, and will gladly forge in his workshop a new bronze breastplate that you can proudly wear in combat, along with the finest shield, spear and sword."

Meanwhile, the Achaean pallbearers solemnly carried Patroclus's corpse, found near the deep trench that the Achaeans had dug, but as that somber funeral procession was happening, Hector attacked the moat like a ferocious tiger leaping upon its antelope prey, and fortunately, Ajax and his soldiers were able to successfully repel the attack and force the Trojans *to ditch* their assault.

Unarmed Achilles, in a moment of sheer madness, foolishly stood on top of the nearby wall and began hectoring Hector, persistently mocking, goading, and ridiculing his avowed enemy's alleged cravenness. But alert Athena cleverly cloaked the Argive General's head in her majestic Aegis, and a glowing halo appeared upon Achilles' crown that absolutely scared the shit and piss out of Hector and his burly, surly bodyguards.

The superstitious Trojans, being completely intimidated by the divine aura, pulled-back to the safety of the city's towering walls, and at the same time, the emboldened Achaeans sought shelter beside *their* recently-constructed ditch and accompanying wall, just as the eternal sun's warm glow gradually sank upon the western horizon.

The Trojans, all individually suffering from either severe diarrhea or chronic constipation as a result of Achilles' supernatural appearance, held a gathering of the minds where the prophet Polydamas, who had a multitude of sexy girlfriends, addressed the assembly, which included King Priam, Queen Hecuba, Helen of Troy, Prince Hector, and Prince Paris.

"Friends and colleagues," Polydamas began his oral commentary. "Here is what I argue is a logical plan for us to initiate. When Achilles held-back from entering the war over a minor squabble with Agamemnon, we had the distinct advantage in the conflict. But now, I dread facing the enraged Argive General and his formidable Myrmidons. If we confront him now, I foresee a terrible massacre of us Trojans occurring."

"Polydamas, what do you suggest?" King Priam asked.

"I wholeheartedly plead, especially with you, Hector. Let us retire to our beloved city and wait-out Achilles' crazed temper-tantrum. Out on the

Troad, our fatigued army is too exposed to *his* animalistic treachery. Our beleaguered troops can guard the city from the surrounding walls' high ramparts. Let's allow Achilles to exhaust his rage, and also fatigue his horses as the lunatic races his chariot in a wild frenzy around-and-around the well-defended city. The irate Phthian warrior will only experience perpetual frustration, and will then return sulking like a denied infant, back to his anchored ships."

"Polydamas, we used to see events and comprehend their nature in a similar fashion," Hector eloquently objected. "But now we're occupying opposite ends of the rainbow. If I interpret your words correctly, in your statement you desire that we should yield-back all the land that we've gained on the Troad by retiring our troops to the city, and that our brave soldiers should stay penned-up like slimy hogs and passive lambs, watching our wealth diminish like a hundred-year-old coot's limp dingle. I say to all my friends, Trojans, and fellow countrymen, that any intelligent person who is present at this meeting who endorses Polydamas's madness is both a traitor and an absolute coward."

"What say you, Trojans!" Hector vehemently challenged the council. "I say that tomorrow, we aggressively attack the Argives; Achilles or no Achilles! Our coordinated advance will dominate the Achaeans! And in conclusion, we'll let the gods determine which side will ultimately vanquish the other!"

With the influence of Pallas Athene, who had committed to side with Odysseus and the Achaeans, not one representative attending the Trojan conclave supported Polydamas's resolution, but instead, by virtue of shouting and raising their right hands, cast their votes for Hector's decisive plan of swift action.

Simultaneously, at the Greeks' somber encampment, a parallel strategy meeting was in-progress. Saddened by the loss of Patroclus, Achilles made an impassioned speech, with his oration's popular theme being that furious military action was necessary to avenge the well-loved hero Patroclus's death. The well-respected Myrmidon General ended his speech with the dire plea, "Someone give me a gold coin so that I may place it inside Patroclus's mouth. The coin will serve as a toll fee for the ghostly Charon to ferry my dear friend's immortal soul, stationed upon *his* barge, across the morbid, underground Styx River, with my dear friend's spirit being transported from the Land of the Living to Hades' dismal Kingdom of the Dead! Dear Patroclus: may you rest in peace among the colorful flowers growing in the Elysian Fields of Hades for all of eternity!"

Women attendants in Achilles' camp entered the funeral tent and washed the gore from Patroclus's corpse, oiled his skin, and administered perfumed salves to his open scarlet wounds. The champion's body was then gently lifted and placed upon a horizontal bier, and then covered with an immaculate white shroud, according to traditional custom.

Meanwhile, Thetis had arrived at the volcanic palace of Hephaestus and made an urgent request to the blacksmith craftsman, who was making wheels for the latest chariot models for Zeus, Ares and Apollo. The master of the flaming furnace was happy to see his unexpected visitor.

"Ah, wonderful Thetis!" Hephaestus warmly greeted. "I'll never forget the time when I had suffered Hera's wrath, and she flung me down from Mt. Olympus. I was but a mere toddler then, but your arms caught my plummet as I was about to plunge into the sea and drown. For your intercession, I am most grateful! What the hell can I do for you?"

After Thetis revealed that Achilles had lent Patroclus his cherished armor only to have it later stolen from the hero's dead body by Hector, Hephaestus, feeling empathy for Thetis's plight, labored for several hours manufacturing an immense shield having five layers of thick solid bronze, and the magnificent defensive item featured an intricate array of bold-relief images displaying Earth, Sun, Sky, Sea, Tits, Erect Penises, Stars and the Moon. And all twelve constellations of the zodiac, along with scenes of resplendent palaces, forts and castles, were also artistically etched upon the shield's majestic surface.

After lighting his forge to an extremely high temperature, the talented-but-lame blacksmith god next meticulously hammered-out upon his incomparable anvil several dozen silver arrows, and a javelin, a cuirass, gleaming shin greaves, and a marvelous bronze javelin for Achilles to use in battle.

Thetis graciously thanked Hephaestus for his prompt and deft assistance; then gathered together the recently formed armor pieces into her sea chariot, and like a predator eagle, swooped over to the distant Troad Plain to deliver the essential weapons and equipment to her still-grieving son.

Chapter 18
"RECONCILIATION OF ACHILLES"

"Well, Eurshiddenme, our pals Eurassisgras, Eurdicisin, Eurcockisnum and I have been really enjoying these dumb-ass moral lessons you're trying to academically teach us inside your new shoddy officer's hut," Eurballsourout praised. "Do you have another fucked-up myth that somehow corresponds with the recent death of Patroclus?"

"Yes, I concur with Eurballsourout," Eurassisgras agreed. "Your original bullshit now sounds like utter horse-shit, which is a step better and higher on the feces scale than your normal chicken-shit! Now Eurshiddenme, tell us a good moral to improve out general morale!"

"If and when we ever get back to Ithaca," Eurdicisin added to the ridiculous conversation, "Odysseus has said that he'll invited us to a big palace party over near his pool. The only problem is that his pool, which we've all been invited to swim-in, is a goddamned cesspool!"

"I had heard a strange rumor that Achilles is a bisexual who had Patroclus as his male Partner!" Eurcockisnum related to his whimsical comrades. "He might even be a secret member of the radical LBGTQRMSV community that Agamemnon, Menelaus, Menapauis, Odysseus, and Ajax have all condemned!"

"As far as I know, that's just only hearsay and not at all true," Eurshiddenme objectively answered. "The two friends always ate meals together, but only had a plate-tonic relationship!"

"But Eurdicisin is right in his blunt criticism of King Odysseus," Eurcockisnum contributed to the peculiar discussion. "I know from experience that visibility is not-too-good under the surface of the king's always-full cesspool! Now please, Eurshiddenme. We promise to remain quiet if you'll quickly divulge to us another one of your model-behavior myths!"

"Okay, guys. Before I had stupidly voyaged with King Odysseus here to Troy," Eurshiddenme confessed, "I was conscientiously studying to be a pedophile priest, and had to listen to major bullshit from the mouths of conceited professors teaching at the Ithacan Impostors Academy, and here's one of my favorite tales that I had learned while being a naïve student there."

"Some ancient Greek myths are popular because the people in them are fucked-up. Even today, people love gossiping and reading about others of their species that are complete assholes, just to make the gossiper or listener feel better about himself or herself. And even four thousand years ago, adults knew about what pains-in-the-ass' teenagers are like, and how the noxious punks' stubborn insistence that they are invincible often leads to predictable tragedy. When acne-faced, hormone-dominated kids think they know it all, then those know-it-alls either wind-up in the local hospital or in the community cemetery. Consequently, it is absolutely amazing that any of us survive those ugly adolescence years to eventually mature into wise adults. As it has been so aptly described, 'It is too bad that youth is wasted on the young'!"

"Now, my military friends, the inventor Daedalus was a genius from antiquity that dared to learn the gods' treasured secrets. The creative Greek was a master architect and engineer who had designed many extraordinary temples, amphitheaters, agoras, buildings, whorehouses, public projects and impressive co-ed' public restrooms. The experimenter was commissioned by the wealthy *cretin'* King Minos to oversee the construction of the Labyrinth, a complex series of underground caves and tunnels situated beneath the monarch's opulent palace on the island of Crete."

"I'll commit to building the Labyrinth for your personal honor and glory," Daedalus told Minos. "But I'll need a lot of foreign material to finish the job. Also, I need to bring along my royal, pain-in-the-ass, punk teenager to keep his ass out of trouble, and to teach the little thug how to value *constructive things,* so that hopefully, the blundering loser successfully makes it to adulthood."

"I know exactly what the fuck you mean!" King Minos concurred. "I need this 'a-mazing' Labyrinth built beneath my palace to keep my monster the *Minotaur* in a safe enclosure. The grotesque creature has got the body of a muscular man, and the head of a formidable bull. Every year, I plan to sacrifice seven young vestal virgins and seven acne-faced *bullheaded* male punks to the *Minotaur* inside my subterranean maze, just to get rid of the know-it-all bitches and the horny bastards, and also to appease the greedy gods," Minos related to the distinguished inventor. "Daedalus, if you're lucky, your asshole kid might be one of the victimized, bullheaded, punk shit-heads to be sacrificed!"

"That's a deal!" Daedalus agreed, warmly shaking the king's already broken hand. "My son Icarus thinks he can do no wrong; the fool defies my authority, and always impetuously attempts taking the 'bull by the horns' when the frivolous asshole should be exercising mature patience and 'discretion', which does not rhyme with excretion."

"Your recalcitrant son Icarus sounds like the typical run-of-the-mill teenage jerk-off to me," King Minos surmised and agreed while examining his crushed right hand. "And Daedalus; I think that *'a minute' tour'* with the *Minotaur* ought to scare the living shit out of your wise-assed punk kid! Ha, ha, ha, ha!"

"After the intricate and complicated Labyrinth had finally been built for the king beneath his expansive-expensive palace, Minos loved its design and its confusing maze-like passages so much that the monarch decided to keep Daedalus on Crete, against the genius's will, to creatively erect other architectural wonders."

"Daedalus, I want you to engineer a great reservoir for Knossus," the tyrannical king insisted. "Since I am one of Zeus's favorite sons, it will be built to honor my omnipotent father, the founder of *my* city! Do I fuckin' make myself' clear?"

"I'd like to stay residing on your ugly, barren, arid, desolate island," Daedalus politely refused, "but I have to return to Athens back on the mainland and give my estranged wife money, or she has threatened me with divorce and with serious alimony payments that are certain to bankrupt my troubled ass!"

"Build me my damned reservoir for the taxpaying people of Knossus, or else, you'll most certainly be fed to the *Minotaur* along with your fucked-up, teenage, punk kid!" Minos boisterously threatened. "Get the message, you' delinquent, egomaniac, lowlife shit-head!"

"Daedalus intensively and extensively worked on the massive reservoir project for several years, but when King Minos had learned that the renowned architect had tried bribing sailors to stash Icarus and himself' inside a ship's cargo hull as stowaways, in order sail to Athens, the Cretan cretin became incensed and mighty pissed-off. Minos had Daedalus and his insolent, know-it-all kid, locked inside a high stone tower situated upon a lofty cliff, overlooking the *Aegean Sea,* which gets older every single and married day."

"From his open-air window overlooking the sea, Daedalus studied the graceful seagulls zipping-around the towering cliffs, looking for human heads to drop their raunchy wet crap bombs upon. The inventor marveled at the birds' elegant flight patterns, as the eagles and vultures circled the stone tower, and the inventor envied the creatures absolute freedom, soaring, drifting, and majestically gliding all over the goddamned cloudless sky."

"Icarus, I have some friends on this island who are willing to smuggle bird feathers and wooden pieces to this tower," the father calmly explained. "We will make sturdy frames that will fit snugly over our arms and shoulders, and next, we'll cover them with feathers, and then fly-off of this Zeus-forsaken-island back to the mainland of Greece."

"Okay, I'll help you Pop," Icarus out-of-character complied. "But only because I need to get back to Athens to shack-up with my old girlfriend, and to escape the danger of that horny *Minotaur* predator, who is said to be gay in addition to being fucked-up. I heard that the big mother wants to screw young boys up the ass with his pillar-sized dick! Let me tell you Pop; I really don't need that kind of 'bull shit' happening to my young asshole!"

"Within six months, all of the necessary materials the accomplished builder had specified had been successfully smuggled into the stone tower, and Daedalus and Icarus diligently manufactured the two sets of wings, using thread and wax to attach the essential bird feathers to the flexible wooden frames. Soon, the determined conspirators had almost-completed their ambitious project."

"Remember Icarus," Daedalus reminded his independent-minded aberrant son. "Don't fly too high or too low. Take the straightest, most moderate course back to the coast of Greece. Follow my stellar lead, and don't deviate, you fucked-up, young-punk deviate!"

"I'll do exactly what the hell I want," Icarus vehemently protested. "And that's all that I'll do, and nothing else. I know precisely how to use these stupid-ass wings without ever having the need for further education from attending *Hermes' Aviation School and Flight Academy!*"

"I wish you wouldn't have such a defiant *mercurial* personality!" Daedalus maturely and vociferously criticized his aberrant offspring. "If you fly too high and propel yourself too close to the sun, the goddamned wax on your wings will melt, and you'll swiftly plummet into the sea."

"Pop, the sun's gotta' be more than seven miles away from the fuckin' Earth, contrary to what you happen to think it is," Icarus argued. "And besides, once I had climbed a mountain and noticed that the higher that I ascended toward the summit, the colder the temperature got! I think you're trying to feed me a lot of nonsensical, superstitious, adult-mythological, non-scientific bullshit about the sun melting my wings!"

"And son," Daedalus proceeded while ignoring his son's arrogant and obnoxious comments. "Don't snafu yourself' and fly too close to the sea. Your wings might become damp and wet from the saltwater waves, and then you'll crash and splash into *Poseidon's* dangerous domain!"

"Pop, the word *don't* ain't in my friggin' vocabulary," the defensive, know-it-all son challenged. "Saying the damned word *don't* to a teenager is just like saying 'I dare you to fuckin' do it'!"

"The following morning, a light breeze accompanied the appearance of dawn, and the two plotters diligently prepared for their clandestine mission. The father and the son donned their portable feathered wings, and Daedalus was the first to leap out of the stone tower's third-story open window. Icarus followed his father's steady example, and soon was also majestically gliding over the rugged mountain cliff, and heading out over the serene *Aegean Sea.*"

"That's the gods' *Hermes* and *Cupid* flying up there!" King Minos's chief counselor erroneously indicated to the astonished monarch. "Even without filing a flight itinerary, those two chums really know how to wing it!"

"Minotaur shit!" Minos yelled and wildly cursed at his principal adviser. "Those nutcase idiots flying around up there are that stupid shithead Daedalus and his fucked-up kid Icarus, desperately attempting to escape my petty despotism!"

"Soon, Icarus became infatuated and enthralled with the extreme exhilaration of flying through the tranquil atmosphere. The excited youth had to test his physical limits zipping, looping, and zooming all over the azure sky in violation of his determined, steadfast father, who maintained *his* straight and narrow course in the direction of the distant Greek mainland."

"I can fly like the gods!" Icarus screamed in absolute delight. "I feel immortal! I feel invincible! I feel like jerking-off!" Icarus was rising and swooping all over the sky, frenetically attempting to gain control of his erratic path from Crete to the Greek mainland, after randomly experimenting with the thrill of flight."

"Daring Icarus evidently flew too high, and the intense heat from the glaring sun made the wax inside his artificial wings gradually melt. The unfortunate lad rapidly plummeted-down to Earth, instantly dying upon impact. The unperturbed and cautious Daedalus looked-back, shrugged his winged shoulders, and then continued his steady flight path to the Greek mainland. 'Father knows best!' Daedalus aptly concluded."

"Is the moral to your fascinating myth the dumb-fuck explanation that younger people like Achilles and Patroclus should always blindly obey the values, teachings, and statements of their parents and elders in authority?" Eusassisgras seriously asked Eurshiddenme.

"No!" Eurshiddenme tersely replied. "The trite moral to this esoteric myth is that a flighty personality will always lead to your demise! Class, my fellow captains, is now officially adjourned!"

* * * * * * * * * * * *

Dawn predictably rose in the eastern sky, and Thetis appeared upon the beach where Archilles lay, conscientiously still guarding Patroclus's body. "Dear child; my son, rest in peace while Patroclus really and truly rests in peace! Sit-up, and let your blue eyes admire this inimitable shield that the blacksmith god has marvelously forged for you in his valley! No man has ever carried such fantastic protection into battle!"

The armor held by Thetis shone so brilliantly that the Myrmidon soldiers standing and bullshitting a half-mile away thought that the intense glare was from a more-miniature second sun that had been recently created.

"You're right, Mother!" Achilles readily agreed. "This shield is quite peerless. But if I now carry it as self-defense against the Trojan forces, the flies and maggots will most certainly land upon Patroclus's limp body and start consuming his exposed flesh!"

"In your absence, I will guard and preserve his corpse by inserting nectar and ambrosia into his lifeless nostrils," Thetis volunteered her specialized services. "It's too bad that I didn't think about shoving the nectar and ambrosia up your friend's nose before he ever engaged Hector on the Troad Plain."

At the Achaeans early-morning strategy session, Achilles apologetically addressed egocentric Agamemnon in front of the Argives' principal officers. "King of Mycenae; let us consider dropping our adversarial enmity toward each other, our lengthy quarrel just being in strife over a single slave girl. I hereby vow that I cease and desist my animosity towards you right now, that is, if you will sacredly promise to do the same towards me."

After a boisterous cheer erupted among the Danaan captains, Agamemnon told the assembled commanders that he too was willing to abandon his disdain, and eagerly welcome Achilles's alliance in savagely fighting Hector and his minions. "Folly has tricked both you and me, Achilles, and the conniving goddess had once hoodwinked Zeus himself," Agamemnon opined. "Then, the Almighty god cast Folly down to Earth, and mankind has grievously suffered ever since the appearance of that harmful female instigator, who perpetually aggravates all mankind with dumb-shit wants such as sex and greed. I'll reiterate the prolific offer that had been stated to you yesterday by Odysseus and his comrades, and upon your acceptance, the earmarked goods will be delivered to your Bireme later today."

"Alright then," Achilles firmly answered. "Let's not dither and dicker any further insignificant chicken-shit that's previously been disguised as serious bullshit! My body and soul burns and sizzles to avenge Patroclus's slaying. I'll not swallow a morsel of food, for I shall fast and make my soul holy by virtue of personal sacrifice! However, if the soldiers need to satisfy their appetites to make themselves stronger for the upcoming battle, then so be it! I crave not food, but instead, I hunger for the anguish and groans of moaning, dying Trojans, with my utmost contempt being especially for that reprehensible rogue, Hector!"

Odysseus departed the assembly of captains with an entourage of men to gather the gifts promised to Achilles by Agamemnon, which included seven chariot tripods, twenty gleaming bronze cauldrons, twelve splendid black stallions, and finally, seven skilled serving women highly-proficient at administering both fellatio and kinky sex.

"Should I include your slave girl Briseis in the count?" Agamemnon asked the leader of the Myrmidons. "Do you still wish to pump her pussy dry?"

"I no longer love or lust for Briseis. Instead, I now wish to screw another recently-arrived slave girl, the gorgeous Ifavagina," Achilles surprisingly revealed. "But no matter how I possessively stare at the girl's alluring body, she completely ignores my obvious flirting. Quite frankly, Agamemnon, I have forgotten all about Briseis and now would love to munch on and pump Ifavagina's love tunnel!"

"What did you say?" Agamemnon yelled in disbelief. "You brazenly say that you want to fuck my daughter, Iphigenia? Be careful with your loose words, Achilles! Your risqué business will soon become your risky business!"

"No, Agamemnon," Achilles angrily corrected the Achaean leader. "I want to screw the new slave girl Ifavagina, not your dyke daughter Iphigenia! But if a vagina comes my way like Ifavagina's vagina, then I might want to pork that new vagina as if it were Ifavagina's vagina!"

Then Ajax wisely piped-up and interrupted the convoluted dialogue. "I hear from camp gossip that Iphigenia's vagina is hairier than Ifavagina's vagina, which is now, for some inexplicable reason, strangely almost bald! But I too have the hots for the new slave girl Ifavagina. I only wish that the bush-less bitch had a boner' to pick with me! Ha, ha, ha!"

Old Nestor laughed at the giant warrior's zany admission and declared: "Ajax; if frail Ifavagina was ever screwed by you, then Ifavagina's vagina would cease to exist. In my humble opinion, I think that Ifavagina would prefer being porked by a thousand-pound grunting and snorting wild boar in heat than be vigorously pumped and maimed by you!"

"True," Agamemnon verified. "Ajax; you are not only an existential threat to Hector and the rabid Trojans; you're also a lethal menace to every female in our camp who wants to get laid!"

Briseis finally learned of Patroclus's death, and rushed-out of her slave hut to mourn his passing. The slave girl knelt-down upon the lonely beach to pray and honor the young hero's shortened life.

'Oh, dear Patroclus; I modestly worship your former idealism and naivete. I never wanted to have sex with Achilles, but always wished to lay in bed with you! I know that you and Achilles had a secret bisexual nature, but now that you are dead, I must confess to Zeus, and all the gods, that Ifavagina and I have our own special relationship going, even though her pussy has somehow recently been denuded of pubic hairs. If and when Ifavagina and I ever luckily return alive to Phthia, we aspire to become entrepreneurial, and open a business to be called the Patroclus Gay and Lesbian Bordello, to fondly and admirably honor your wonderful virgin memory.'

* * * * * * * * * * * *

Achilles was also lamenting the death of Patroclus as the Phthian heir donned his new armor that had been skillfully manufactured by Hephaestus. 'I think of all the dead I've known in addition to your friendship, and I know, dearly-departed Patroclus, according to foretold prophecy, that I'll soon be reunited with everyone deceased down in dark and dismal Hades,' Achilles lamented. 'I had thought that I would perish first here at foreign Troy, but you have beaten me into the hereafter. I care no longer for my future throne back in Phthia, nor do I ever think about all of the riches that Agamemnon has offered me for my allegiance to his and Menelaus's cause in this despicable war. All I think about is reuniting with your spirit in the swirling and mysterious darkness of subterranean Hades!'

Meanwhile, upon the summit of radiant Mt. Olympus, Zeus was asking Pallas Athene if the benign goddess had abandoned Odysseus and the Achaeans. "Go and imbue Achilles with nectar and ambrosia so that your new Greek hero will have sufficient power, stamina and energy in his limbs to emerge successfully in his impending combat with Hector. To tell you the truth, dear daughter, I'm beginning to like this defiant fellow Achilles myself!"

Achilles proudly mounted his chariot, which was hitched to Xanthus and Balius, two magnificent horses reputed to be divine in heritage. Amazingly, Xanthus spoke profound words to Achilles.

"Master; my keen extra-perception senses tell me that your prescribed doom draws near, despite your valorous intent to avenge Patroclus's death at the bloody hands of Hector, which most certainly has been inspired by interfering Lord Apollo. You're hearing this vital analysis right from the horse's mouth! Balius and I can only assist you in your quest, but we cannot save your ass from the encroachment of death, and we foresee your imminent rendezvous with King Hades and Queen Persephone! Stop being a stupid shit and go back and sulk inside your military hut!"

"Asshole equine!" Achilles rankled and yelled at the phenomenal talking steed. "I don't need to wear jockey shorts to comprehend that what you are commonly saying, I already am well-aware!"

Chapter 19
"THE GODS BATTLE"

As Odysseus's five knuckleheaded captains prepared to again confront the formidable Trojans in frivolous hand-to-hand, spear-to-spear combat, fastidious Eurballsourout asked his immediate superior Eurshiddenme for some moral inspiration and some fundamental rationale for fighting the "irrational war" for greedy King Agamemnon of Mycenae, and for equally avaricious King Menelaus of Sparta.

"Look guys," Eurshiddenme speculated and stated. "Here is the only moral justification that I can offer. If covetous people aren't punished by the gods in this world, then I submit that the violators will definitely find their deserved penance after death in Hades."

"I need more motivation to continue fighting for stupid-ass selfish causes," Eurdicisin added to the preposterous discussion. "Even if I receive a small sack of gold as my compensation for fighting for Menelaus and Agamemnon, that miniscule pittance will be meager consolation for my family if I get my balls castrated by an errant Trojan javelin, and as a result, can't sire any punk kids to raise back in Ithaca."

"Eurdicisin is right," Eurassisgras confirmed. "Agamemnon, Menelaus and Odysseus are tiny pawns on Almighty Zeus's gameboard, and even worse, we five assholes are minor pawns on Agamemnon, Menelaus, and Odysseus's less-important gameboard! No matter how you evaluate circumstances, we're being rooked by power-hungry kings and unfaithful queens. Don't worry, Eurshiddenme!" Eurdicisin cautioned. "We won't heckle you if you're sincere in your candid answer to us. But instead, give us some reason to die other than to become deceased for asshole narcissistic Agamemnon, for vindictive Menelaus, and for arrogant Achilles!"

"Yes; give us a good example that sinful dipshits playing with our frail fate will be punished in the end, either in this world or the next," Eurcockisnum begged Eurshiddenme. "I mean, I have low self-esteem to begin with. Give me some consolation for fighting for sex-driven royalty, when I suffer from chronic erectile dysfunction with my flaccid dingle, and also with me carrying useless barren testicles. Unlike Eurdicisin, I'm already impotent, and I don't need to be castrated by any fuckin' errant javelin in order to be sperm-less with a goddamned hollow-weenie!"

"Yes, I urge you high-ranking sir; tell us a decent story that will inspire us to fight and die," Eurassisgas requested of Eurshiddenme. "We promise to remain reticent and will try to relish your suspect rhetoric!"

"Well men, here's today's rendition as told to me by an about-to-die lesbian prostitute who had suffered from osteo-arthritis in her permanently stiff clit, and also from flat, punctured, deflated tits," Eurshiddenme prefaced. "Midas was King of Phrygia in Asia Minor, and most people living inside and outside Phrygia didn't give a fast fart about the egotistical ruler, or about any of his irrelevant, imperial bullshit. Despite the public's apathy about their royal guardian, Midas was extremely wealthy and very powerful, because he taxed his subjects to death and used their labor, and also their money, to break almost everyone's balls or puncture their tits. The emperor never took any crap from anyone, preferring to pursue his own foolish inclinations, making hasty and irrational judgments without the consent of his distinguished transvestite advisers, whom *he* thought were simply charlatans and demented assholes, instead of being harmless, deviant transvestites."

"One day Dionysus, the always-drunk Greek god of wine and frivolity, was traveling through Phrygia with his entourage of naked nymphs and retarded satyrs, who were creatures that happened to be half-man, half-goat, and fully fucked-up. Anyway, one member of the troupe was Salenus, an old, fat, bald-headed prick who was barely sober while nodding his noggin and seated upon his lazy donkey, which all of a sudden smelled some ass's ass a mile away in King Midas's royal stables."

"The donkey surreptitiously lagged behind, and then strayed from the caravan of merrymakers, who continued to party without even realizing that the old fat fart and his mount were missing from their elite company. The independent ass took Salenus's ass west, and an hour later, arrived at King Midas's incomparable rose garden, where Salenus's ass fell off *his* ass and tumbled into an *asinine* clump of thorny, asshole rose bushes."

"The King's alert gardeners discovered Salenus bleeding and laughing upon the ground, and the common laborers helped the comical, drunken idiot stagger to his feet and think of what words to say. Meanwhile, the good-natured gardeners searched in vain for Salenus's eight other asses."

"Where the fuck am I?" the chubby, bald-headed old codger inquired. "Who wants to fuckin' tickle my armpits and scratch my balls with both ends of an ostrich feather?"

"The notorious revels of hiccupping Dionysus had become common knowledge throughout Phrygia, and the alert gardeners perceptively recognized that Salenus was one of the wine-god's intimate colleagues. The landscapers wrapped a wreath around *his* neck, consisting of assorted flowers, and also assorted and discarded marijuana butts, dragged his corpulent carcass up the palace steps, and gracefully dumped the intoxicated Salenus upon the marble floor. Greedy King Midas was then quickly summoned to royally entertain his new eminent guest."

"The King introduced himself to famous Salenus, who was still so inebriated that he believed *he* was speaking with a male prostitute in a nearby city ghetto. Midas was thrilled that one of Dionysus's close acquaintances had visited *his* opulent palace, and the monarch insisted that Salenus stay for a feast that would rival any that Dionysus himself had ever attended or provided."

"You must stay and enjoy my fine hospitality! I say hospitality because after you get done a full week of biological partying, drinking, eating, and screwing, you'll fuckin' wind-up in my royal hospital," Midas told the still-dysfunctional Salenus. "In this country, there is always feast and never famine! And when we run out of food, we suck on each other's genitals and then merrily lick our sticky fingers."

"That's perfectly wonderful!" Salenus exclaimed, while groggily staggering-around and habitually hiccupping. "My throat, my stomach and my loins are all famished! Bring on the strippers, the switch-hitting lesbians, and the goddamned male couch dancers, you stingy, parsimonious bastard!"

"Much preparation and attention to palace detail was done for the impending celebration, with servants flitting-around setting tables, carrying wine jugs and baskets of food, and placing sweet-smelling, ancient aphrodisiac elixir at strategic places."

"A fantastic orgy followed, which lasted for ten whole days and nights, until all the male attendees ran out of sperm fluid, and all the women's hairy, pink honey-wells went dry. Lyres and pipes were played by female minstrels having their menstruals, so the musicians were exempted from participation in the orgy, and when not tooting-away, had to sit all by themselves at a designated "periodic table" where they had some "good chemistry and lousy biology" to share, while periodically taking their daily physics."

"Midas next conducted Salenus through the festooned halls to the King's favorite palace bath, where the two frolicked and toyed with each other like a pair of horny homosexual chimpanzees. Those flirtatious activities went on for another two whole days, until Midas collapsed on the mosaic tile floor from sheer exhaustion, and inebriated Salenus had drunk all of the dirty, scummy water from the hot tub, thinking and believing that it was sweet-tasting wine mingled with aphrodisiac elixir."

"Dionysus heard about Midas's wild celebration, and arrived at the King's palace to retrieve his wayward friend Salenus. When the god of wine learned of the wonderful hospitality Midas had extended to *his* "salubrious comrade", Dionysus promised to grant the illustrious monarch any gift *he* so desired, either reasonable or extravagant."

"The King's heart possessed many non-virtuous, negative qualities, such as lust, greed, pride, hedonism, and vanity. So naturally, *his* exploration of pleasure was predicated upon satisfying one or more of those particular self-destructive vices. Midas's mind was still-fatigued from all of the ten-day biological indulgence, along with the two-day private orgy with Salenus, so the king's selfish mind was now in total disarray, a facsimile of his obese, bald-headed guest's erratic thought patterns."

"King Midas's cerebrum envisioned the golden cups that his intoxicated revelers had dented and hurled upon the palace marble floors, and the ruler thought about *his* golden honeycomb that the famous Greek architect Daedalus had engineered for the king's honor. 'Those drunken, shit-faced imbeciles have ransacked my entire palace, have vandalized my cherished golden honeycomb, and have smashed or ruptured all of my treasured golden possessions,' the disenchanted emperor imagined and concluded."

"Dionysus," Midas answered the quasi-deity, who preferred reveling with scumbag mortals down on Earth rather than associating with *his* condescending, almighty, pompous peers on *Mt. Olympus*. "I wish to have golden statues of you and Salenus manufactured to commemorate your fine visit to Phrygia, and to pay tribute to your amusing friend's memorable stay ay my ornate palace." The King then realized a once in a lifetime very *golden opportunity*. "Therefore, Dionysus," Midas continued as the greedy bastard finally announced the true reason for his veiled plan. "Give *me* the power to transform everything that I touch into solid gold. This unique gift will protect me from gold diggers, from goldbrickers, and from itinerant *Golden Fleecers*. The Midas Touch will be like my own personal golden parachute, sheltering me from potential poverty, even though I don't know what the fuck a parachute is, let alone a goddamned golden one!"

"I suggest that you give the weird matter some more thought," Dionysus solemnly and soberly advised, while cautioning to his new acquaintance the importance of serious deliberation and rational discretion. "Don't do anything 'rash', for I have no ointment or lotion that can cure major skin irritations!"

"Kings of Asia Minor tended to be obstinate and stubborn after committing-to and announcing their intentions, so Midas was adamant about his innermost desire. "Dionysus, this is my grandest wish," the egomaniac selfishly maintained. "I would like to be conferred with the *Golden Touch.* Now, I insist that you keep your promise and afford me *that* particular luxury!"

"Okay Your Motley Majesty; you win the debate!" Dionysus replied and conceded, shaking his immortal head left and right to demonstrate his obvious skepticism and objection. "When Salenus and I exit your magnificent gardens, the *Golden Touch* will go into effect. But always remember, dear Midas," the god of wine austerely lecturer. "The only things' that should be golden' are silence, sunrises, sensational sunsets, and your later years, you totally duplicitous idiot."

"Ten minutes later, Midas became so exhilarated from the official implementation of *his* new magical power that the emperor couldn't decide what object he should touch first in order to convert the item into solid gold. The covetous king chose a branch of a tall oak tree in the garden, located not far from the palace wall, and after Midas touched the tree's largest limb, its leaves slowly made a spectrum transformation from green, to yellow, and then finally to pure solid gold."

"These stellar leaves are better than the ones Daedalus and his son Icarus had manufactured inside the royal workshop!" Midas marveled and uttered. "They are worth a small fortune, and I have only begun to proliferate my already great wealth," the nutcase king laughed. "I can't wait to fuckin' touch the royal falcon and make it into a golden eagle! Ha, ha, ha!"

"Midas was now the greatest and most demented king in all the ancient world. He soon honored his next inclination, which was to stoop-down and touch his garden's well-manicured lawn, and the blades of grass instantly converted into strands of gold. The euphoric fellow next grabbed an ordinary stone, and the small rock astonishingly transformed into a lump of pure solid gold. The now-ebullient monarch next touched a familiar root crop vegetable growing in his private garden, and the nondescript object immediately turned into *twenty-four 'carrot' gold."*

"The joyful King was extremely delirious upon contemplating his new-found ability. Midas playfully held-out his hand, and eagerly sprinted past a row of six white marble pillars, and after the excited gold-magician touched each separate one, the columns all magically changed into solid gold. The ecstatic ruler jubilantly hypothesized that he would make his entire palace into a beautiful gold edifice, but then, the royal magician considered that the six golden pillars were a nice contrast to the majestic white marble structure that rivaled any god's temple in either Greece, Egypt, Philadelphia, or anywhere else in Asia Minor."

"Then, crazed Midas had an inspiration. The enthralled king grabbed a golden delicious apple from a fruit bowl and held it up to his lips. 'This apple is already *golden,*' the gold collector mused. 'I wonder what will happen if I attempt biting into it'."

"The anxious King zealously bit the apple, and much to his dismay, chipped two of his formerly perfect-shaped front teeth. 'How stupid I was!' Midas acknowledged. 'I should've asked Dionysus to grant me the *Golden Touch* in just my left hand, so that I could use my right hand to eat, to write draconian edicts, and to fuckin' jerk-off. I must experiment more to evaluate the extent of this remarkable gift. Then, I should be able to ascertain whether it is or is not an evil, wretched curse masquerading in disguise'!"

"The regal King ordered his royal servants to set their master's table, and Midas amusingly entertained himself by converting the dishes, saucers, cups, and tablecloth into pure gold. The object-transformer accidentally touched the table, but then realized that it had been pure gold *before* he had acquired the phenomenal *Golden Touch.*"

"When Midas's chatty, gossipy servants had finally exited his personal dining room, the apprehensive king tampered some more with his newly-acquired special talent. He gingerly grabbed a slice of bread, and inserted one end into his mouth. The emperor nearly lost several incisors from *their* crunching-down upon the flat, solid metallic surface. The King suddenly became extremely terrified by his 'new damned and accursed power'."

'I will attempt biting, chewing, and swallowing a tiny morsel without using my hands!' the worried ruler theorized. 'If I just use my lips, I ought to be able to eat that second ordinary slice of bread on the table. Thank *Olympus* my lips don't fuckin' have fingers!"

"The frustrated King bent-over, and used his nose to move the slab of bread closer to his mouth. Then, the experimenter bit into the slice, but it too had become solid gold. Midas's emotions quickly shifted from disappointment, to anger, to shock, and then finally, to exasperation. "What the fuck's goin' on here!" the aggravated monarch yelled-out to his intimidated servants, who fearfully perceived their flamboyant master's petulance, and together hid behind the six golden pillars inside the botanical garden. "If only I had waited and thought the entire situation through," the King imagined and regretted. "Then, I would've wisely wished for the *Golden Touch* to only exist on the index finger of my left hand! Shit! Now I can't even finger Mrs. Midas's wet love canal! On second thought, that's not such a bad fuckin' idea!"

"Midas reached for a 'goblet' of wine, but soon the gold collector became aware that he could neither drink from nor *gobble it*. The liquid gold solidified inside his mouth and throat, nearly choking the incensed imbiber to death. In a fit of rage, the distraught king violently spit-out the solidified golden chunk, finally fully fathoming the futility of his extraordinary gift of touch."

"This is fuckin' insane!" Midas loudly exclaimed. "If I hold my dick while I'm taking a piss," the worrier orally considered while speaking to a wall mirror, "then my bird will turn into a fuckin' goldfinch, and my balls will transform into golden nuggets. Holy shit!" the emperor cried-out as he instantly experienced *social insecurity.* "And I'm still two decades away from my goddamned Golden Years! And if I feel or scratch my ass with the *Golden Touch*, my ass will become a *golden tush,* and I'll be shitting-out gold bricks that will scrape the feces right out of my corroded colon, and also clear out of my abused semi-colon!"

"Out of sheer desperation and extreme anxiety, the now-penitent ruler lifted his cursed hands up in the air and earnestly prayed, "Oh great and wise Dionysus. Forgive my terrible greed and my lustful need for perpetual ostentation. Please show me mercy by removing the *Golden Touch* that *you* have so generously conferred upon your humble suppliant!"

"A familiar voice descended from the sky and instructed, "Midas, you would've been better-off if you had discreetly requested a dozen additional assholes to complement the big one you already carry around with you. Go to the mountain of Tmolus', who as you know, was a minor god that had been punished by being transformed into a solid precipice. Bathe in the nearby stream," Dionysus's voice loudly directed. "And then the *Golden Touch* will be miraculously washed-away. And the next time a powerful immortal asshole like me offers you a special favor, make sure you have assessed all of the *goddamned* consequences. Show more prudence and less impudence, you' stupid, ingrate, fucked-up jerk-off!"

"Midas was very grateful to Dionysus for providing him with the appropriate solution to *his* terrible dilemma, but in his haste, the distracted king heeded the wine god's instruction, but unfortunately, ignored *his* sage advice. The possessor of the Golden Touch journeyed to the mountain of Tmolus, cleansed his entire naked body in the gentle shallow stream, and soon noticed that the sand at the bottom of the narrow river reflected a bright gold color that has been that exact particular hue ever since."

"The Phrygian King was absolutely delighted to have been returned to a normal mortal existence. However, Midas still retained much of his former arrogance, vanity and greediness. The stubborn fellow soon resented, and then despised gold, as well as all of the other trappings associated with massive, limitless, decadent wealth."

"Confused Midas soon became a quasi-environmentalist, appreciating the sounds of babbling brooks, along with singing meadows and whispering pines. The mentally-disheveled ruler often distanced himself from his splendid palace, from his gossipy staff, from his marvelous festivals, from his fancy embroidered robes and tunics, and from his fantastic harem of fifty horny harlots, all sporting hyperactive eager beavers. While partaking in *his* dedicated "communion with nature", Midas coincidentally neglected the important political and economic affairs presently going haywire inside his burgeoning-but-chaotic empire."

"Now, the satyr mini-god Pan had made himself a pipe to play, and it just so happened that the minor deity of amusement was cavorting-around in the woods near Mt. Tmolus. Pan delighted in playing his new flute when the woodland fellow wasn't exercising, thrusting, or having his own impressive skin flute sucked on by some blind forest nymph that always craved oral gratification while providing sexual satisfaction in return. Hence, the well-endowed satyr had the appropriate nickname 'Peter Pan'."

"As a result of Pan giving his new flute a major blow-job because he had just received one from the aforementioned blind forest nymph, the beasts and the other creatures of the woods became very active and happy, making exotic sounds and enchanting dissonance, in addition to loudly farting all over the 'Fuckin' Forest'. Midas encountered Pan in the deep woods and requested that the goat-god continue playing *his* alluring melodies for hours and hours, until the chirping birds, the buzzing bees, and the squealing squirrels all developed chronic laryngitis and genital atrophy."

"Phoebus Apollo, god of music and the lyre, will be proud of my new musical instrument," Pan told Midas. "I'll be glad to serenade you and the forest animals until my lips grow weary, or until the end of the world arrives, or until my dick falls off, until the cows come home, or until whatever fucked-up event happens first!"

"But if Midas possessed one major fault in addition to his abundant greed, his vanity, and his arrogance, it was the fact that the king never learned when to keep his big mouth shut. "Great!" the idiotic emperor-turned-idiotic-naturalist answered the forest satyr. "I'll ask *Olympus* in a prayer that Apollo and *you* should compete in a musical contest, and that the honorable Tmolus will judge who is the more skilled musician. The pleasure of listening to the music will be much more satisfying than possessing the accursed *Golden Touch,* or even better than having a dozen additional assholes to crap out of!"

"Now naturally, Tmolus himself' was a woodland deity, and would be biased toward selecting Pan while discriminating against Apollo's musical ability. The god of music's harmonies had a classical rhythm that edified the *Olympus residents*, that extolled Greek heroes, and that praised dignified, rational virtues such as justice, truth, honesty and generosity."

"But Pan's revolutionary music suggested emotional expression, along with freedom of thought, loose ethical and immoral human behavior, and the pursuit of basic physical pleasure. It was a competition between "mind and conscience versus heart and body," and Pan had the definite advantage as far as Tmolus was concerned, because Tmolus used to enjoy getting laid, getting blown, working his erect stick, and wiping his ugly asshole a thousand times a day. Hedonism appealed much more to Tmolus than intellectual activity ever had, so imaginative and creative Pan was destined to emerge victorious in his not-so-amicable rivalry with arrogant Apollo."

"But Tmolus soon discarded his favoritism for Pan, and also, his prejudice against Apollo. He awarded the coveted 'laurel wreath prize' to the god of music, being fully aware that Apollo was a dangerous *Olympus god,* and possessed far greater clout among the immortal "Powers That Be" than the less influential Pan had acquired. "I don't want to be a friggin' immobile mountain for all eternity," Tmolus said to a neighboring ridge named Cliff. "I don't even have hands or a throbbing dick to jerk-off with!"

"Midas, however, was not quite as prudent and as diplomatic as Tmolus had been. He too was biased in favor of Pan, and had completely shut and covered *his* ears when Apollo had been singing and playing his splendid lyre. The tyrannical king was quite spoiled, because in the past, when *he* yelled "Leap," his courtiers and servants would always request "How high"? And then the obedient subordinates would always habitually jump to the exact precise height that the dictatorial emperor had arbitrarily stipulated."

"No one has dominion over the way I think!" Midas selfishly muttered to his reflection in a nearby crystal-clear forest stream. "It's now time for me to speak-up for what is legitimately the forest god's triumph over that pompous *Olympus* loser Apollo!"

"The self-centered King of Phrygia came-out of his self-induced stupor and vehemently protested to the heavens that Pan had decisively won the musical competition, and not Apollo. Tmolus indignantly peered-down at Midas, wishing that 'the asshole should incinerate himself in a nearby active volcano's hot crater'. Perceiving Tmolus's rejection of *his* boisterous verbal appeal, Midas beckoned to Apollo, furiously criticizing the 'unfair judgment that had been rendered by Tmolus'."

"Go suck a wet one, you dumb fuck!" Apollo nastily retorted. "Oh, you fucked-up mortal King; you must most-certainly have defective ears," the archer god continued. "I now feel compelled to give *them* their true shape." The falsely victorious god' of music, medicine, literature and the lyre swiftly whirled-around, and then proceeded northwest toward venerable *Mt. Olympus,* thoroughly convinced that *his* final judgment pertaining to 'that asshole Midas' was far too lenient'."

"Midas raised his hands up to his long, furry donkey ears and screamed-out to the sky, "Great Zeus in heaven! I've been given an asses' ears. At least Apollo could've granted me a long donkey's dick to go along with these exaggerated furry ears!"

"Upon returning to his palace after his bizarre Mt. Tmolus and woods' escapades, Midas felt ashamed of his animalistic appearance, and wore a large purple turban to camouflage his abnormally large and embarrassing ass's ears. The Ruler attempted to explain to his perplexed advisers and counselors that wearing the purple turban was a privilege that only the King could exercise, and the chief consultants were happy to hear *that* dumb-shit proclamation, because no one in the court desired to look so horribly unstylish and unfashionable as the 'fucked-up eccentric Monarch' did'."

"After the King's hair grew so long that his tresses and braidy-bunches had to be sheared and trimmed, Midas summoned the services of the royal barber, who was also a royal gossiper, and a royal pain in the ass's ears."

"Cut and groom my straggly, shaggy tresses," King Midas sternly commanded. "And if *you* dare tell anyone of my secret, you'll have to sleep with the royal zoo's 'twelve dozen' female gorillas when the apes are all in heat. Can you think of any punishment more fuckin' *gross* than that?"

"The royal barber was tempted to relay the King's personal problem to almost-everyone the fellow saw or met, but *he* intensely feared he would be mauled and mangled by a hundred forty-four aggressive, sexually-aroused, affectionate, female gorillas. Consequently, the intimidated barber quietly bit his tongue so often that it was now two inches shorter than it normally would be. 'I don't know what's worse,' the barber painfully thought and anguished. 'Being emulsified by twelve-dozen, horny, female gorillas, or sleeping with my corpulent five-hundred-pound wife; that choice is really a very tough decision. I'll now have to seriously think about to decide which lousy option to pursue. The ugly gorillas are looking better and better in my mind every damned minute!' the neurotic barber concluded. 'And besides that, crazy King Midas also might get pissed-off at me, and send my ass all the way to a distant fabled place called America to fuckin' become in the distant future a Yankee clipper'!"

"In bed, the troubled barber tossed and turned, and his obese wife rolled over on top of him, thinking that the poor hair-cutter desired sex, when actually, all that *he* wanted was more oxygen. The paranoid barber even made mysterious noises and nebulous utterances in his deep-snoring sleep, and when *his* subconscious was about to reveal the King's awful 'donkey ear secret', in desperation, the diminutive barber would beg for more sexual gratification, and his steamrolling wife would accommodate his irregular request at least five times every single night, until the guy was steamrolled flat as a pancake."

"Feeling as flat as a table, one afternoon the bedraggled barber strolled-down to a distant meadow to take a leak in a waterlogged pond. When he noticed that no one was in the vicinity to observe his *private* behavior, the barber then stuck his head inside a groundhog hole to relieve his extreme tension, by then shouting profanities into the cavity. A belligerent woodchuck surfaced, quickly bit a chunk of flesh out of the bad-luck barber's scalp, and then burrowed back down to its dark den."

"'I'll have to dig my own hole to get the necessary relief that I seek," the aggrieved hair trimmer said to himself. "I will not despair, despite my great apprehension! I fuckin' never want to be a goddamned Yankee clipper in that imaginary future fantasy place called America!"

"It required six minutes of assiduous excavation, but then the resolute barber finally accomplished his prime objective. Without hesitating, the hair-trimmer pressed his head inside the newly-created hole and bellowed, "King Midas has ass's ears! King Midas has ass's ears!"

"The excavated hole eventually filled-up with scummy stagnant pond water, and several weeks later, a colony of wild reeds began growing all around the cavity's circumference. When the thin reeds sprouted even higher, the growths rustled as the wind briskly blew between them. A court messenger happened to stop at the distant "pissing pond" to take a leak, and then *his* ears sensed a rather peculiar refrain. The young courier dashed to the King's majestic palace and alerted everyone he knew of the strange articulations originating from "an enchanted hole" down near the isolated palace swamp."

"A hundred or so curious imperial employees darted-down to the secluded pond area to observe and listen to "the most fascinating phenomenon ever". As the crowd gathered nearer to the hole that had been dug by the neurotic barber, the naughty reeds were melodically whispering and repeating, "King Midas has ass's ears, and King Midas's ass has ass's ears, too! King Midas has ass's ears, and King Midas's ass has ass's' ears, too!"

* * * * * * * * * * * *

"That was a great inspirational story!" Eusballsourout excitedly commended Eurshiddenme. "King Midas is probably paying for his sinful greed down I Hades as we speak. And his fucked-up kingdom of Phrygia was in Asia Minor, not too far from Troy!"

"And if we don't annoy the gods' fickle dispositions, we'll be rewarded in Hades by resting forever in the tranquil flower fields of Elysium," Eurdicisin constructively contributed to the myth's evaluation, "rather than being harshly punished for all eternity like Tantalus and Sisyphus in King Hades and Queen Persephone's dreadful Area of Atonement."

"Fuck toxic Agamemnon and Menelaus in pursuing their selfish ambitions here at Troy," Eurassisgras spoke-up. "If I can save my soul in the next world, if there is a next world, I'll behave myself now in this world and then hope for the best!"

"I can identify with King Midas's curse. I'm glad that I'm not the only one who has had trouble with his dangling dingle, so let's proceed and go kill some deranged Trojans, and then luckily get killed ourselves," Eurcockisnum assessed and verbally concluded. "Maybe I'll be able to have a two-dimensional erection and a pair of virile testicles while whirling and swirling around down in dark lackluster Hades!"

"I think that we should collaborate in order to corroborate a viable plan of action," Eurballsourout pragmatically suggested. "If we can't become victims of homicide while fighting on the Troad, then perhaps we can commit mass suicide to escape this fucked-up war, and then take our chances as renegade spirits down in Hades!"

"I hope you ridiculous clowns enjoyed this morning's moral lesson!" Eurshiddenme remarked, before offering a brief prayer to Pallas Athene. "Let us not procrastinate in activating our new-found ethical campaign. Even if we lose this fuckin' Troad battle and get killed in the process, we'll die ethically knowing that we have morality and religion on our side!"

* * * * * * * * * * * *

In Zeus's resplendent marble temple atop Mt. Olympus, the all-powerful deity called an emergency session of his family for the purpose of reviewing current developments in the historic Trojan War.

"Some of you immortals have chosen to support the Greek side, namely you Athena, Hera, Poseidon, Hermes and Hephaestus, while on the other hand, you Aphrodite, Apollo, Ares and Artemis have come-out in support of the Trojans. Now mind you," Zeus emphasized and paused. "Even though you are immortal, and that nectar and ambrosia keep you that way, there is ample evidence that human-made weapons such as bronze spears and swords can cause you gods pain and injury, and perhaps if striking one of your vital organs, might even kill you! Nectar and ambrosia, and the immortality that those two ingredients provide, can only protect you so far!"

Several minutes later, Achilles went on a hostile killing rampage, and was weakly challenged by Priam's young son, Aeneas, who was swiftly whisked-away by Zeus, because the king god desired for the Trojan prince to escape from Troy and eventually establish a vast empire to the west. The intense battle raged-on, as the clattering of solid bronze weapons, and the accompanying clamor of screaming warriors permeated the air. During the melee, Achilles had violently knocked Hector to the ground, and the incensed maniac would have killed his avowed foe right then and there, but Phoebus Apollo quickly interceded and shrouded the Trojan warrior in a thick, mysterious mist, which effectively prevented berserk Achilles from gaining final sweet revenge for his beloved and fallen Patroclus. The leader of the fierce Myrmidons could not be appeased. Achilles remained furious about losing his most trusted friend, honorable-but-quixotic Patroclus.

Chapter 20
"ROUTING OF THE TROJANS"

Eurshiddenme, Eurballsourout, Eurassisgras, Eurdicisin, and Eurcockisnum paced at a short distance behind Achilles and his Myrmidons when Odysseus's head captain alertly spotted what appeared to be a shallow cave upon a low hill where the five mischievous Argives could easily hide and watch the about-to-occur conflict unfold from a distance.

Ten minutes later, Achilles and his forces were successfully driving the Trojans to the confluence of three rivers, the Scamander, the Salamander, and the zig-zagging Meander. The fleeing Trojans, fearing for their precious testicles, frenetically dashed into the Scamander, when the other half of the intimidated enemy darted toward the closed gates of Troy.

The avenging Myrmidon chief entered waist-deep into the river, and Achilles deftly slaughtered thirteen unlucky Trojans, and *his* following vanguard captured twelve other young enemy troops, and then expertly bound their hands behind their backs with thick leather belt-straps. The enemy hostages were to be taken to the funeral pyre of Patroclus to be executed as Achilles had earlier sworn to his soldiers, prior to the burial of the fallen Myrmidon hero.

But then, a garrulous Trojan named Lycaon, a son of King Priam, who Achilles thought he had killed in a previous encounter years before, appeared on the opposite shore and was surprised to again confront the Greek General face-to-face. Immediately, the Trojan felt a frantic need to supplicate himself.

"Spare me, great Achilles," Lycaon shouted out of sheer fright, yelling so loudly that Odysseus's five cowardly captains in the distant cave could easily eavesdrop his appeal. I shall not attempt to scam you, Great Greek, here in the Scamander. Instead, I beg you to spare my lackluster life. If you recall," Lycaon pitifully panted, "you had many years ago sold me for a hundred quality bulls. If you again ransom me now, my father Priam will pay three times *that* colossal sum! Almighty Zeus has put me into your hands, and I believe that our coincidental meeting is not of my volition!"

"It looks like Achilles has taken this enemy bullshitter by the horns and refuses to listen to some cornball bum steer," Eurballsourout laughed.

"Yes; it's deja-moo all over again," chortled a delighted Eurassisgras.

"Pretty soon that bullshit Trojan will be lying in the mud and soon becoming ground-beef for the buzzards!" Eurdicisin coughed and then snickered.

"It's way *past your* bedtime, Mr. Trojan! Stop cow-towing to Lord Achilles!" Eurcockisnum added to the zany litany of dumb-ass puns.

"Stop fuckin' punishing my ears!" Eurshiddenme ordered his four dunce-like subordinates. "We've all heard that kind of feckless bullshit pleading before, coming from other captured human cattle that were begging Trojan chattel!"

But Achilles was drastically adamant about disposing of pleading Lycaon. "In the past, I had captured enemy prisoners and sold them to other nations as slaves. But Lycaon, that practice had been done before Patroclus had been killed by your sibling Hector. Even someone as strong and gallant as I will someday die! I say, pathetic Lycaon: this is your arrived-moment of fatal demise! Now, be voraciously devoured by famished fish seeking their next delicious meal!" Achilles's voice boomed as the impatient attacker thrust his bronze sword into the center of Lycaon's heart.

The river god Scamander naturally sided with the geographically-local Trojans. At that precise moment, Pallas Athene appeared upon the scene as a flat image at Achilles side, and the goddess mentally transmitted to the awesome hero's brain, 'Fear not, handsome; Athena is on your side and has your back.'

Achilles heard a commotion and splash occurring behind him, and became exceedingly angry when he observed a huge Trojan wading into the three-foot-deep water to boldly challenge the avenger of Patroclus.

"Let us not bandy or banter silly words!" the newly arriving-warrior yelled his last sentence as Achilles's lethal spear entered the soldiers' chest and exited through the bragging Trojan's spine, and then protruded out his back.

Being pissed at the quick and sudden outcome of the short-lived duel, the upset river god caused a high wave surge to generate, which chased Achilles out of the cold water, rapidly pacing onto the steep bank, and then another two-hundred-foot sprint had the Greek General safely standing upon the hot desert plain.

"My mother Thetis told me that my fate was to die at Troy, but I prefer being killed by Apollo's silver arrows rather than merely drowning by means of a miniature tidal wave!" Achilles bellowed to the cloud-covered sky. "I'm not a clumsy toddler who accidentally slips into a local mountain stream."

At that moment, Pallas Athene again appeared as a flashing flat image at Achilles's side, and telepathically planted another brief message inside his vulnerable brain. 'Fear not, intrepid Greek! I assure that you will not become dead by drowning in river torrents!'

Noticing her special hero in jeopardy from a second even more massive tsunami about to crash onto the river bank, Hera, also favoring Achilles, spoke to her lame son, the blacksmith god Hephaestus. "Your unfaithful wife Aphrodite has aligned with her lover Ares against Achilles and the Argives. Follow my instructions carefully. Make the weak river god know the power of Olympus by having him suffer from unfamiliar waves of spectacular wind flames!"

"Hephaestus used his knowledge of forming fire and created a conflagration so immense that it cremated all of the Trojan corpses lying upon the river bank, and also upon the nearby plain; the blaze also parched trees, shrubs, weeds, cactus and wild desert flowers throughout the entire vicinity. And then, the fish submerged inside the heated river were also scorched and scalded, as the biased river god quickly surfaced and loudly pleaded for mercy.

"Stop this raging inferno, Hephaestus! I surrender and submit to your supreme authority! I withdraw from the fighting and wish to return to the river bottom in peace! Hera: I beg you; convince your crazy pyromaniac son to stop his wild activity! I now promise that I shall cease helping the Trojans wage their crusade against the invading Argives!"

Inside the nearby cave upon the hill, Odysseus's five Greek officers were observing and listening to the ongoing solicitation of the river god, crying and appealing to Hera and her arsonist son, Hephaestus.

"That bastard river god never before ran into a maniacal fanatic like Lord Hephaestus," Eurballsourout attested to his four colleagues. "The river god used to only have water on the brain, but now the fucked-up loudmouth has become a real hot-head!"

'True," Eurassisgras concurred with Eurballsourout's assessment. "Thanks to Hephaestus, the asshole river god is really in hot water now! Ha, ha, ha!"

"Achilles must really have the dumb-dick river god all burned-up!" Eurdicisin indulgently laughed. "The name of *that* river should be changed from Scamander to Hot Springs!" Eurdicisin added.

"We ought to throw some tulips and daffodils into the tremendous river inferno and have a fantastic florist fire!" coughed Eurcockisnum, nearly splitting his vibrating gut wide open.

"This is the river god's main claim to flame," Eurshiddenme indulgently jested. "That flammable river god is no longer quite as flame-boyant as he had been only fifteen-minutes ago!"

"Holy Harpies shit!" Eurballsourout exclaimed. "I used to think that all of this mythology nonsense was total fantasy, but after seeing the impressive, muscular blacksmith Hephaestus appear before my very eyes and almost-incinerate the bizarre river god, I'm rapidly becoming an avid believer!"

"Me, too!" Eurassisgras chimed-in. "I always thought that when our ancestors dug-up ancient bones and fossils, probably of incredible creatures that lived thousands, or perhaps even millions of years ago, that our predecessors had made-up fictional accounts of what kind of mythological animals those discovered bones and fossils represented; and then inventing imaginative creatures like Gorgons, such as Medusa, or like Scylla and Charybdis, or like…."

"The Sphinx, the Seven-headed Hydra, and Hades' vicious three-headed dog Cerberus," Eurdicisin academically added.

"Not to mention the smelly-fish-crotched Sirens, those big-breasted mermaids that sing and attract voyaging mariners' ships, and entice the vessels to crash into their jagged jetty, or even the legendary Cyclopes of yore could have been some real prehistoric animal instead of a mythological monster!" Eurcockisnum was inspired to articulate and then elaborate. "Or, perish the thought; even the very dangerous Chimera, or what about the legendary Kraken, supposedly terrorizing and killing innocent sailors navigating in foreign, northern waters!"

"Okay men, I'm glad you now see the merits of the mythology I've been futilely attempting to indoctrinate into your mini-minds," Eurshiddenme congratulated his underlings. "But on the contrary, those bones and fossils were not of prehistoric beasts as you've so falsely surmised, but actually those remnants and vestiges are of early mythology creatures that I've been inculcating into your miniature cerebrums. These excellent examples of mythology monsters are precisely why we must certainly obey, fear, and daily pray to the gods of Mt. Olympus, with our special homage starting with honoring Almighty Zeus and Pallas Athene."

* * * * * * * * * * * *

"Enough Hephaestus," beautiful Aphrodite demanded of her ugly husband. "You've completely scared the hydrogen and the oxygen out of the obnoxious river god. But don't violate Zeus's strict code of ethics. There is no need to further harm an immortal, even a minor one, like the insignificant local river god you've just terrorized, in defense of a mere mortal such as Achilles! Retire to your workshop, and who knows what might transpire later tonight? As you've often proven with me, your glamorous wife Aphrodite, opposites surely attract!"

Meanwhile, outside the gates of Troy, upon the Troad Plain, other gods were involved in their own rare disputes and imbroglios. Chauvinistic Ares threw his javelin at Pallas Athene yelling, "This is what the hell you get for motivating Diomedes to slash my exposed hand!"

The javelin deflected off of Athena's raised shield, so the favorite daughter of Zeus grabbed a large rock, hurled it at Ares, and the flung object hit the god of war in the helmet, and with its impact, knocked the contemptible bully onto the hard ground.

"That's for your overall stupidity!" Athena, a woman's rights advocate, yelled at the god of war lying still and fecklessly whimpering like an infant upon the desert sand, almost unconscious. "Fuck with me one more time Ares, and you'll never fuck a mortal woman ever again! I guarantee it!"

Aphrodite zoomed upon the scene to render benevolent assistance to the fallen Ares, and Hera, noticing that development transpiring, and remembering Paris selecting Aphrodite over her and Athena in the beauty contest at Thetis and Peleus's wedding, the vindictive wife of Zeus instructed Athena to kick Aphrodite in the twat, and then punch the goddess of love and beauty's ass lying flat upon the Troad Plain.

As Athena surveyed the damage done to whimpering Ares and to unconscious Aphrodite, the brave goddess hollered down to them: "Let all who decide to help amorous Paris and the rabid Trojans become as hapless and as incapacitated as you two defeated wimpy dumb-shits!"

Meanwhile, a short distance away, Poseidon and Apollo were about to slug-out their personal differences in broad daylight. "Just consider Apollo, how my brother, Mighty Zeus, compelled you and me to build these high walls surrounding Troy. Now, here today, we meet as determined enemies outside those same walls, and although it is not yet dusk, I intend to knock the living daylights out of you!"

"We are both immortal, Poseidon," Apollo objectively contended. "And I refuse to fight with you over the petty concerns and squabbles that prevail among mortal men. Let the asshole humans settle their own grievances without our direct involvement."

Artemis, the goddess of the hunt, was disappointed at her archer brother's recent exhibited cowardice. But the goddess of the bow and arrow was then confronted by Hera, who commanded, "Artemis; you kill deer and mortals efficiently, but don't you ever pretend that you can oppose me!" And with those imperative words, Hera lost her temper and beat the living and dead shit out of insolent Artemis.

Hermes was soon intercepted on the battlefield by the goddess Leto, the mother of twins Apollo and Artemis, whom Zeus had made pregnant. Hera had accumulative jealousy and contempt for Leto, and had cast the sultry bitch out of Zeus's white marble temple upon Mt. Olympus.

"Listen Leto," Hermes cautiously greeted his immortal female adversary in the ongoing war. "I've seen what the hell Hera has done to Aphrodite, to Ares and to Artemis, so if you don't mind, I'll pretend I'm a rabbit without a tail and hightail it the hell to a much safer place."

Now, all of the gods and goddesses had wisely decided to evacuate the oddball battle scene with the exception of Apollo, who stayed secluded inside the city walls to ascertain that Achilles would not destroy Troy until Fate had ordained for *that* destruction to happen.

At dusk, King Priam and Queen Hecuba surveyed the Troad Plain from the palace ramparts just above the Scaean Gate, and the royal pair witnessed their panicked army stampeding toward the narrow, open portals below.

"Hold the gates open until all of our soldiers have entered," Priam yelled-down, "and then bar and bolt the doors immediately to keep brutish Achilles and his prehistoric Myrmidons from entering and killing us!"

After the Troad battlefield was clear and empty of the regularly clashing armies, Odysseus's five zany officers decided to evacuate the cave on the hill, and amble back to their camp next to the Ithacan king's Bireme.

Upon exiting the dark cavern, their noisy departure had aroused a huge brown bear that had been hibernating in the hollow's narrow interior. The awakened carnivore growled at the screaming cowards, soon rushing to attack the shrieking intruders. Eurassisgras was the last to reach the cave's entrance, but the clumsy fool tripped over a misplaced tree branch and tumbled to the cave's rock floor. Amazingly, the uncoordinated asshole still was holding his spear upright, and as the agitated bear leaped in the air, the spear's tip penetrated the animal's underbelly, and most of the creature's guts were soon hanging out of its severed stomach. In a matter of seconds, the ferocious bear ceased breathing.

"Holy shit that's quickly plopping-out of Zeus's asshole!" Eurballsourout exclaimed to Eurassisgras. "You saved all of our lives from utter extinction. That fierce ursa was a definite existential threat to our mortality."

"You'll certainly be celebrated as a spectacular hero back at camp!" Eurdicisin praised. "Even Odysseus will honor your sensational bravery!"

"Sometimes you get to eat the bear," Eurcockisnum orally philosophized, "and sometimes the bear eats you!"

"If that ferocious bear hadn't accidentally jumped upon your lucky spear," Eurshiddenme insisted, "then Eurassisgras, your ass would definitely have been grass if that beast had mowed you down! You were extremely fortunate to accidentally spear that bellicose beast in its soft belly with your trusty bronze weapon!"

Chapter 21
"DEATH OF HECTOR"

Odysseus's five colorful captains gutted the remaining organs from the deceased bear's underbelly and together, carried the animals' edible remains outside the cave's entrance. Eurshiddenme beckoned to and flagged-down a donkey cart that was in the area picking-up dead Achaean warriors lying upon the Troad Plain, to be later honored in a mass funeral service scheduled for that afternoon. The bear's carcass was casually tossed onto the back of the wagon, and the driver transported the former beast into the Argives camp, followed by the five zany hunters ambling behind on foot.

"I'm extremely proud of you brave men," Odysseus commended his stooge-like captains. "Killing that mammoth predator is equal to slaughtering five dozen charging Trojans!"

"It was not easy," Eurdicisin deftly prevaricated. "In fact, General Odysseus; the whole relentless fight was rather unbearable. But in the end, the five of us managed to triumphantly persevere."

"That's right," Eurshiddenme disingenuously fibbed and injected into the preposterous conversation. "Several hungry, feral male lions showed-up to greedily steal our fabulous prize, but we valiantly fought-off the cantankerous carnivores with our lethal bronze swords and spears. Honestly, Odysseus; the whole ordeal was rather frantic and life-threatening!"

"Well, you intrepid men are to be commended for your admirable audacity, and as an earned reward, I'll give you tomorrow off so that you can fully rest from your arduous experience," the Ithacan King praised his new-found audacious underlings. "But be prepared to engage the enemy after your brief hiatus from combat."

"Thank you, Sir," Eurcockisnum replied, tongue-in-cheek. "Eurballsourout almost got his three testicles clawed-off, but then our comrade valiantly attacked the bear with his spear when the angry beast growled and stood on its massive two feet. The entire scenario was quite surreal!"

"Well, killing this enormous bear will be an inspiration to the legions of troops who will certainly marvel at your incredible accomplishment, and fully appreciate your remarkable demonstration of Achaean valor,"

Odysseus lavishly congratulated his loony subordinates. "Surviving that terrifying, unanticipated rendezvous with such a dangerous creature is without a doubt an enviable badge of courage to be honored by all our amazed troops, and your illustrious achievement is obviously so outstanding that you men don't even have to tell me how many Trojans you've successfully massacred this cloudy afternoon!"

"Sometimes you kill the bear, but most of the time, the bear kills and eats you!" Eurassisgras impressively summarized and conveyed to Odysseus in a wonderful canard plagiarism of himself. "I only wish that there were four other ferocious bears in the general vicinity for Eurshiddenme, Eurdicisin, Eurcockisnum, Eurballsourout and myself to savagely kill, and later have a tremendous feast for a hundred or more famished troops."

The following morning, Hector stood alone outside the Scaean Gate to boldly defend Troy against on-a-mission Achilles in singular combat, in a crucial winner-take-all death match.

"Hector, my reckless son," King Priam shouted-down from the high wall overtop the citadel's main gates. "I implore you not to face that maniac Achilles all by yourself! That rampaging savage has killed so many of my sons, and I regret to publicly announce that I have no more sperm juice in my shriveled-up loins to produce any more fucked-up offspring."

"Listen to your beleaguered father," Queen Hecuba shouted-down to mentally-possessed Hector. "It has been prophesied that after you are killed and Troy crumbles, succumbs, and falls, Priam's feeble body will be torn apart by his own hungry hunting dogs near the bark of the historic barking olive tree."

"I care not for ordinary olive trees, or for the shallow words of senile old fuck prophets," Hector defiantly yelled-up to his petrified parents. "I care only about settling my score with Achilles!"

"But Hector," Queen Hecuba begged and pleaded. "Show more regard for your family, for your relatives, and for your besieged city. I had diligently nursed you with my tiny breasts when you were just a little sucker, and then and there I should have known your aggressive nature when you bit my nipples right off my chest without even having any damned teeth in your mouth!"

The passionate entreaties from Priam and Hecuba's lips went unheeded, and surreptitious Hector waited like a venomous snake huddled inside its lair for its human enemy to approach. 'I shall either save my countrymen and my city, or sacrifice my life and legacy in glory to the incensed

Achaean madman! This is my singular choice to decide now!' the Trojan champion reasoned. 'And to my devoted wife Andromache, it's now or never, my own true love'!"

"Hector, let's cut to the chase!" Achilles yelled as the Greek hero sprinted forward to encounter his worthy opponent face-to-face, and even though ice-making had not yet been invented, the Trojan prince suddenly got cold feet, turned-around, and hustled in the opposite direction, then being frenetically pursued by implacable Achilles.

Three times the pair dashed around the entire city walls, but then Achilles had a sudden brainstorm. 'I'll turn around, run in the reverse route, and I'll eventually again confront cowardly Hector face-to-face, since the scampering asshole is so frightened that he never turns-around to gauge my closeness in the chase. My gazelle legs are much faster than his rabbit's feet!"

During the superhuman sprinting event, Athena was active providing stamina to Achilles, and Apollo was supplying strength and endurance to the fleeing Trojan prince. But then, Almighty Zeus felt empathy for Hector's losing plight, since Priam's obdurate son had performed myriad sacrifices paying homage to the chief Mt. Olympus deity. "I've a mind to salvage Hector from Achilles's lust to avenge Patroclus!" Zeus uttered to Athena. "My heart has dual allegiances in this intriguing struggle!"

"What in Hades are you possibly thinking?" Pallas Athene challenged her omnipotent patriarch. "Fate has determined that what we are presently witnessing should materialize, and it is now in progress! According to prophecy, Achilles is about to butcher and maim Hector before the prince's alarmed parents appalled eyes, and all of the residents of Troy are irrefutably doomed!"

"I'll put an end to this bizarre death debacle right here and now," Zeus declared to Athena. "Hand me my scales of justice to decide a resolution to this dilemma! I'll arbitrarily put my finger on one side, and its weight will affect what blind Fate has already decreed!"

Zeus held-up his golden scales and placed his index finger upon Hector's left-hand side, which indicated that the unlucky Trojan would die with his losing side of the five-ton scale being depressed and lowered. But then, entering out of a dense mist, a Trojan ally sauntered-up to Hector and greeted his very surprised old friend and confidante.

"My brother, Deiphobus; you have come to give me aid and comfort as we both fight the crazed Achaean maniac!" Hector gleefully acknowledged. "Two against one certainly evens my chances!"

"Priam and Hecuba had begged me to stay upon the palace ramparts with them, but I could not witness you dying at the hands of the awesome Achaean champion. Oh brother, what a mess this is! Please take satisfaction in these propitious words: I pledge with all my honor and heart that you will not combat Achilles alone!"

"Achilles," Hector confidently greeted his avowed adversary, face to face. "We will now fight to the death, but I propose a bargain for you to consider, and for Zeus and his majestic family to also consider. If I shall be victorious over you, I shall strip you of your armor as a coveted trophy, but I'll not mutilate your body any further. I'll respectfully return your corpse to Agamemnon and to Menelaus for proper burial! Will you promise to do the same for my remains?"

"Fuck you, Hector!" Achilles stubbornly cursed and belittled his foe. "We are like rival lions from separate prides vying for dominance. No truce or settlement will exist between us! This is a wicked and desperate fight to the death, and nothing more!"

The combatants stood erect, twenty feet apart. Achilles hurled his deadly spear at Hector, but missed his aim as the Trojan ducked-down like a mallard paddling its webbed feet upon a pond and then dipping its head underwater. But then, Hector vigorously tossed his spear at Achilles, which deflected off of the inimitable solid bronze shield that Hephaestus had manufactured for Thetis to give to her son. The duel had reached an impasse.

"Quick Deiphobus!" Hector shouted, holding out his empty hand. "Give me *your* spear to hurl at my obstinate opponent."

But Deiphobus was no longer present, and it was at that moment that Hector realized than Zeus, influenced by Athena, had played a cruel ruse upon his tricked psyche. 'Although I am aware that I'm fooled by an Olympus prank and am destined to die, let future generations tell and revere my glorious story!' Then Hector screamed, "Let's get it on, bastard Achilles!"

A mammoth two-opponent battle ensued, and after ten minutes of loudly clashing swords, Hector's chest was greatly pierced by Achilles's spear, and the Trojan warrior collapsed to the Troad's hot sand to utter his final words.

"The gods are watching your bitter wrath unfolding, and your time is coming soon. The sand in your hourglass, arrogant Achilles, does not match the sand upon this arid plain, and my hazy mind foresees Apollo and Paris gladly eliminating your petulant ass from earthly existence!"

Achilles triumphantly stripped Hector of his enviable armor, and contrary to the royal Trojan prince's wishes, the Phthian heir and his Myrmidon officers repeatedly slashed and penetrated the fallen hero's body with their sharp spears. Achilles, showing ultimate spite and rancor, then tied leather straps around Hector's bloody heels, and attached the dead Trojan's feet to the rear of his colorfully-decorated chariot, and next proceeded to parade and drag his former nemesis around the entire walled city seven consecutive times.

Much to the horror and grief of Hector's wife Andromache, his parents King Priam and Queen Hecuba, Prince Paris, Helen of Troy, and the entire shocked residents of the whole damned city, Achilles ostentatiously displayed his vast contempt for his principal Trojan foe.

The one who suffered the most sorrow from Hector's horrible demise was his inconsolable wife, Andromache. 'That monster Achilles has callously and brutally abused my husband's body, which is no longer recognizable,' the sorrowed spouse uncontrollably sobbed and evaluated. 'I curse that I had even been born to have to suffer this inhuman emotional pain. And our only son, infant Scamandrius, being terribly unlucky through no fault of his own, being left an unfortunate fatherless orphan; and me a widow, *our* combined futures being helplessly wasted-away, a fatherless child and a husbandless spouse. My son,' Andromache contemplated and wept, 'will be shunned and ostracized by other inconsiderate boys who will shout insults about *his* father's inability to save Troy, along with its many defensive bastions, from suffering immediate poverty and ruin. Scamandrius will be bullied and ignobly ridiculed by his ruthless peers, who will mock and chide my boy, saying that *his* incompetent father had failed Troy, and had made its tremendous wealth disintegrate into pitiful bankruptcy.'

"Thus, did aggrieved and melancholy Andromache sadly mourn, and at that mirthless moment in time, so did all of Troy weep with her.

Chapter 22

"FUNERAL GAMES"

"That bear meat we consumed last night was absolutely delicious," Eurassisgras declared to his four happy-go-lucky captain comrades. "Maybe within the next week, we can find another cave and cub a few clubs, er, I meant 'club a few cubs' to obtain some more tender protein."

"I've heard some gossip around the camp that Achilles is planning some exciting games and contests to honor Patroclus," Eurballsourout mentioned to his half-interested colleagues. "I was thinking about entering the javelin throwing event, but then I realized that I have a slipped discus in my lower back."

"When I was a kid, I used to be able to hit a bulls-eye in nursey school tossing a broomstick spear," Eurdicisin claimed. "But then I had a bad nightmare that the bull's eye was closely watching me, and that the bull was going to gore my tiny ass in a gory manner."

"I would voluntarily enter the archery contest," Eurcockisnum related to his four associates, "but when I shoot an arrow, my style is to bend-down, so if I pull the arrow too deep across the bridge, I'm afraid that I'll become even more bow-legged than I already am!"

"Say Eurshiddenme," Eurassisgras addressed his higher-ranked captain. "How about reaching deep into your mythology repertoire and telling us a good story that involves an athletic contest, perhaps even a racing event, to get us thinking about the upcoming Patroclus games. The guys and I will not interrupt your impromptu presentation, because we realize that you get your testicles twisted whenever we do!"

"Okay, you' junior jerk-offs, who only have calluses on your right hands," Eurshiddenme observed and related. "I do have a pertinent tale that matches-up perfectly with the athletic contests that have not yet been posted. Here it goes."

"A beautiful young girl, Atalanta, was a rapid-running speedster, and the daughter of King Schoeneus of Boeotia. Atlanta also was a highly-skilled archer who was desperately searching for a suitable *beau*. Although Atalanta was also very fast afoot, her dim-witted father King Schoeneus was not too swift."

"Atalanta had pledged to the Olympus gods that she would only marry a man that was a faster sprinter than she was. In fact, the girl was speedier and more fleet-footed than any naval *fleet* known to the ancient world. Young, horny, ambitious youths from all over Greece often arrived in Boeotia to race against the speedy doll, and each failed asshole left the city-state kingdom disappointed and defeated."

"King Schoeneus eventually got so pissed-off at all of the foolish parasitic gigolos showing-up in his isolated land, seeking fame and fortune, that the ruler made an explicit proclamation: "Any dumb-fuck jerk-off with a death wish that comes to Boeotia to challenge my daughter Atalanta to a foot race will be condemned to death at the hands of the official executioner, immediately after losing the contest." And then the volatile King Schoeneus turned to his beautiful daughter and said, "Atalanta; we need fewer male *racists* in Boeotia, so I made this special law to discriminate against the dirty, intruding, foreign bastards," the elderly, cantankerous, ill-tempered, totally soulless monarch preached to his lovely offspring."

"One fine morning, an impractical youth name Hippomenes arrived in Boeotia from an unknown *fishing village,* that really knew how to catch sea bass, the remote, unidentified hamlet being situated on the other side of the vast mountain range. The happy-go-lucky young man was really a worthless, idealistic vagabond that appeared in the unhospitable country, only because his aimless aspiration in life was to wander all over the general topography without ever accomplishing a single damned thing."

"Why is everyone in attendance shouting over there near the pissed-off King?" Hippomenes asked a local resident. "Has a ferocious rogue lion maliciously scratched *their* tender balls, tits and fat asses'?"

"No curious stranger; four young men have recently challenged the King's daughter Atalanta to a foot race, and when the dumb fucked-up aliens lose, they will be promptly slaughtered by the royal executioner," the jubilant spectator disclosed to Hippomenes. "We Boeotians are basically cannibalistic and sadistic. We then, according to the King's new edict, will barbecue the four doomed losers' butchered flesh, and have a great picnic feast with lots and lots of delicious grilled meat! That's why everyone is cheering and prematurely celebrating their next nutritious meal!"

"Unlucky idiots!" Hippomenes answered, referring to the bold male challengers, and not to the carnivorous citizens of Boeotia. "How foolish the cocky assholes are to risk their lives simply for a permanent piece of ass and the acquisition of great wealth," the critical wanderer commented to the excited bystander, while they both watched the four young men limbering-up their leg muscles for the start of the all-important 'life-or-death race'."

'This girl Atalanta must be a witch, a powerful enchantress, or a rich bitch with an ideal snatcheroo,' Hippomenes speculated. 'She might even be an evil sorceress, who possesses the ability to attract so many unfortunate distant young men to their deaths. This remote desert place Boeotia seems like a fools' paradise. I'm not so sure that I want my life abruptly abbreviated, simply over stupid things like money, prestige, power, good sex, and beauty.'

"Soon, the talkative and callow visitor observed Atalanta approaching, and his dingle began throbbing and bobbing under his orange tunic. 'That deadly witch is really a tough-looking bitch!' Hippomenes noted and rhymed. 'My blood-drained brain is so empty and light-headed that I feel like racing her myself right this very moment'."

"The trumpeters' shrill signal to commence the race gradually broke the naïve young man's highly focused infatuation. On the count of three, the five contestants zoomed-off their starting blocks, but Atalanta soon moved-out into the lead with her gorgeous light-brown tresses blowing and waving over her shoulders in the morning wind."

"Hippomenes further evaluated all possible circumstances. 'I hope those four male participants lose the damned race! That way Atalanta will still be available for me to vanquish in a future sprint,' Hippomenes selfishly thought. 'I'll simply eat a pound of baked beans tomorrow morning and take-off like a falcon out of Hades, making a run to the first outhouse just beyond the finish line. But right now, I must admit, I've never attended a real-life human barbecue before,' the itinerant youth acknowledged. 'And strangely enough, I must admit that I'm enthusiastically looking forward to voraciously eating and licking other men's meat'!"

"Atalanta easily and deftly crossed the finish marker, and won the race by a wide margin. King Schoeneus placed a victor's laurel wreath on his athletic daughter's head, and announced to the boisterous crowd that a barbecued meat smorgasbord would be set-up in one hour after the royal executioner', butchers and chefs completed their particular tasks."

"The moody, fickle King looked-down on the throng and spotted the ever-plotting, lazy Hippomenes, while the almost-hypnotized traveler kept his eyes fastened on the very charming Atalanta's heavy breathing chest. 'These friggin' races are killing my military draft,' the highly-mercurial King grieved and mentally weighed. 'That's four more soldiers I could've easily enlisted into my personal bodyguard'."

"But soon, the irritated King's daughter's attention turned toward the young newcomer, and the big-breasted girl immediately discerned that the lad would not be satisfied until he became un-mystery meat for a future 'Bountiful Boeotian Beef and Ale Barbecue'."

"Speak, oh visiting youth!" Schoeneus boomed at the thoroughly-entranced Hippomenes, who was busily admiring the King's daughter's firm tits and vivacious curves. "Tell us what brings you to Boeotia, as if we all don't fuckin' already know! Can't you get laid in your own fuckin' town, or what?"

"Your voluptuous, curvaceous daughter only races wimpy faggots to achieve athletic fame," Hippomenes arrogantly criticized. "She has not gone up against any man that has superior physical prowess like I possess. I am a son of Poseidon, the immortal sea god," Hippomenes boasted. "And if I lose and am executed and barbecued by you friggin' assholes, then my Big Daddy will seek vengeance by deluging Boeotia with a major tidal wave coming over yonder mountains, and efficiently and egregiously drowning all of you raunchy bastards and bitches as if your second-classed city was inhabited by a colony of filthy rabid rats!"

"You might want to re-think the possibility of actually losing a race," King Schoeneus gulped and whispered to his extremely talented daughter. "This young sucker seems to mean business, and I'm intimidated by his threat that we'll all suddenly drown out here in this desert community, right in the middle of fuckin' nowhere. I wonder if the fool has the wherewithal to do what he claims?"

"Don't worry, father!" Atalanta supportively answered. "I'll easily defeat his ass, and we'll just call his bluff about Poseidon being his father and causing a major aquatic catastrophe! And if I am to drown to death, I can think of no person on this planet whom I'd rather do it with than you, Big Royal Daddy-o!"

"But the swift Princess, in her vulnerable heart, also didn't desire to see the young handsome visitor become the next-day' menu's barbecue entrée. "Brave, stupid, foolish, horny asshole," Atalanta personally addressed Hippomenes. "Either Apollo, Hermes, or maybe even Zeus must be envious of your muscular physique, and each wants to see you aptly eliminated from the rolls of the living by voluntarily becoming 'dead meat'. I suggest that you not rendezvous with your imminent doom, and wisely retract your announced intention of racing me," the gorgeous girl begged. "When a simpleton such as yourself races against death and fate, the invincible almighty gods' opponent, namely me, always wins! I implore you', handsome stranger," the fair maiden continued. "Abandon your unreachable dream and leave Boeotia as soon as possible. The afternoon four-door-chariot to Corinth leaves in two short hours."

"No go, my fair lady," Hippomenes courageously replied. "For I shall enter tomorrow's race and wager my mortal life, just for the privileged opportunity to be your dedicated husband. I cannot live with sadness and cowardice, once I have gazed upon your slender beauty, and lustfully admire your firm, hard tits that stick-out from your magnificent chest like perfect dual female erections!"

"Atalanta fearfully stepped-away from her fascinating, fascinated challenger, bent-down to adjust her right sandal, and waited for her stern, psychotic, dominant father to answer the eager stranger's brazen remarks. Seconds later, the egomaniac King cleared his parched throat and gave the predictable response."

"Face your destiny at noon tomorrow, young fool!" the King definitively stated. "Prepare to meet your ultimate downfall, you outrageously covetous, wet-behind-the-ears neophyte! Tomorrow you fuckin' die!"

"Hippomenes left the belligerent King, *his* stunning daughter, and the fanatical barbecued beef banquet and ale crowd, and hurried into the woods to first vomit, and then take an extended dump, in that exact sequence. After the youth mechanically wiped his sore butt with dried leaves and prickly-painful tree bark fragments, the intrepid stud studied the sandy course upon which he and the swift girl would compete. 'Perhaps I spoke too prematurely without analyzing the whole situation properly,' the young fellow regretted. 'Maybe I'm even a bigger asshole than everyone actually thinks I am? A premature decision is almost as bad as a goddamned premature ejaculation'!"

As Hippomenes raised his eyes to the cloudless blue sky, the ambitious adolescent saw a remarkable heavenly figure drifting afar on the horizon, and then quickly moving towards him at breakneck supersonic speed. "Sacred *Mt. Olympus!*" the amazed and presumptuous youth gasped and exclaimed. "It's Aphrodite, goddess of beauty and love, come to give me guidance, confidence and a certain erection!"

"Greetings, dear Hippomenes," the almost-impeccable goddess saluted with her right hand raised over her head, showing an abundance of ugly underarm hair. "You have the stout heart of a *hippo,* Greek for 'horse', and a case of the *meanies,* like no other human presently alive on this whole damned Earth!"

"Then, you've come to succor me and give me strength and courage?" the lad inquired, as Hippomenes avariciously peered at the goddess's wonderful solid breasts. "I'm a little deficient in abstract qualities like love and beauty, so I often think with my blood-engorged penis, rather than with my brain-drained noggin that's devoid of fabled Type-O Negative red fluid."

"You must win the impending race and wed the King's comely daughter," Aphrodite insisted to her new-found champion. "Here, inside this scruffy bag my left hand is holding, are some valuable tools that will aid you in your current dilemma. I hope you find them practical, and figure-out how the Hades to effectively use each of them!"

"Hippomenes opened the dirty, blood-stained, goatskin bag and examined the weird array of objects stashed inside, while majestic Aphrodite continued her rather odd discourse. The young champion conscientiously listened to the gorgeous goddess's authoritative and imperative rhetoric."

"I was just recently visiting distant Africa, and have taken three golden apples from the immortal tree that grows near the northern mountains, along with the sturdy thick foot-long branch that the golden fruit had matured upon," the goddess loquaciously explained to her chosen hero. "Since I am an immortal *Olympus* deity, I have a license to do what the Hades I like with complete impunity, whenever I feel motivated to act. And incidentally my dear mortal," Aphrodite orally proceeded. "Here is a little utilitarian gift from your sea god sponsor Poseidon; it's a small six-inch-long trident attached to a circular belt, fastened midway around."

"What am I to do with these rather wonderful-but-peculiar items?" Hippomenes urgently asked. "Sell the golden apples on the immortal bough, and use the trident as a fork during a future Boeotian barbecue?"

"That's where your noteworthy imagination is supposed to kick-in," the goddess impatiently-and-vaguely revealed. "Use your limited brain capacity, and implement the unique things in the bag, along with the souvenir trident in a creative manner. But I'll mercifully give you a good hint," Aphrodite declared out of pity for her new favored champion. "Put all five gifts inside your tunic, and your essential clue is: 'Four to rod, and one to prod'! Get it, my favorite, thick-skull Earth asshole! 'Four to rod and one to prod'." And without providing any more helpful directions, the beautiful deity then *vanished into* thick oxygen, which hadn't adequately learned to diet properly, and therefore, naturally would have ordinarily been *thin air.*"

"Four to rod and one to prod!" the inquisitive youth kept introspectively thinking and then repeating. "There's only one thing those fuckin' words, constituting a really dumb riddle, could possibly mean."

"The next morning, just before noon, Hippomenes first placed and next fastened the trident belt around his lower abdomen, so that the three-pronged fork would slam against his buttocks when he would run, and painfully "prod" the youth forward in his quest for the finish line. Then, the visitor to Boeotia ungracefully shoved and stuffed the long-branch and the three-attached, large golden apples down his girdle inside his tunic, making it appear that his genitals were ten times bigger than their normal, non-aroused size. Hippomenes then awkwardly walked towards the King's official starting line, as everyone in the gallery gawked, scoffed, jeered and pointed at *his* very exaggerated sexual and highly-visible, lower abominable abdominal apparatus.

'Look at his grand protruding dick and massive balls!' Atalanta thought in sheer astonishment, as the thoroughly-amused spectators all roared and heckled with laughter. 'With equipment like that, this city doesn't need any damned fire department to put out raging infernos!'

"And then, the angry tiny-pecker King Schoeneus, who didn't have the balls to do what Hippomenes had audaciously enacted at the starting-line, raised his imperial right hand for silence. "Hear me one, and hear me all. This gullible, idiotic, poverty-stricken youth Hippomenes seeks to gain my daughter Atalanta's hand in marriage by winning the upcoming foot-sprint against her. If the empty-headed fool somehow is victorious, and escapes the axe of the official royal executioner, then we'll all have to turn vegetarian this afternoon at the King's fruit and produce buffet, along with the accompanying ceremonial country salad bar!" the King reminded his peevish and suddenly irate subjects. "Let the dolt Hippomenes's death be a clear message to all other silly, frivolous youths that have the crazy notion to think that they can run faster than my winged-footed little girl!"

"Then, determined Atalanta crouched-down in her regular starting position, but being encumbered by all of the paraphernalia stuffed inside *his* burgeoning girdle, poor beleaguered Hippomenes could only stand there and wish that the King would immediately articulate the numerical countdown to begin the race. 'Four to rod and one to prod!' the trustful, callow boy kept thinking over and over again inside his puzzled and befuddled mind. 'Four to rod and one to prod!' Soon, the familiar shrill-sounding trumpets were blown, and the King sanctimoniously gave the traditional three-number countdown."

"The young male challenger managed to maintain his initial dash side by side with his highly-skilled opponent, despite the handicap of having five uncomfortable objects jiggling-around inside his uncomfortable girdle. But about one-third of the way into the five-hundred-yard sprint, Atalanta began distancing herself from her tenacious rival. The girl then felt sorry for her inferior pursuer, so she slowed-down sufficiently for Hippomenes to run alongside of her. The princess's right hand accidentally touched *his* exaggerated crotch, and that unexpected wild sensation momentarily stunned and aroused the ordinarily very competent female athlete."

"Hippomenes instinctively used his innate intelligence, removed one of the three golden apples from under his tunic, and tossed it several hundred feet ahead, so that its falling would attract the attention of his spirited competitor. As the distracted young lady bent over to pick-up the priceless golden apple, the ambitious champion approached her behind from behind, and rammed the sturdy protruding tree branch into his rival's crotch, directly-up her butt hole, making Atalanta shriek with both pain and pleasure."

"The revitalized wannabe' champion removed his artificial dork from his formidable female opponent's tail-end, and then conscientiously continued sprinting towards the nearby finish line, with the six-inch-long trident repetitiously goosing and penetrating his severely-lacerated buttocks all the way. Atalanta got over her momentary aberrant sexual deviation, and again hustled-back into the thick of the race. The fleet-footed girl was quickly catching-up to her inventive challenger, as Hippomenes neared the booing, jeering, incensed, carnivorous crowd assembled at the finish line."

"Much to everyone's disappointment, Hippomenes had won the race *by a rod,* or by a massive fake hard-on, and also had simultaneously won the right to ask for King Schoeneus's permission to marry *his* royal attractive daughter. When the chagrined King announced to the already-dissatisfied throng that a vegetarian buffet was to be served in an hour, all of the disgusted spectators belligerently pelted the royal asshole with pebbles, stones, and rocks, and then the agitated crowd angrily left the area in both miserable and disenchanted frames of mind to demonstrably boycott the lousy vegetarian smorgasbord."

"Then, ecstatic Hippomenes secretly reached-down into his girdle and removed the long sturdy branch with the two remaining golden apples still attached. He happily handed one of them to Atalanta, and romantically said to his prospective bride, "A golden apple a day keeps rabid cannibalism away!"

"Atalanta pulled-up Hippomenes's orange tunic, looked-down inside his pink girdle, and innocently-but-humorously exclaimed, "Where's the beef, you dumb-ass meathead?"

'That was a positively terrific story," Eurassisgras lavishly praised Eurshiddenme. "Speaking for my delighted comrades, we were all thoroughly impressed. I think you've satisfactorily made your four attentive listeners into devout athletic supporters!"

* * * * * * * * * * * *

Two parallel events were simultaneously occurring as the Achaeans were lamenting Patroclus's passing, and the Trojans were sorrowing for their dead Prince Hector. Achilles insisted that a large funeral feast should be prepared, featuring butchered pigs, oxen, sheep, and rams, all roasted and barbecued over roaring pit flames. Getting ready for the grand banquet in honor of Patroclus, the Myrmidons all rinsed and scrubbed the dirt and blood from their arms and legs, but Achilles rested and dozed-off on the beach sand, without washing any of the grime from his corroded kin.

In Achilles' strange dream, Patroclus vaguely appeared, praising his master for honoring him with such a glorious feast. "My spirit is waiting upon the banks of the underground Styx, and impatiently hovering for the ferryman Charon to paddle his barge to this shore, and transport my soul to Hades and to Persephone's dismal Kingdom of the Dead. I only hope that my soul will be able to reside in the daffodil Fields of Elysium, and not in the Area of Atonement where the unhappy dead are doomed to an eternity of perpetual punishment. Once my body is burned upon my flaming funeral pyre, then I'll be able to finally hail Charon for my bleak river crossing into dark and mysterious Hades. And thank you, friend Achilles, for placing the gold coin in my mouth to cover the expense of Charon escorting me across the macabre Styx to Hades."

Achilles awoke from his subconscious manifestation and reached to embrace Patroclus's vanishing ghost, but the nebulous apparition evaporated into the thin air around it.

After the great feast had concluded, the following morning, Patroclus's lengthy funeral procession meandered around Troy's walls for the purpose of displaying Greek tradition to the astonished Trojan witnesses. Then, upon the beach near the Achaean camp, Achilles cut his long locks of hair and placed them inside Patroclus's joined hands. Upon the elaborate pyre built of massive logs and firewood, sacrifices to Zeus and his immortal family were sacredly consecrated, with dead hunting dogs, sheep, bulls, rams, hogs, and the twelve captured and recently-slaughtered Trojan youths lying prone beneath Patroclus in the gruesome mass cremation scene.

In the meantime, Hector's body lying near the Argives' camp was not touched by either wild dogs or buzzing insects, for the prince's corpse was shielded by Apollo, and also protected by Aphrodite, with the goddess applying nectar an ambrosia anointing the many gashes and wounds. In the distance, the roaring fire from Patroclus's funeral pyre leaped and danced high into the night sky in what appeared to be fences of flames, as the zealous Myrmidons sang and repeated in chorus, "Good, good, good, good libations!"

Daylight broke over the eastern horizon, and at noon, the Greeks, in honor of Patroclus, participated in the magnificent athletic contests in respectful commemoration of fallen Patroclus. Diomedes had won the chariot race with the beautiful white horses he had confiscated from Prince Aeneas of Troy. The fist-fighting contest was owned by the famed boxer Epeis; and Ajax and Odysseus's wresting match resulted in a tie decision, with both grapplers rolling around upon the hard sand, locked together in solid, dual bear hugs. Showing remarkable stamina, Odysseus next was a favorite contestant in a footrace event, where the Ithacan King easily emerged victorious. Polypoetes of Thessaly, who only spoke in the words of many Greek poets, was triumphant in the shotput competition, and saddened Achilles came in second to Meriones in the close archery rivalry, shooting the wings off of a pigeon, which was acting as a sitting duck, the abused bird being tied to a high pole.

"Alright, worthy men," Agamemnon commanded and ordered. "The sporting games have officially ended. Let us now return to our separate huts, tents and campsites, for tomorrow, we'll again savagely engage the mendacious Trojans in mortal combat! Let's all get a good night's sleep, so that tomorrow, we can scurry out onto the Troad battlefield and win one for the fallen gipper, er, I mean, for the fallen Bireme skipper!"

Chapter 23

"RANSOM OF HECTOR"

For ten long nights, Achilles tossed and turned in his straw bed, not being able to soundly sleep. And each night, the lonely warrior ambled along the incoming surf until rosy-fingered dawn made her grand appearance upon the eastern horizon. Early that morning, the son of Peleus would drag Hector's corpse around Patroclus's mounded tomb, and then out of sheer frustration, leave the non-decaying body, which was still shielded and protected by Apollo and Aphrodite, lying face-up upon the hot desert sand.

Seeing King Priam being insufferably miserable over Hector's demise, perceptive Zeus shrewdly dispatched Iris, Goddess of the Rainbow, to the Trojan monarch's regal palace to placate and advise the despondent ruler.

"Take heart," Iris spoke to the inconsolable monarch. "Zeus pities your great depression. I urge you to now venture into the Achaean camp of Achilles and offer him extravagant gifts. Bring along an elderly courier, for Achilles will honor Zeus's Law of the Suppliants and not harm old-age visitors who enter his military domain! He will perceive you and the aged herald as non-threatening encroachers! And take with you a sturdy wagon to carry your opulent gifts to Achilles as ransom for Hector's body, and perhaps to then transport your son's remains back to Troy for proper religious services and burial."

"But what guarantee is there that I and my aged herald will not be captured and killed by the ruthless Argive sentinels?" Priam asked his goddess visitor.

"Lord Hermes will guide you safely through harm's way to Achilles' hut, and the son of Peleus will greet you respectfully, for even he fears Zeus's retribution to anyone who violates the sacred Law of the Suppliants."

After Iris had vanished from the palace throne room, Priam told Queen Hecuba that he was going to visit Achilles to retrieve Hector's body in exchange for a sizeable ransom. The harried Queen answered, saying that her husband had gone insane for suggesting such a dangerous scenario to ever be attempted.

"Achilles has killed several dozens of you sons, and shows no evident shame or mercy. Husband, you jeopardize your life for considering direct involvement in such a perilous mission! Stay home with me where you know you will see the sun both rise and set tomorrow in its daily journey around the Earth!"

'If any Trojan said to me' what I have just said to you," Priam replied to his worried wife, "then I too would accuse the speaker of being crazy. But I had conversed with the anonymous goddess face-to-face, and I trust her words of wisdom. Now I shall call faithful Idaeus to accompany me to the Achaean camp."

Several other non-lackadaisical-but-adept servants were summoned to assist in gathering the treasure trove of gifts to be offered as ransom in exchange for Hector's corpse. The items included twelve extravagant jewel-studded robes; twelve full-length cloaks obtained from the palace cloak room; a dozen soft-fabric-but-rugged carpets; twelve linen capes along with a dozen matching tunics; ten Troy-pound bars of gold; six gleaming chariot tripods; four huge bronze cauldrons, and finally, a platinum partridge and a purple pear tree. All of those fabulous gifts were carefully loaded into the rear of the transportation cart, and Priam was at the reins of his own personal royal chariot, while senile Idaeus sat and controlled the horses pulling the wagon loaded with the expensive gifts.

As the melancholy king and the obedient herald approached the Achaean wall, an Argive sentry demanded that they halt their forward progress. "Let's flee while we can still get away!" Idaeus pleaded to Priam. "We can die only once in this pathetic life!"

"No, my herald! We must comply with the commands of the anonymous goddess who had appeared to me earlier this evening!"

"Where are you two old coots going so late at night?" the Achaean guard cautiously asked. 'Tell me the truth, and if I believe you, I shall allow you to safely pass through the locked gate into the Argives' camp!"

"I am Priam, father of slain Hector," the Trojan king all-too-honestly answered. "Those valuables in yonder wagon are to be offered to Achilles as ransom in exchange for my son Prince Hector's body. Tell me, kind sentinel. Has Achilles butchered my son and fed his flesh to wild hunting dogs?"

"No, King Priam! I think some gods' mercurial whims are truly at play. No maggots or flies have invaded your son's body. But every day, in his mania, Achilles drags Hector's remains around the mounded tomb of

Patroclus, who had been slain by the Trojan prince, as tribute to *his* dearest friend!"

"Benevolent guard, please take this golden chalice I'm holding as a deserved gift for assisting me with valuable information about my son Hector," Priam cordially requested. "You deserve some minor reward for your cooperation."

"Are you testing my loyalty, King Priam?" the faithful sentinel replied. "This golden cup is meant for my master, Lord Achilles, whom I both fear and respect. But now that I understand the true nature of your mission, I shall allow your chariot and your wagon to pass through the wall's gate. But first, I shall unbar the bolted door to ensure your safe passage into the Achaean camp."

A circular fence as high as a twenty-foot-palisade had been constructed around Achilles's modest hut, and a heavy beam acted as a bar that required three strong soldiers to lift in order to gain access to the Phthian heir's humble headquarters. A tall figure stood in front of the obstacle and announced to Priam, standing upon his chariot's platform, "I am no mortal Achaean soldier. Instead, I am Hermes the Messenger, sent by Zeus himself to lead you inside to speak with sorrowed Achilles. Be sure to kneel at the gallant warrior's knees, and refer to yourself as being a father who has lost his beloved son, as Peleus would feel at losing Achilles. That sort of soap-opera melodramatic rhetoric will soften *his* heart."

Although the time of night was late, Priam courageously entered the hut and approached Achilles and his stunned captains, who were amazed to see an old man nervously encroach into their private conference.

"Who the hell dares to trespass into my residence? Are you animal, vegetable or mineral? You look older than the hills, and more-feeble than my wrinkled-faced and decrepit father, King Peleus!"

"Mighty Achilles! Hear my desperate plea. I am about the same age as your father, who still maintains a glimmer of hope that you will return to your native land alive. But my life has been riddled and cursed by ugly fate, for I am Priam, father of deceased Hector. Before this tragic war, I had fathered fifty sons with ten different women. Apathetic Ares has taken most of them away to reside as flitting spirits inside Hades' and Persephone's dark underground realm. Now my withered testicles are so soft that they soon will be tender-loins. It has now been twelve days since you had emerged triumphant in a tragic death battle with my dear son, Hector. Think of how your father Peleus would feel if he had lost you! I would like to pay you a king's ransom to retrieve my dear son's body for a proper religious burial. For you see, mighty Achilles, we are all victims of fate, and we must not violate Zeus's supreme will, or else suffer dire consequences."

"You must indeed have entered into my secured compound with the aid of some sophisticated god or goddess," astonished Achilles replied. "And I now believe that you are indeed Priam, aggrieved father of Hector and Paris."

"Fear the whimsical gods and their terrible wrath, dear Achilles, for we' are indeed mortal, and suffer *their* occasional anger and their volatile sensitivities."

"Zeus and his criminal family have no cares themselves, and must amuse their fickle desires by constantly manipulating us and frustrating our fragile lives," Achilles sagaciously answered. "Zeus has two jars sitting upon his mantel; one good and the other evil, and the all-powerful deity mixes ingredients from each, or from both, and the all-powerful alchemist produces an outcome that his mercurial mood wishes at any given moment."

"Yes, most certainly, young handsome hero. Your father, like myself, had been blessed with wealth, glory and influence. Yet, he too is worried about losing his only son, and sorrows at the concept of *that* prospect ever occurring, if established prophecy does regrettably materialize. And here you are, fighting in a foreign land, all because greedy Menelaus of Sparta wants to retrieve his irresponsible wife from my stubborn son Paris, and take Helen back to Sparta against her will. Both you and I are unfortunate victims of such bad and selfish decisions of others."

"I pity you, King Priam, for you, like myself, have suffered excruciating emotional anguish caused by ignorant assholes. You have exhibited much daring in coming here, risking death, and showing me that you truly possess a heart of iron. I admire your conviction and your implacable sense of purpose."

"Oh, great Achilles, give me back my Hector, so that he can have a proper burial, and so that you can avoid retribution from Olympus for violating the mighty gods' sacred laws. Please accept my valuable gifts from my personal treasury, offered as worthy ransom for my dearly beloved son's corpse."

Remarkably, obstinate Achilles acceded to Priam's strange request, and then acting like a suave host, invited the herald Idaeus into his hut to warm by the fire, and next sent key personnel outside to unload the array of gifts from the transportation wagon, leaving only two shrouds as cloaks to envelop Hector's body for shipment back to Troy. Achilles then directed two skilled servants to thoroughly cleanse and wash the abused corpse, and then wrap Hector's purified remains inside the expensive silk shrouds.

"Do not cry or weep, dear Priam," Achilles advised, "for nearby soldiers might hear your distress and report your presence to Agamemnon and Menelaus, who might warrant your capture and have you executed. But as long as you remain reticent, you are under my full protection and discretion."

An hour later, after Hector's corpse had been cleansed and adequately prepared, Achilles lifted the shrouded body and carried it to the cart that would be driven by Idaeus back to Troy before daylight.

"Before departing back to your palace, let us eat to consummate our fond bond and our agreed-upon firm resolution. You have astutely negotiated fairly and convincingly, King Priam, and I admire your wisdom, and envy your judgment."

"And likewise, I admire your courage and also your acute perception of reality," Priam complimented and returned. "I would like to sleep several hours before dawn shows its appearance to the east. Please provide beds for my loyal herald and me to rest until then. Your assistance and your empathy will be greatly appreciated."

"I will honor your noble intent," Achilles amenably replied. "The fighting on the Troad will not resume for nine days while you and your countrymen mourn Hector. And after your son's sacred burial, fighting will flare-up again when your grief and honorable intentions have been fully satisfied."

Then, Priam and Idaeus slept in a utilitarian back room while Achilles, still a virgin, slept with Briseis and Ifavagina, who were also recent secret lesbian lovers. In his light sleep, Achilles pondered that if avaricious Agamemnon ever learned of Priam's stay inside Achilles' hut, the Trojan King would have to pay at least three times the ransom that he had already provided to the already-rich Phthian heir.

Several hours later, dependable Hermes, exclusively assigned by Zeus, supervised Priam and Idaeus's safe return passage across the arid Troad Plain, with the pair easily accomplishing their trip back to the high walls of Troy. Priam's vigilant daughter, Cassandra, who possessed the gift of prophecy, was the first to see her father and his herald approaching the citadel's Scaean Gates. Soon, thousands of the city's residents and troops emerged from their domiciles to celebrate Priam's daring and accomplished venture into the camp of the Achaeans to successfully repossess Hector's body for decent burial.

Hector's remains were solemnly and somberly carried into the palace's temple sanctuary, where pitiful diriges were sung, mourning the intrepid prince's death along with acknowledging Priam's son's subsequent journey down to King Hades and Queen Persephone's ominous and mysterious Kingdom of the Dead.

Chapter 24
"THE TROJAN HORSE"

After King Priam had paid Achilles the extraordinarily handsome ransom for repossession of Hector's body for proper burial, and after Patroclus's death had been adequately appeased by Achilles and his' by-the-book Myrmidons, another terrible battle ensued on the Troad Plain where the hero Achilles was killed by an arrow shot by Prince Paris that had been guided by Phoebus Apollo, hitting the Greek archer in the tender heel of his right foot, which was the most vulnerable part of his anatomy, and hence, today's medical reference has evolved into commonly used nomenclature, "the Achilles tendon".

After noble Achilles had been born, his sea goddess mother Thetis had magically dipped his infant body into the Styx River, holding his inverted form by one ankle. Hence, the Greek champion was only vulnerable in *that* one heel, and that is precisely where devious Phoebus Apollo had furtively guided Paris's famous fatal arrow.

The *Trojan War* had taken nearly ten-long-years to fight, and the lengthy conflict was finally won when Odysseus, the notorious brilliant schemer and infamous ball-breaker, had two immense Wooden Trojan Horses constructed, and then had the best Greek warriors situate the separate structures outside the main gates of Troy, which was strategically located at the Hellespont Channel between Greece and Persia (now Turkey).

"How big does this Wooden Horse have to be?" King Agamemnon asked the designing genius Odysseus. "Give me a basic idea of its final dimensions and total weight."

"According to my schematic, the Wooden Horse should be at least ten-foot-wide, twenty-foot-long, and twenty-five foot high, and its capacity in its hollow stomach should be able to easily accommodate twelve-to-twenty of our best warriors."

"How about the approximate weight of this monstrosity?" the leader of the Achaeans asked Odysseus.

"I estimate it to be at around two tons, but that's without any soldiers hidden inside," the Ithacan king informed.

The Trojan army officers insisted that the Trojan Horses should remain outside the city gates, but the superstitious priests and priestesses had idiotically claimed that the Greeks had left the peculiar structures as respectful gifts to first honor and appease the gods, and second, as tokens of a final peace with Troy, and gullible King Priam foolishly had his guards drag the immense devices, which were built on large rollers, into the city proper.

The first wooden horse contained fifty horny, kinky Greek harlots that were instructed to exit down a hidden ladder at a designated time of night, and then directly proceed to flirt-with and expertly service free sex to the nearby, sex-starved Trojan guards.

While the aroused guards were humping and pumping the nymphomaniac Greek whores, a dozen of the finest Greek soldiers had been confined and impatiently waiting inside the second more famous Wooden Horse's interior.

As a sidebar coincidence, Helen of Troy had approached the second horse and walked in a circle three times around it, and then raised her hand to curiously feel the recently-built equine's hollow underbelly.

Inspired by always-scheming Aphrodite, who had staunchly advocated the Trojan cause, Helen's melodic voice called-out, naming the best undigested Greek occupants among the concealed Danaans who were hidden inside the horse's abdomen, and Menelaus's stealthy wife amazingly spoke-up like an accomplished ventriloquist, sounding exactly like the voice of each soldier's Greek spouse.

Helen's estranged husband Menelaus was seething inside the horse's belly, sitting right next to clever Odysseus. Two of the fanatical interior combatants, Diomedes and the Spartan king, were eager to get-up and wildly charge outside the wooden wonder in response to their wives' voices, and all dozen heroes felt compelled to answer back their spouses' alluring beckoning from where the soldiers were sweating and huddling inside the artificial equine.

Diomedes and several others felt compelled to reactively scream-back imprudent replies to Helen's vocal imitations, but nimble-witted Menelaus and Odysseus held the others' destructive compulsions in check to preserve their secret mission from Trojan detection.

All of the scared-shitless Achaeans sitting inside the Wooden Horse's belly managed to keep their chatty mouths shut, except for fucked-up Anticlus, who was the only one about to raise his throat's vocal cords, and the imbecile had felt a dire death-wish to answer Helen's alluring summoning.

Odysseus instinctively and firmly clapped his hands upon Anticlus's mouth, and held the numbskull in a gorilla grip before then puncturing the stupid shit's already-abused testicles with a sharp dagger. In short, heroes Odysseus and Menelaus deftly kept their dual grips upon Anticlus's choked neck, and also upon the rogue's bleeding balls, until Athena again appeared upon the scene, and escorted Helen away from the second Trojan Horse, presumably being led to ultimate safety.

One by one, the dozen Greek heroes descended the concealed hidden ladder, and quickly killed the fifty Trojan guards while the preoccupied in-heat sexpots were busily screwing and happily climaxing inside the fifty insatiable, horny Greek harlots.

The hero Odysseus had ingeniously thought-up the stellar ideas of the dual *Trojan Horses,* basically because the perpetual schemer wanted to return to Ithaca and pump his old lady, Queen Penelope, whom the faithful, itinerant king had heard was being wooed by two-dozen or so totally-worthless suitors, walking around the rugged island with massive hard-ons. And thus, after inventing the infamous dual Horses, Odysseus was about to make the transition from the ten-year Trojan War to his incredible ten-year odyssey adventure, finally returning home to his native Ithaca.

About the Author

Jay Dubya is author John Wiessner's pen name and also his initials (J.W.) John is a retired New Jersey public school English teacher and he had taught the subject for thirty-four years. John lives in southern New Jersey with wife Joanne and the couple has three grown sons. John is the creator of fifty-eight books.

Jay Dubya has written adult satires *Fractured Frazzled Folk Fables and Fairy Farces* and *FFFF and FF, Part II. Black Leather and Blue Denim, A '50s Novel* and its sequel, *The Great Teen Fruit War, A 1960' Novel* and *Frat' Brats, A '60s Novel* are adult-oriented literary endeavors constituting a trilogy.

Pieces of Eight, Pieces of Eight, Part II, Pieces of Eight Part III and *Pieces of Eight, Part IV* are' short story/novella collections featuring science fiction, paranormal and humorous plots and themes. *Nine New Novellas* is the companion book to *Nine New Novellas, Part II, Nine New Novellas, Part III* and *Nine New Novellas, Part IV*. And *So Ya' Wanna' Be A Teacher* is a satirical autobiography describing the author's thirty-four-year educational career in American public schools.

Ron Coyote, Man of La Mangia is adult humor and the work is an imaginative satire/parody on Miguel Cervantes' Don Quixote, published in 1605. *Mauled Maimed Mangled Mutilated Mythology* is a work that satires twenty-one famous ancient tales. *The Wholly Book of Genesis* and *The Wholly Book of Exodus* are also adult satirical *humor. Thirteen Sick Tasteless Classics, Thirteen Sick Tasteless Classics, Part II, Thirteen Sick Tasteless Classics, Part III* and *Thirteen Sick Tasteless Classics, Part IV* are adult satirical rewrites of famous short fiction.

John has also authored a trilogy of young adult fantasy novels, *Enchanta, Pot of Gold* and *Space Bugs, Earth Invasion. The Eighteen Story Gingerbread House* is a new collection of eighteen diverse and creative children's stories.

Jay Dubya likes '50s rock and roll music and he also enjoys pop' songs by the Beach Boys, Fleetwood Mac, the Eagles, the Rolling Stones, ELO, John Mellencamp and by John Fogerty.

Author Biography

Born in Hammonton, NJ in 1942, John Wiessner had attended St. Joseph School up to and including Grade 5. After his family moved from Hammonton to Levittown, Pa in 1954, John attended St. Mark School in Bristol, Pa. for Grade 6, St. Michael the Archangel School in Levittown for Grades 7 and 8 and then Immaculate Conception School, Levittown, Pa. for Grade 9. Bishop Egan High School, Levittown Pa was John's educational base for Grades 10 and 11, and later in 1960, the aspiring author graduated from Edgewood Regional High, Tansboro, NJ. John then next attended Glassboro State College, where the future author was an announcer for the school's baseball games and also read the nightly news and sports over WGLS, GSC's radio station.

John Wiessner had been primarily an English teacher in the Hammonton Public School System for 34 years, specializing in the instruction of middle school language arts. Mr. Wiessner was quite active in the Hammonton Education Association, serving in the capacities of Vice-President, building representative and finally, teachers' head negotiator for 7 years. During his lengthy teaching career, John had been nominated into "Who's Who Among American Teachers" three times. He also was quite active giving professional workshops at schools around South Jersey on the subjects of creative writing and the use of movie videos to motivate students to organize their classroom theme compositions.

John Wiessner was very active in community service, being a past President of the Hammonton Lions Club, where he also functioned for many years as the club's Tail-Twister, Vice-President and also Liontamer. John had been named Hammonton Lion of the Year in 1979, and in 2009, the community helper earned the prestigious Melvin Jones Fellow Award, which is the highest honor that a Lion can receive from Lions International.

John also was a successful businessman, starting with being a Philadelphia Bulletin newspaper delivery boy for two years in the late 1950s in Levittown, Pennsylvania. After his family moved back to New Jersey in 1959, John worked at his grandparents and his parents' farm markets, Square Deal Farm (now Ron's Gardens in Hammonton) and Pete's Farm Market in Elm, respectively. He later managed his wife's parents' farm market, White Horse Farms in Elm for three summers.

Also, in a business capacity, for 16 summers starting in 1967 John Wiessner had co-owned Dealers Choice Amusement Arcade on the Ocean

City, Maryland boardwalk and also co-owned the New Horizon Tee-Shirt Store for eight summers (1973-'81) on the Rehoboth Beach, Delaware boardwalk. In addition, "Jay Dubya" was a co-owner of Wheel and Deal Amusement Arcade, Missouri Avenue and Boardwalk, Atlantic City. And then, for 18 summers beginning in 1986, John had been the Field Manager in charge of crew-leaders for Atlantic Blueberry Company (the world's largest cultivated blueberry farm), both the Weymouth and Mays Landing Divisions.

After retiring from teaching in 1999, writing under the pen name Jay Dubya (his initials), John Wiessner became the author of 58 books in the genre Action/Adventure Novels, Sci-Fi/Paranormal Story Collections, Adult Satire, Young Adult Fantasy Novels and Non-Fiction Books. His books exist in hardcover, in paperback and in popular Kindle and Nook e-book formats.

Google: Jay Dubya books